SECRETS
D'AMOUR

She was standing close enough to him for the tips of
her breasts to touch him through her thin chemise and
for the deliciously warm smell of her body, mingled
with her expensive perfume, to titillate his senses in a
manner he found irresistible. He felt under her chemise
and grasped a handful of the soft flesh of her belly in a
way that was half desire and half exasperation. And
soon his hand found its way down inside her knickers,
to feel her thick curls and then to caress between her
thighs.

'No . . . I really must go,' she whispered, her mouth
touching his cheek. 'You'll make me late . . .'

By the same author

PLAISIR D'AMOUR
JOIE D'AMOUR
FOLIES D'AMOUR
MYSTERE D'AMOUR

SECRETS D'AMOUR

Anne-Marie Villefranche

Nexus

A Nexus Book
Published in 1990
332 Ladbroke Grove London W10 5AH

Reprinted 1992

Printed and bound in Great Britain by
Cox & Wyman Ltd, Reading, Berks

ISBN 0 352 32396 5

SECRETS D'AMOUR

Foreword

Anne-Marie Villefranche's stories of the very unconventional love-affairs of her friends in the Paris of the 1920s have become extraordinarily popular, not only in France itself but throughout Europe and right around the world, from North and South America to Japan. It is for the amusement of her large and cosmopolitan audience that this fifth volume of her work has been prepared for publication.

As appreciative readers are aware, Anne-Marie's favourite form was the *conte* – the long short story of about 7,500 words. In her hands this was ample to sketch in a pair of lovers, often mismatched, and their background; to relate the improprieties of the relationship that developed between them; and to describe the outcome – usually scandalous and always unexpected.

There were occasions when the intricacies of the affair that had caught Anne-Marie's interest could not be contained satisfactorily in so short a compass. An instance is the story of Armand and Madeleine in this volume. To overcome the problem in her own inimitable way, Anne-Marie composed a series of nine connected stories about the same people. Together they make up a full-length novel, but they can also be read separately as complete stories in themselves.

The reader may therefore choose to begin at the beginning with the first story, *Diversions on a Staircase*, and follow the unfolding sequence of events through to its conclusion in *Secrets Revealed*, or to take any story in the book at random and enjoy it for its own sake.

Those familiar with Anne-Marie's earlier published

works will recognise several of her friends in this volume. Armand Budin, for example, appeared first in *Plaisir d'Amour*, pursuing a lady who tried out the abilities of would-be lovers on her maid first. In *Joie d'Amour* he and an acquaintance discovered by chance that they were unknowingly sharing, on a regular basis, the favours of the same ambitious young lady. In the present volume, Armand plunges into a passionate love affair with Madeleine Beauvais, the estranged wife of his cousin, having learned nothing from previous escapades.

The complex affairs of Madeleine's sister Yvonne have also been written about at some length previously. In *Joie d'Amour*, when she was still Yvonne Daladier, she deserted a devoted lover for a more promising one, only to be left penniless when he turned out to be a swindler. In *Folies d'Amour* she was on the point of becoming engaged to a suitably wealthy man when a comically indecent misadventure with a fortune-teller put a stop to this affair.

The present volume finds her a few years later, now Yvonne Hiver, having in the meantime succeeded in her ambition of marrying a rich man and becoming the mother of two children – none of which prevents her from embracing other and younger lovers. I will not trace here the antecedents of other men and women involved in the shameless events which make up the narrative of this volume, but leave to the curious reader the pleasure of identifying them from the earlier books.

Jane Purcell, London, 1988

1

Diversions on a Staircase

Madeleine Beauvais was tall, slender and beautiful – and it would be no exaggeration to say that her husband's cousin Armand was half in love with her. He visited the Beauvais apartment often, for the pleasure of seeing her and talking to her. He thought about her every day, and sometimes, perhaps when he'd had a little more champagne than was good for him, he fantasised about her. Human nature being what it is, it need hardly be said that these fantasies of his were of a certain kind – in them Armand gave himself the privilege of stripping off Madeleine's clothes and indulging his passions in a variety of shameless ways on her elegant body.

At twenty-nine Madeleine was at the peak of physical perfection. She had an oval face with delicately prominent cheekbones, a long fine nose and a generously broad mouth. Her hair was of a fascinating walnut-brown shade and, though it was cut fashionably short, it seemed to float about her head in shiny and perfumed delight. When her women friends described her as very good-looking, they generally shrugged their shoulders to convey that they did not entirely understand what men found so interesting about her. The truth was that no man could fail to be instantly aware that there was about her a certain invisible aura, impossible to define, perhaps, but which had much to do with a concealed sensuality.

Not that she was in any way provocative, of course. As a married woman of good background and breeding she dressed and conducted herself within the bounds expected. Yet in some subtle manner, her physical presence hinted at a secret enthusiasm and capacity for love beyond the ordinary. It could be recognised, by those susceptible to such nuances, in the tiny gestures of her hands when she talked, and in the way she turned her wrist. It was in the graceful way she crossed her silk-stockinged legs when she sat, and in the round curves of her little breasts and hips under her beautifully-styled clothes.

The many men like Armand Budin who experienced the exquisite attraction that seemed to linger about Madeleine like a delicious aroma always understood each other perfectly well. There was not one of her acquaintance who would not have been delighted beyond words to have an opportunity of taking her clothes off one afternoon and making love to her. But alas, she was known to be utterly, devotedly and remarkably faithful to her husband Pierre-Louis, even though they had been married for eight years.

Naturally, over that long a time there had been young men enough – and middle-aged men too – who in private had revealed to Madeleine the strength of their feelings for her. And from that they had gone further and given her indications of their aspiration to be permitted to become her lover. They had expressed to her their desires, according to their individual temperament and understanding, and these varied from romantic declarations of undying love that seemed to demand no more than to hold her hand and press a chaste kiss to her cheek, all the way up the scale to robust statements of a burning passion to kiss her breasts until she fainted from pleasure.

There was one particularly bold fellow, Claude Bonheur, who had disgraced himself by succumbing to his hungry desire for Madeleine. He was a good-looking man of twenty-five or so, tall and blue-eyed, a lawyer by profession and, in any normal circumstances, with all a lawyer's caution. But at a party in the Beauvais' apartment he became a little too exhilarated by a combination of champagne and his need to possess himself of Madeleine's charms. This intoxicating mixture carried him far beyond the limit of good manners required in polite society. When he found himself momentarily alone with her in some corner of the apartment, he seized the opportunity to clasp her tightly round the waist and rubbed himself rapidly against her.

It is to be presumed he did this in the hope that the firm touch of his ramrod against her belly, even through layers of clothes, would inflame her passion to the point where she would refuse him nothing. Observing that he was a little drunk, she asked him to let go of her and tried to push him away, and so end the matter without further unseemliness. But when he held on and rubbed against her harder and faster, as if determined to discharge his excitement into his underwear, it was not Madeleine's passions that he aroused but her anger – to the point where she smacked his face and rebuked his impudence very sharply.

The truth was that, without exception, every one of the aspirants for her favour were turned away with a firmness that admitted no ambiguity. Imagine then the astonishment and the delight of Armand Budin when it came to him in a moment of revelation one evening that he could have Madeleine – have her whenever he wanted, have her naked on her back on his bed for his pleasure, just for the asking! The force of the realisation was almost overwhelming – a tremor ran through his body and his breath caught in his throat, almost as if she were already spread beneath him, his belly on her and his moment of gratification arriving.

Except that, knowing Madeleine's character as he did, it was utterly improbable that she should indicate her readiness to surrender her body to him. It was as improbable as if he had been informed that he had won a million francs in a lottery – on a ticket he had forgotten that he had even bought. But he had bought a ticket, so to speak, in that two or three years previously he had made his interest known to Madeleine in a manner that was so charming that she had been flattered rather than annoyed. So much so that she had discouraged him with almost as much grace as if she were accepting his advances.

There was nothing particularly special about the occasion on which Armand made the astounding discovery that the virtuous Madeleine would now welcome his approaches. He was one of a party of a dozen friends, including Pierre-Louis and Madeleine, enjoying an evening at *Les Acacias* nightclub. Though Armand had attained his thirtieth birthday some months previously, he had not troubled himself with marriage and therefore he took along as his partner for the evening one of the many pretty women he knew, Dominique Delaval – an elegant young woman who *had* been married, but found it inconveniently restricting after two or three years and was married no more.

The band played American jazz music, the champagne flowed, the friends gossiped about other friends, the time passed very pleasantly. Armand danced several times with fair-haired Dominique and, for the sake of courtesy, once with each of the other women in the party. It was Dominique's vivacity, no doubt, as well as the generous proportions of her half-covered bosom, that ensured her instant popularity with men in general – especially married men. During the course of the evening each of the men in Armand's party demanded the pleasure of dancing with her.

One of them, Armand took note, felt himself free enough from observation among the couples on the crowded dance-floor to move his hand down from between the elegant shoulder-blades exposed by Dominique's backless evening frock, and feel her bottom through the clinging tangerine silk chiffon. It was not just a friendly squeeze – Vincent kept his hand there for the entire time they were dancing. Nor was he content to let his hand rest lightly on Dominique's bottom, as if to steer her, though with unnecessary intimacy, through the jerky steps of the dance. So far as Armand was able to make out in the brief intervals when the general movement on the floor permitted him to see Dominique's back, Vincent's treacherous groping hand

4

was moving continuously – to stroke and squeeze the delectable cheeks concealed by Dominique's frock.

It had to be admitted that the temptation was very great. The graceful rotundities of Dominique's bottom were so exquisitely shaped that if a sculptor could reproduce them in pink marble his work would be acclaimed a masterpiece and given pride of place in the Louvre. Not, of course, that this marvellous endowment of hers was shaped of anything so cold and unyielding as marble – under the satin skin of its cheeks there was a wealth of warm and pliable flesh that was an unfailing delight to grasp. These long delicious oval delights swelled out the back of her dress in a way that made the hands of every man who saw her itch to squeeze them.

This Vincent Moreau who was committing so displeasing an act of familiarity had been a good friend of Armand since they were at the lycée together. When he brought Dominique back to the table, Vincent's face was noticeably red, even in the near-darkness of the nightclub, and there was an obvious bulge in his black evening trousers. He took the chair next to Dominique and whispered to her, his mouth almost touching her diamond-studded ear, while he refilled her glass. Under cover of the table he put his palm on her silk-stockinged knee and, with the dexterity of long practice, started to ease his hand up her thigh under her frock.

To be sure, in the dim lighting of nightclubs multitudes of men put their hands up women's frocks, night after night. There is, in fact, a widely-held theory that this is the true purpose of nightclubs – and that the drinking and dancing are no more than means of facilitating the progress of male hand up female thigh. But Vincent's pretty wife Brigitte was sitting opposite him across the table, and it has for long been scientifically established beyond possibility of contradiction that, on the day she gets married, a woman develops a mysterious psychic power. It warns her with a cold tingle down her spine of the instant her husband touches another woman's treasures even if, at the time, he is right across the other side of Paris.

Before Vincent's hand could cover more than half the voluptuous journey from Dominique's knee to the top of her silk stocking, Armand put an end to a folly that might quickly degenerate into embarrassment, by pulling Dominique to her feet and leading her back to the dance floor. It was not precisely that he was jealous; he knew well enough that he was by no means the only man on terms of intimacy with Dominique. But he thought it unmannerly of Vincent to attempt to seduce her under the eyes of her partner for the evening – and even more ill-mannered to behave like that under his wife's nose.

The proper thing would have been to ask Dominique for her telephone number and call her tomorrow to arrange a meeting, if Vincent was so taken by her. His excessively open approach showed a lack of respect both for his wife and for Armand. After all, it was certain enough that Vincent would have played the outraged husband if Armand had had the temerity to slide his hand up Brigitte's thigh under the table to touch the *bijou* which Vincent regarded as his property! The incident passed and was forgotten, except by Brigitte, who gave Vincent a cold glare and ceased to speak to him for the rest of the evening.

It was when the party were leaving the club at two in the morning that the truly breathtaking instant of revelation arrived for Armand. The dozen friends were standing cramped together in the tiny entrance foyer, sorting out their coats and hats. Pierre-Louis was tipping the cloakroom attendant, and Armand took Madeleine's impressive evening wrap with the sable collar and draped it over her bare shoulders. There was no intent in his mind beyond the ordinary courtesies. After all, in a quarter of an hour he would be at Dominique's apartment and, shortly after that, locked in naked embrace with her.

Yet, the nature of men being as it is, he could not resist a quick glance over Madeleine's shoulder as he

6

held the wrap for her. She was wearing a chic little sleeveless cocktail frock of white satin, scooped very low in front to reveal the division of her breasts, and belted loosely around her hips. There was a long string of pearls about her neck, wound round once close to her eminently kissable throat, and then dangling in a second loop to the level of her breasts. And it was at those delicious little pomegranates that Armand glanced, over her bare shoulder and down the loose front of her frock.

The subtle and expensive perfume Madeleine had dabbed behind her ears, under her chin and in the valley between her breasts rose to Armand's nostrils and affected him so powerfully that he experienced a sudden stir inside his trousers. He forgot all about Dominique and the pleasures that awaited him; his easily aroused passions were suddenly centred on the unattainable Madeleine. It must be understood that it was very crowded in the tiny foyer, with twelve of them all together, putting on hats and coats and gloves. Perhaps that was the reason why Madeleine moved a little step backwards towards Armand while he helped her into her beautiful dark green evening wrap with the sable fur collar.

As everyone knew who had ever seen Madeleine Beauvais on a dance-floor, she had long and elegant legs, and she was very nearly as tall as Armand. With her back so close to him, her head was near enough to his face for his nose to be tickled by the soft waves of her dark brown hair. And he had only to sway forward the merest fraction – unnoticed in the general movement around him – and incline his own head just a little, for his lips to touch the bare nape of her neck in a kiss so light and fleeting that, he thought, only he knew that he had bestowed it. This briefest of touches on her skin whipped up his fast-rising emotions even further, so that in his fantasy it was not the nape of her neck his lips brushed against but her mouth.

A moment later he was startled to realise that he was not the only one who knew he had kissed Madeleine as delicately as a butterfly hovering above a flower. Not that the actions or words of any of his friends gave him reason to think that – it was something much more personal in nature. Through the long evening wrap he was holding up for Madeleine, so that it hung between their bodies like a thin curtain, he felt her bottom press itself against his loins. And not merely a brief accidental touch either she was rubbing her bottom against him with gentle deliberation.

The surprise of it made him utter a soft little gasp and he responded to her gesture at once by pressing his belly and loins against her. There could be not the least doubt of it – she wriggled her bottom against him even more firmly, sending delightful sensations through him. And all the while he was staring down the front of her white satin frock at the roundness of her unconfined pomegranates and their dark red buds. Her hands came up to take the wrap from him and drape it round herself, so covering the delights he was staring at, and her fingertips touched his fingers briefly.

The contact of their hands was casual in the extreme, or was meant to give that impression to any other person in the foyer who might have noticed it. But to Armand it was as if a live electric wire had brushed across his hand and sent a current of thousands of volts coursing through his body. His loins jerked convulsively against Madeleine's bottom and he gave an almost inaudible sigh of astonishment, his mouth close to her ear. She moved a little away from him and half turned, to look into his eyes while she thanked him for holding her wrap. There was a half-smile on her face that let him know that she had been aware of what was stiffening rapidly inside his trousers when he jerked against her.

And, unless Armand was being deceived by false and eager hope in the subdued lighting of the foyer, there was an expression in virtuous Madeleine's velvet brown eyes that indicated her willingness to let him press his baton against her on some future occasion, when it was at full stretch. To clinch matters, in case he thought that perhaps the champagne was causing him to read too much significance into a harmless and accidental contact of her bottom against him, she touched his upright part.

That is to say, she moved the hand that was hidden inside her long green wrap until the back of it pressed against him. And more that that – when she saw the look of intense pleasure that flitted over his face, she turned her hand under the all-concealing wrap and squeezed his adjunct between her fingers for an instant, before she turned away from him. After that there could be no mistaking her intent: she was extending to Armand a friendly invitation to demonstrate to her, on some suitably private occasion, his abilities as a lover.

All this – from the moment when Armand held up the fur-collared wrap for her to the moment when she moved away from him to take her husband's arm – lasted no more than three seconds by the clock. For the friends standing around them, putting on their coats, there was nothing whatsoever to see or take note of. Yet for Armand it was as if he had conducted a long, delightful and illicit courtship of Pierre-Louis' wife, with all the usual kisses, declarations of love, warm embraces, avowals of passion, touches of delirious pleasure. All of which culminated in the sure and over-whelming knowledge that the utterly, devotedly and remarkably faithful Madeleine was, after eight years of marriage to Pierre-Louis, his for the taking.

What could have brought about this astounding change of attitude on her part was totally beyond his conjecture, though the exciting possibilities that it offered were well within the reach of his imagination. From the very first time he had ever seen her, when she became Pierre-Louis' fiancée, he had been conscious of her subtle aura of sexuality. After the marriage, and through the years since, he had observed this indefinable quality of hers grow more and more powerful, as if she were a beautiful fruit ripening in the hot sunshine of Pierre-Louis' marital attentions. All that was required now was to stretch out his hand!

It is of course well known that love never exists without secrets – the delicious little secrets that draw lovers even closer together and which must be preserved from the knowledge of any other person. In the three seconds of their remarkable silent courtship in a nightclub foyer, a tremendous love-secret had come into existence between Armand and Madeleine – a secret that would have not only dismayed her husband but would have amazed all the others present, even cynical Vincent, who for years had been hinting to Madeleine, without receiving the least encouragement, that he was the man for her.

Though he could hardly be aware of it himself, there was a slightly dazed expression on Armand's face and his hands were trembling as he helped blonde Dominique into her black evening coat. With goodbyes said all round, cheeks kissed and hands shaken, he got into a taxi with her and gave the driver the address of her apartment. His mind was still whirling with the secret of Madeleine's gesture while the taxi drove through almost empty streets, and it was more from habit than desire that he put an arm round Dominique's shoulders and held her close while he kissed her. She lay against him contentedly while he unbuttoned her soft black cashmere coat and slipped his hand inside to fondle her breasts.

Dominique was a fuller-bosomed woman than Madeleine; she had, so to speak, a pair of juicy Charenton melons under her frock, rather than Madeleine's sweet pomegranates. In consequence, Armand's desire to feel her bare flesh was frustrated, as so often before, by the deep brassière she wore to support her bounty. He abandoned the attempt on her breasts until such time as he could strip her naked, and instead put his hand up her frock to stroke her thigh above her gartered stocking-top. The skin was so smooth and soft to the touch that his pointer, stiff since Madeleine had pinched it between her fingers through her wrap, bounded inside his trousers. He slid his hand higher up Dominique's thigh, into the lace-edged open leg of her silk knickers.

'But what an impatient man you are!' Dominique whispered.

Needless to say, she was not complaining about what he was doing to her, for she moved her knees apart a little to be sure that his fingers could more easily reach the curly-haired folds of soft flesh between her warm thighs.

'You excite me too much, Dominique,' he murmured. 'I can't wait. An hour ago in the club, when I saw you dancing with Vincent, my blood almost boiled. I was half out of my chair when he brought you back to the table.'

'And what did you have in mind?' she asked softly.

'It was in my mind to knock him down and drag you out into the street to make love in the nearest dark doorway.'

Dominique's gloved hand rested lightly on his thigh. She chuckled a little at his words and trailed her fingertips along the hard swelling in his trousers.

'You really *are* excited, *chéri*!' she exclaimed softly. 'Is it because you saw Vincent trying to stroke my bottom?'

Dominique was not being entirely straightforward in the way she put her question. Vincent had not merely tried to stroke her bottom on the dance-floor, he had succeeded in full measure. He had felt her fleshy cheeks through her frock and knickers so very thoroughly that their curves, size and texture and the deep crease between them would be imprinted permanently on his memory. She had made not the least effort to discourage him, for the best of all reasons. She was a sensual woman who enjoyed having her bottom stroked, but apart from that, Vincent was a good-looking man with a more than adequate income and not overly devoted to his wife, as his actions had shown.

He was, in fact, the type of admirer Dominique liked to have about her in good numbers, so that she was never without someone pleasing she could call upon to take her out to dinner or take her to the theatre or take her dancing or take her to bed. In her private scheme of things, Armand fitted into the same category as Vincent, with the added attraction that Armand had no wife to distract his attentions,

'When I saw him fumbling at you I was on the point of exploding with jealousy,' said Armand, though he was speaking to convince himself as much as Dominique.' There was nothing for it but to take you instantly back on to the dance-floor and feel your gorgeous bottom myself – to wipe away the memory of his perfidy. And as you can feel, I have been desperately excited ever since.'

His answer was as lacking in frankness as her question had been. True, he had stroked Dominique's bottom a little when they had danced together, but the sensation had been mildly pleasing rather than furiously arousing. His present state of high excitement was due entirely to his brief and entirely unexpected little episode with Madeleine.

'But I am flattered, my dear,' said Dominique.

She chuckled again as she eased open the buttons of his trousers and slid her gloved hand inside to take hold of him. Armand trembled at the touch of soft kidskin against his hot flesh. On leaving the club he had hung his long white silk evening scarf round his neck but he had not troubled to put on his overcoat. It lay folded across his lap, concealing the slow movement of Dominique's hand inside his open trousers. It was her turn to sigh in pleasure when his fingers fluttered inside her warm little alcove and she tugged his pommel right out of his trousers, so that she could clasp its length in her palm.

Naturally, though Dominique derived as much enjoyment from arousing Armand as he did from arousing her, she was careful not to let their play go just that little bit too far. Not from any misplaced motives of decency or modesty, of course, for she was possessed of no more decency and even less modesty than Armand. But she did not intend to allow his physical tension to release itself until the stiff part she was caressing was warmly ensconced in the proper place for it – between her legs. And that would be when they reached her bedroom and she could spread herself comfortably on her back.

She heard Armand's fast little intake of breath as his pangs of delight increased in intensity, and immediately she let go of him. She brought her hand up to his face and ran a gloved fingertip along his black pencil-line moustache and then stroked his cheek while she kissed him to stifle his soft moan of disappointment at being abandoned high and dry. Her mouth was open against his and her wet tongue flicked at his lips.

Under the caress of his fingers in her slippery little opening, she too had advanced far up the slope of pleasure. And in turn, Armand refused to permit her to reach the peak at the top of her slope, close as she was to it. With only a few more movements of the hand inside her knickers he knew he could precipitate her crisis – her hot tongue reached into his mouth in a silent and yet urgent plea to complete her pleasure – but his fingers ceased to flicker over her secret bud.

He did not remove his hand from between her legs, as she had removed her hand from him. He left it where it was, but motionless, not permitting her tension to disperse itself in the least, but also not letting it rise any higher. 'Torturer!' she gasped into his open mouth, her fleshy thighs clamping tight on his hand, to urge him to resume his play. But she knew very well that he would do no such thing for a while, for this was a game they had played with each other many times before. They played it together in taxis driving about Paris by night, in the darkness of theatres and cinemas, in boxes at the Opera and at orchestral concerts.

They had tantalised each other to the very brink of climactic explosions while listening to the music of Poulenc and Honegger, to name but two, and while watching a variety of modern dramas on the stage, and newly-released films at the cinema on the Champs-Elysees. The trick was to stop dead two seconds before the crisis so that the victim was left frantic with unresolved desire. And then, after the soaring emotional temperature had cooled down a little, usually the victim would seize the opportunity to retaliate, but sometimes the aggressor would resume the finger-play.

It happened at times that either he or she misjudged the other's condition and stopped just a second or so too late. This had brought about some memorable convulsions, as when Dominique at the ballet had shrieked in the sudden ecstasy that Armand had unwittingly induced during a performance of *Scheherezade*, at the very height of the colourful whirlings on stage. And there was an occasion when Armand had been carried right over the edge by a moment or two of excessive stimulation and had delivered his rapture into the palm of Dominique's hand during a much-admired film of Jean Renoir.

A glance through the taxi window showed Dominique that they were almost at their destination. Nevertheless, it was her turn to retaliate, and more than that, it was a matter of pride to take her revenge on Armand. She slid her hand back under the folded overcoat across his lap, where his fore-limb thrust upwards out of his open trousers. Instead of raising his expectations once more by the mundane clasp of her gloved hand, in a moment of inspiration she took one end of the long white silk scarf draped round his neck and wrapped it quickly about his quivering pride.

'Oh, oh, what are you doing, Dominique?' he gasped at once.

'Wouldn't you like to know,' she whispered into his ear, her fingertips rubbing him through the silk of the scarf.

She kissed him again and a strand of her blonde hair fell forward across his face. The soft touch of it against his cheek imparted one more deliciously excruciating twist to Armand's tightly-strung nerves and brought him within a heart-beat of a total loss of control. In his soaring arousal he tried to turn his hand between her thighs to get it free, so that he could tease her bud again. But Dominique held her legs very tightly together, preventing him from reaching her vulnerable spot, while she tormented him with delicate cruelty through the silk of his own scarf.

'Oh, yes – I'm sure you'd love to,' she murmured fiercely, 'but I'm not going let you, not even if you beg me!'

But even as she said the words, she was afraid that she had let him go too far. His back went rigid against the taxi seat, his legs jerked straight out in front of him, and Dominique expected to feel the wet surge of his passion through the thin scarf and her fine kid glove. And at that very moment the taxi swooped into the kerb and braked noisily to a stop that almost threw them to the floor, while the driver announced in a surly voice that they had arrived.

Poor Armand had very nearly arrived at another destination – but not quite. Dominique's hand was gone from him, her thighs had released their grip and she pushed his hand away from her as he sat up, drawing in deep breaths in a supreme effort to calm himself. There was no opportunity to button his trousers over his wildly shuddering stalk: the driver had turned to stare at him while he told him the fare. Armand was compelled to get out of the taxi very awkwardly, his overcoat folded over his arm in an attempt to conceal his embarrassment. He paid the driver one handed, while Dominique stood on the pavement and grinned at his discomposure and her own victory.

The concierge was long ago in bed and Dominique's apartment was on the first floor. She pressed the switch that put on the electric light and she and Armand went up the stairs side by side. He was breathing as heavily as if he were climbing a mountain rather than a flight of stairs, and his free arm was about her, his fingers trying with feverish persistence to grip the flesh of her waist through her clothes. She took quick advantage of his condition to slip her hand down between his body and the folded overcoat hanging from his bent arm as concealment, until she touched his exposed part and took hold of it. She chuckled at its furious jump in her gloved hand.

15

'I won that bout, my friend,' she said, giving him a long and cheerful squeeze. 'You were so close to the edge that two more strokes of my hand would have finished you.'

'No!' Armand gasped, his face pink with emotion.

'But yes!' she retorted. 'Even now it wouldn't take much.'

'Dominique . . . no!'

In the euphoria of the moment, she completely misunderstood the significance of his exclamation. She took it as a simple denial of her claim to victory, instead of the emergency warning it really was. She gripped Armand's equipment tightly, to prevent any unwanted accidents before she could get him into her apartment and lie down with her legs apart to enjoy the culmination of what she had started in the taxi, but as she was about to discover, the situation was not as she believed. Side by side they climbed three more steps to the half-landing, where the stairs turned, and it was then that Armand's raging passions became too strong to be contained for even another minute.

He pulled away from Dominique's gripping fingers and, before she was able to form any idea of what he intended, seized her by the shoulders. He whirled her round to face away from him and pushed her violently towards the banister, so that for a moment she thought that his mind had become deranged and that he was going to hurl her over.

'Quick, quick,' he was moaning. 'Help me, _chérie_!'

She was too alarmed to hear his words properly, let alone make sense of them. In his desperate condition Armand had set in train events too urgent – and perhaps too bizarre – for Dominique to comprehend immediately. She was also off-balance and reached forward anxiously with both hands to grasp the wooden railings and save herself from falling – and thus unwittingly assumed the ideal position for what Armand wanted to do to her. He flicked her unbuttoned evening coat and flimsy frock up over her back and dragged

16

her loose lilac knickers down her thighs with trembling hands, his breath rasping.

'No!' she exclaimed sharply, understanding at last that she was to be ravaged, not murdered. 'This is ridiculous, Armand. Twelve more steps and we'll be in the apartment.'

He had bared the soft pear-shaped cheeks of that marvellous bottom of hers – so realising the ambition of every man who had danced with her that evening – but his emotions were too fraught for him to fondle them. He merely thumped himself against her naked delights so strongly that her fear of being pitched head-first over the banister became acute. One of her high-heeled shoes had been twisted half-off when he whirled her in front of him and she tottered unsteadily, feeling her ankle giving way. She lifted her foot off the floor to get rid of the shoe altogether, and Armand immediately forced her legs apart and got his hands between them.

'This is a stupid game, I don't like it,' she said in high dudgeon, trying to glare at him over her shoulder.

She held on tightly to the banister with one hand, while with the other she reached behind her to try to get hold of her knickers and pull them up again. But matters had gone too far by then for any effective protection against Armand's urgent desires: her knickers were round her knees, her darling commodity fully exposed to whatever violation was burning in his mind, and his feet between hers prevented her from closing her legs.

She gasped to feel his joined thumbs abruptly split the fleshy peach he had uncovered, and again to feel the quivering touch of his hard spindle against her inner thigh. She tried to drag herself forward, away from him, but by then he had an arm round her waist and his hand down between her legs from the front to hold her open. 'No Armand!' she protested, as she felt him slide up inside her with one long hard push.

'This is ridiculous,' she repeated with asperity, 'stop it at once!'

Ridiculous indeed – and inappropriately timed – this

uninvited insertion may have seemed to her, but to Armand it was a matter of life and death. Her little game in the taxi with the silk scarf had aroused him to the verge of frenzy and her tight grasp as they climbed the stairs had sent his deepest emotions plunging completely out of control. The act of sliding into her warm and velvet depths was enough in itself to bring on his crisis. At the very moment of her protest against his entrance, while his fingers were still hooked into her to prise her open and without so much as a single thrust of his loins, he flooded her with his passion.

'I don't believe it!' she exclaimed indignantly, while he jerked against her bare bottom in the after-throes of ecstasy.

'Je t'adore, je t'adore . . .' he was murmuring in content.

Although her natural first reaction to the onslaught had been shock and outrage, Dominique was a woman who much enjoyed playing sensual games, particularly with Armand, whose own zest for such diversions was equal to her own. And now that the hurricane had blown itself out, she bore him no grudge, in fact she was amused by the results of her little trick with the scarf. And apart from that Armand's spontaneous and tremendous discharge had been undeniably impressive. She knew few women who could precipitate so tumultuous a response from their men-friends. And when Armand's hands stroked her bare belly, her own temporarily suppressed excitement started to mount again.

The electric time-switch installed by a thrifty landlord to save himself money turned off the light and suddenly it became very dark on the stairs. So much the better, thought Dominique; at least anyone coming home late would not see her with her underwear round her knees and Armand's spike in her from the rear! She pulled away from the intrusive item in question and turned around inside Armand's encircling arms to press herself warmly against him.

18

'Dominique, you are superb,' he whispered gratefully.

She put a hand on the back of his neck to pull his head down so that she could kiss him. Her other hand was holding his wet handle, to let him know that she had forgiven his impetuosity. He felt up the back of her frock and clasped the flawless cheeks of her bottom, as if in homage, a satisfied worshipper at the shrine on which he had made his offering. Dominique's kiss became more demanding, but did not immediately elicit the response she desired: it seemed that Armand was content to stay on the stairs for the rest of the night! But Dominique's need for solace was growing rapidly and she wanted to get her clothes off and be adored properly.

'I knew I'd won the bout,' she said, her tone affectionate. 'There was no need to rape me on the stairs to prove it. Are you calm enough to get the rest of the way to my apartment?'

But she was wrong to believe herself the victor of this evening's little game. It was impossible for her to know it, of course, but what had really set Armand's passions aflame and deprived him of his senses was the love-secret that had established itself between him and Madeleine. The touch of Dominique's fingers in the taxi had been no more significant than the last ripple on the surface of an river in spate that causes it to burst its banks and flood the countryside.

Armand's hard plunge into Dominique's warm flesh and his instantaneous paroxysm of delight was not the hot-blooded compliment to her irresistible charms that she believed. The truth was that in the delirium that had taken possession of his faculties, he had been completely insensible of the fact that it was her body he was making use of. At that moment he thought that he was delivering his frenzied tribute to the woman he desired most in all the world – Madeleine.

Such moments of total madness are rare. For the tranquillity of society in general, perhaps it is as well. A little later, in bed, Armand was very conscious that it was Dominique to whom he was making love. She was very desirable, of course, lying naked on her back while his tongue teased the prominent buds of her breasts and her hands roved caressingly across his back. The bedside lamp was off and, though the curtains were open, the room was very dark. Even so, no light at all was required for Armand to be sadly aware that the belly he was kissing was not Madeleine's, and the plump wet mound where his fingers were dabbling – that too was not Madeleine's.

The hand that reached for his stanchion, with all the familiarity of well-established acquaintance, was not the same hand that had squeezed it for an instant through his trousers in the foyer of *Les Acacias*. If only it were! His emotions were so overwrought that he believed that he would have discharged his rapture into that hand the moment it took hold of him! 'It's so hard!' Dominique exclaimed, stroking him vigorously, and Armand gave a silent little sigh of regret that it was not Madeleine tugging at him to lie between her parted legs.

Naturally, his equipment was ready to perform its pleasurable duty, for what man's would not be, in bed with Dominique naked? He mounted her quickly, his belly on hers, and slid into her warm and welcoming receptacle. But it was with Madeleine that his raging fantasy concerned itself while he rode rapidly up and down. He imagined that Madeleine's long legs were crossed over his back and Madeleine's heels were kicking in delight against his jerking bottom. The breasts squashed under his chest were Madeleine's, he persuaded himself, the hot mouth clinging to his mouth was Madeleine's.

When his moment of crisis arrived, he fantasised that it was into Madeleine's soft belly that he was pouring his ecstasy, and that the marvellous little cries and moans of gratification he heard were Madeleine's. Yet for all that, in spite of the climactic release he had enjoyed, when eventually he eased himself off Dominique and lay beside her to hold her in his arms, he experienced a feeling of vague disappointment.

'That was *very* nice, Armand,' Dominique said in a contented tone, almost like a kitten rubbing its furry head against him.

To be sure, she suspected nothing of the love-secret for which he pretended to himself, even during those most intimate moments when he was penetrating her, that it was not her but another woman he was enjoying. It could even be said, with truth, that Dominique derived a considerable benefit from the secret that was overshadowing Armand's enjoyment of her sumptuous body. She had hardly recovered from their first bout before his stem was stirring again in her hand, his lips were hot on her breasts and his fingers between her thighs. Indeed, the power of his fantasy stirred him to great endeavours that night and Dominique was the grateful recipient of his false and deceptive passion twice more before he let her go to sleep.

After this intense and repeated gratification, her sleep was profound, but sometime during the night she felt herself being dragged back to reluctant consciousness by an insistent movement between her legs. Her eyes blinked open for a moment. The room was still dark. She was lying on her back, her legs apart, and the covers had been thrown aside to expose her naked body completely. She brushed her hand over her belly to flick away whatever it was that was disturbing her rest – and she touched a head. It was Armand, of course, crouching between her legs his tongue thrust deep inside her well-used recess.

'But what are you doing?' she asked in a voice blurred by sleep.

'Making you wet, *chérie*,' he answered, pausing in his task.

'No – no more, Armand. I am too tired.'

'Just once more,' he murmured. 'I'll be quick, Dominique.'

'Not now,' she said drowsily, pushing at his head to make him stop. 'Go to sleep and leave me alone.'

'I *was* asleep, but I dreamed we were making love. You were wearing a long white satin night-gown with a long slit over your belly for me to put my hand through and feel you. And just as I was climbing on to you, I woke up tremendously excited.'

'Mm,' she sighed, sliding back into sleep now that his tongue was no longer troubling her most sensitive spot.

Naturally, Armand was not telling the truth. His dream had been of Madeleine, and it was her soft little belly he had dreamed he was feeling through the long slit in her white garment. And in spite of the repeated satisfactions he had taken with Dominique before they both fell asleep, the dream had been so vivid that he awoke with his unruly limb straining for immediate relief and rubbing itself against the satin bed-sheet. As the shreds of his dream vanished, Armand guessed with an inner laugh that if he had not woken up when he did, his determined part would have jerked against the smooth sheet until it poured out its passion.

It was impossible not to take it in his hand and console it a little, but it refused to be comforted and made it very apparent to him that nothing short of a full outpouring of its desire would calm it sufficiently to permit him to go back to sleep. And though Madeleine was not available, beautiful Dominique lay naked on her back beside him, though oblivious of his need. To rouse her was to invite at least the possibility of a refusal; it seemed the better course to uncover her very gently and prepare her to be penetrated before she knew what was going on.

That she had woken up and categorically refused his attentions counted for nothing to a man in Armand's condition. He waited until a tiny half-snore advised him that she was again asleep, and poised himself on hands and knees high above her naked body. Slowly, oh so slowly, hardly a centimetre at a time, he lowered his loins until the tip of his baton lightly touched the thin thatch between her thighs. He moved a fraction and felt it touch the lips he had made wet and slippery with his tongue, and she stirred a little in her sleep and muttered something unintelligible.

With the utmost caution, he eased himself forward just enough to be certain that he was precisely positioned at the mouth of her entrance. The contact with her warm flesh had started his impatient object twitching and the movement caused Dominique to stir again, and oh, disaster! Armand felt her begin to turn on to her side to get away from what was disturbing her. At once he drove straight into her velvet depths and, still balanced on hands and knees so that no other part of his body touched her, flicked in and out at break-neck speed.

'*Mmf*!' she spluttered, waking with a start, 'What?'

By then the deed was done – Armand's passion surged into her belly and, before she was conscious enough to identify the sensations that had dragged her from sleep, he had finished and pulled out and was lying beside her, trembling happily in the after-glow of his gratification.

'Armand,' she said, her hand shaking his bare shoulder, 'I had such a strange dream. What did you do to me?'

'There, there,' he soothed her, taking her in his arms, 'it's all right. Go back to sleep, *chérie*.'

His satisfied part soon lost its stiffness and he fell asleep cuddling Dominique to him. But even after his stolen nocturnal bliss, he was aroused from his dreams soon after daybreak by the long contact of her warm, bare bottom against him. And moments later Dominique, now well-rested and more receptive, was half-awakened most pleasantly by the sensation of her plump cheeks being fondled. She was on her side, with her knees drawn up and her back to the perpetrator, and in her half-dream she neither knew nor cared who was causing her these delightful thrills.

She lay still, drowsily enjoying what he was doing, and in due course she felt gentle fingers probing the fleshy petals between her thighs in the most delicate manner imaginable. A tiny sigh escaped her lips as the questing fingers touched her secret rosebud and ascertained that it was moist and ready. In another moment a hand under her thigh raised it and the fingers opened her wide for something thicker and longer to insinuate itself slowly up into her. She murmured, 'That's so nice,' when she felt arms round her and hands playing with her soft melons.

By now she had reached a sufficient level of consciousness to remember that it was Armand who was sleeping with her that night and she pushed her bare bottom against him to help him in deeper. The tip of his wet tongue was in her ear while he bounced lightly to and fro against her luxurious cheeks until he and she reached their climactic moments together. Dominique had not opened her eyes during this little early morning episode. She lay passive throughout, quivering to the adorable sensations. As soon as her thrills faded she went back to sleep – even before Armand had withdrawn from her.

Of course, if she had been able to guess the thoughts in his mind while he was pleasuring her – the fantasy behind his closed eyelids that he was embedded in Madeleine – Dominique would have been furious, she would have screamed at him to get out of her apartment, pushed him naked down the stairs and thrown his clothes over the banister after him. But happily for her, his secret remained unsuspected. Dominique slept on calmly until midday, her blonde hair across her forehead and one round and crimson-tipped breast fully exposed by the way the rumpled sheets were disposed and by her scorn for night attire.

But to her surprise, when she at last woke up, Armand was not alongside her in the warm bed, to kiss her and murmur, *'Bonjour, ma chérie,'* as he always had on past occasions when he had stayed with her. She rang for her maid to bring her breakfast coffee, and was astonished to hear that she had seen him going very quietly out of the apartment door at eight that morning! The maid set the tray across Dominique's lap and made herself busy about the room, picking up the short tangerine evening frock, the silk stockings and the crumpled lilac knickers that lay strewn on the carpet from the night before's hasty undressing.

Propped up comfortably on her pillows, Dominique sipped her coffee, a hand down inside the bed to rest between her thighs in fond reminiscence of the pleasures of the night and of the dawn.

I wonder why Armand got up and left so very early, she was thinking. *He couldn't keep his hands off me last night – I think he even had me in my sleep, unless it was a dream. I'm sure he's fallen in love with me.*

2

The Ambiguity of Surrender

When a woman, and especially a married woman, looks at a man with a certain expression in her eyes, he understands that she has decided to accept him as her lover. The intimate delights of her body are to be made available to him and, in return, he is expected to make her feel adored and cherished – in addition to being pleasured. To Armand this seemed obvious and straightforward enough when Madeleine looked at him in that way, but to transform the unspoken promise into the delicious reality of naked little breasts to be kissed and long slender thighs parted for his triumphant entry – this proved to be complicated and frustrating.

The first time that he tried to telephone her to arrange a meeting, her husband Pierre-Louis answered, and it was necessary to invent some more or less convincing reason why Armand wanted to speak to him. At the second attempt, later that day, the maid answered the telephone and informed Armand that Madame Beauvais was out. Armand thought it prudent not to leave his name, in case the maid delivered the message to the husband instead of the wife.

When he tried again the next day, he was at long last successful in speaking to Madeleine. But to his consternation, the tone of her voice was as cool as if her deep brown eyes had never looked at him with a secret offer of delightful surrender shining in them, or as if the back of her hand had not brushed lightly across the front of his trousers when no one was watching. For Armand, in his dismay, it was necessary to proceed most warily. He suggested that they might meet for a drink in some pleasant spot when she was out shopping, or perhaps even lunch, if she had the time.

To a man whose desire was so intense that he had left another woman's bed for her – with no intention of ever going back – these suggestions were ridiculously inadequate and unsatisfactory. But it was all too obvious that Madeleine had reconsidered, in the light of day, some implications of her actions in the nightclub foyer. Perhaps a little too much champagne had made her normal defences collapse and permitted him to see the forbidden desire concealed in her heart. And yet, thought Armand, of all the men she knew, it was he who had been given that brief glimpse of what lay behind the veil of conventionality.

That notwithstanding, he had the distinct impression from Madeleine's tone that to pursue matters at present would be to meet a vigorous and perhaps final rebuff. It would be far more productive to let matters take their own course, let her feel that his devotion was permanent but not obtrusive, and wait in hope that before too long her curiosity – to say nothing of the secret desire she had let him catch sight of – would overrule her scruples and bring her into his arms.

But however deferential his approach, it made no difference at all. Madeleine said that she was too busy for even the briefest of meetings with him and there was something in her voice – a certain remoteness – that suggested that she could think of no reason in the world why he had telephoned her with these inappropriate invitations. Virtue and fidelity, it seemed, had reasserted themselves very powerfully in her heart. It was with a feeling of disappointment that Armand put down the telephone. His self-esteem had been as thoroughly deflated as the part of him that had risen unrequested when he lifted the telephone to speak to her.

It is a commonplace to say that women are well known for changing their minds. Only two days after her disheartening response to Armand's approach, she telephoned him at nine in the morning to say there was something important she would like to consult him about. The chilling remoteness was entirely absent from her voice this time, she spoke warmly and as a friend. Indeed, there was a certain unmistakable quality in her voice and words that hinted at something beyond friendship. It was the equivalent of the expression in her eyes that had said to him, *Yes, you can have me*. As soon as he heard it, Armand was sure what she wished to consult him about.

She arranged to come to his apartment in the rue de Turbigo at three that afternoon and, for both of them, it was a day that changed the course of their lives. While he was waiting for her in a fever of impatience, Armand felt that a great benediction was about to be bestowed upon him – and such is male pride that he believed he thoroughly deserved it. He was, after all, the most charming and accomplished lover that he knew. And this was confirmed yet again by the fact that Madeleine had chosen *him* after rebuffing so many would-be lovers during her eight years of marriage to Pierre-Louis.

Only an extremely vain man – and of a romantic disposition – could entertain such thoughts, of course. That Armand did so is a testimony not only to his conceit but also to the unusual attraction that Madeleine exercised over men. After all, Armand had not reached the age of thirty unmarried without enjoying the intimacies of enough women to know that, brunette or blonde, well-fleshed or slender, with melons or pomegranates, passive or boisterous in bed, women are made to the same basic design all over the world, for so has a wise and benevolent Providence arranged matters for the delectation of men.

And men too, give or take a few centimetres here and there, are also constructed to a common pattern. From this it follows that the number of ways in which men and women are capable of giving each other pleasure with their bodies is limited. The impossible *Kama Sutra* and other books of Eastern gymnastics may catalogue the details of sixty-four different ways and give them poetic names, but the majority of Europeans are content with half a dozen at most, and some unimaginative people with just one, and that the most obvious of all.

Suffice it to say, that elusive and least well-defined of all the emotions – *love* – which can elevate the most ordinary physical transaction between men and women into a truly divine experience, is not concerned with the agility of lovers. Nor is it dependent on appearances, for beautiful women often take ugly men as their lovers, and handsome young men can be found anywhere who are ecstatically devoted to extremely plain women. And as for character, that has nothing to do with it, for everyone knows instances of good-hearted men or women involving themselves to insanity with partners of poor repute.

Not that love, as such, figured at all prominently in Armand's thoughts while he was waiting for Madeleine to arrive. Burning desire, of course; ecstatic pleasure, ah yes; immense gratification – again and again! But after that, who could say what might develop? In Armand's philosophy it was best to enjoy the passing moment without troubling about what might follow; such matters had a way of arranging themselves, he had found. There were times when he had fallen passionately in love with whichever young woman he was interested in just then and to be in love had made him deliriously happy – once for as long as six months.

He lunched early in one of the little restaurants he used regularly near his apartment: a light meal and no more than half a bottle of good Burgundy, and just a little cognac with his coffee. Back in his apartment, he stripped and showered, using expensive toilet soap that left a faint and pleasant trace of its perfume all over his body. His implement started to twitch in his hand when he covered it in creamy white soap-suds and though he tried to direct his attention elsewhere, it grew long and stiff until it stood upright under the warm water cascading down from the shower-head.

'Not yet, you idiot,' he addressed his rearing part. 'You must be patient for another half-hour. Lie down again and sleep until Madeleine arrives – you will need all your energy then. I promise you complete freedom to do whatever you want to her.'

Far from calming his wilful companion, the promise only made things worse – it jerked up and down under the spray, its red-purple head unhooded and swollen with pride.

'No, no, no – I utterly refuse to give in to you! You must wait!' Armand exclaimed, outraged by the thought that had insinuated itself slyly into his head.

To demonstrate beyond the possibility of argument who was the master, he reached for the shower control, gritted his teeth and twisted it hard, bringing an agonising deluge of ice-cold water down on his impudent mutineer. He stood it for as long as necessary – perhaps half a minute – until all rebellion was quelled and what had been rearing its head as high as his belly-button now dangled shrunk and defeated, before he turned the water off and dried himself.

He dressed with great care, aiming at presenting himself as debonair and dashing, elegant and yet not too formal. In addition to making the right impression on Madeleine, he wanted clothes that he could take off quickly and with minimum fuss – few things make a woman more impatient than waiting naked, excited by kisses and caresses, while her lover struggles with shirt-buttons or shoe-laces. Armand put on a pair of pale green and white striped silk shorts, and looked right through his wardrobe before making up his mind. His eventual choice was an ivory-coloured silk shirt, with *café-au-lait* trousers and a beautifully-cut single-breasted mohair jacket in tobacco-brown.

He chose a tie and a handkerchief to match for his breast-pocket, stood in front of the long mirror in his bedroom and studied the result. He was pleased with his appearance. His pencil-line black moustache was neatly trimmed and added a certain distinction to his upper lip, his hair arranged itself in curls round his temples and the back of his neck, curls that many a woman had found irresistible and had entwined her fingers in while he kissed her – all too often fingers which bore another man's gold wedding-ring in addition to the usual diamonds.

Women are not expected to be on time, and only a complete idiot would look for punctuality from a desirable young woman making her way to a man's apartment for a rendezvous of love. To arrive at the appointed hour would be to admit to him that her passions were as strong as his – perhaps even stronger – to confess without words that she was on fire to feel his mouth on hers and his hands on her breasts. All this may very well be true, but no woman of the world would put such power over herself into a lover's hands.

Self-esteem, to say nothing of an outward show of imaginary modesty, requires that a woman comes late to a meeting with her lover. By this means she tries to convey the impression that she is there not for any pleasure of her own but that, in her generosity of heart, she is bestowing a great favour on the importunate man by condescending to meet him in private. Understanding this, Armand was not in the least surprised when Madeleine arrived a quarter of an hour late. The autumn weather was not cold, but she wore a superb full-length silver-fox coat and a little black cloche hat with a diamanté clip pinned to it above one ear.

Perhaps after all there was a cold little breeze along the pavement of the rue de Turbigo, for Madeleine's cheeks were flushed a charming pink. And again, it may have had nothing to do with the autumn weather, but have been an indication of the hidden fire in her heart. Armand hurried through the greetings as quickly as good manners would permit, his impatience worse than ever now that she was actually in his apartment. He kissed her gloved hands one after the other and then, when she took her gloves off, he kissed both hands again, this time on the soft palm and then on the inside of her wrists, where the fragrance of her delightful perfume almost made his head swirl.

31

He stood behind her to help her out of her beautiful fur coat and before he had time to hang it up, she turned and pressed her body against him, put her arms about his neck and kissed him warmly. He had the bulky coat over one arm and could use only one hand to caress her back through her clothes. But when, her mouth still clinging to his, she unwound an arm from his neck and felt down between their bodies until she was touching the long hard bulge in his trousers, he let the fur coat fall to the floor and employed both hands to knead the graceful cheeks of her bottom.

Less than two minutes later they were in the bedroom and she allowed him to enjoy the enormous pleasure of undressing her. Under her silver fox she was wearing an elegant long-sleeved jumper of fine wool, knitted in diagonal stripes of white and black, and a charcoal-coloured skirt that fell in thin pleats to a finger-breadth above her knees. The jumper was pulled in tight round her waist by a broad belt of shiny black patent leather held by an elaborate round gold buckle. She pulled off her cloche hat and threw it and her gloves on to the nearest chair, then held out her arms to Armand in a charming little gesture that meant *I am yours to do as you please with*.

Endowed by a beneficent Providence with long and slender legs, Madeleine was almost as tall as Armand. They stood together by the side of the broad bed, her beautifully coiffed head inclined upwards only a very little to be kissed. He held her oval face between his hands while he showered endless kisses on her full-lipped mouth and on her eyes, on her thinly-plucked dark eyebrows and on her broad and smooth forehead. As may well be imagined, by then the rebel inside his trousers was clamouring silently for the opportunity to do what he did best. But this was not a moment to be hurried and Armand had almost kissed her breathless before his hands touched her breasts, perfectly outlined by the clinging of her jumper.

Ah, that dizzying instant when a lover's hand clasps a soft breast and his breath sighs out through his mouth in wordless appreciation! In Armand's considered view it was astonishing that, while almost every painter who had ever held a brush had taken great pleasure in depicting on canvas his mistress with bare breasts, not many poets had celebrated in verse the joys of feeling a woman's warm globes. One exception was Verlaine's memorable poem, *Foursome*:

Breasts where hands gorge themselves with pleasure,
Heavy breasts, powerful, proud and teasing,
Rolling and swaying, and knowing they've beaten us,
With a sideways loving look at our subjection.

But Verlaine was a special case and apart from him, the lack of interest in breasts by poets could be regarded as little short of disgraceful.

When Armand's gentle fingers had learned to his satisfaction the shape of Madeleine's succulent pome-granates and she was leaning against him with knees that trembled a little, he reached for the buckle of her belt and explored it for a second or two before finding the secret of the clasp. He undid it and let the belt fall to the carpet. But before he could thrust his hand up inside her expensive jumper and perhaps, by the forcefulness of his ardour, pull it out of shape, Made-leine moved a step back from him, crossed her arms and eased it over her head herself. She need not have felt anxious, as it happened, for Armand was very far from being a clumsy beginner in the delicate art of undressing pretty women. But Madeleine had been a faithful wife for eight years and was, if it may be so expressed, out of touch with the niceties of being han-dled by a lover.

Armand unfastened the waist-band of her skirt with skilful fingers and let it slide rustling down her silk-stockinged legs to the bedroom floor. She stepped out of it and got rid of her highly-polished black shoes with casual flicks of her slender ankles, and Armand gave a long sigh of bliss and stared at her in rapt admiration. As well he might, for she too had evidently devoted some thought to what she should wear in order to enchant and impress him on this occasion of incalculable significance. In consequence, the underwear she had chosen for him to see her in was of a simple and yet breathtaking beauty.

In intentional contrast to the black and white severity of her outer clothes, she wore a chemise of delicate carnation-red silk, cut straight across the top to show off the division of her breasts. It had the narrowest of ribbon-straps over her softly-rounded shoulders and was tailored so closely to her body that the points of her breasts could be observed pushing against it and the graceful curve of her belly was perfectly moulded by the silk. On the front of the chemise, adorning the space between the outward-thrusting points, an intricate design of flowers, buds and leaves was hand-embroidered.

'But you are adorable!' Armand whispered.

In spite of all his experience of women and facility with words, for a moment or two he was hardly able to speak coherently for the strength of the emotions unleashed in his heart by the sight of Madeleine in her underwear. She smiled at the few words he murmured and accepted them as a tribute since, for all their banality, they are exactly what every woman expects and demands to hear from her lover.

The prettily stitched hem of her chemise was a hand-breadth below the join of her long thighs, so that a little of her open-legged knickers of matching carnation-red silk could be seen. And while Armand stood lost in unaccustomed reverie, she slipped off her chemise and let him see that the floral design was repeated down the sides of her knickers, from waist to leg. She stretched out her arms to him in welcome and at once he was on his knees at her feet, his lips pressed against the warm flesh of her belly, his arms round her legs and his hands up inside her underwear to hold the satin-skinned cheeks of her well-shaped bottom.

There were no comparisons in his mind at that moment – no balancing of the enchantments of Dominique's soft oval cheeks that he had rubbed himself on so luxuriously in her bed, as against the refinement of Madeleine's taut round cheeks that he held now. Indeed, in his exhilarated frame of mind he had totally forgotten Dominique and could think of no one but Madeleine. With a lover's eye for detail, he noticed that the top edge of her flimsy silk garment was at the level of her belly-button, half hiding it and half showing it, but in any case drawing attention to it.

With a hand trembling slightly from an excess of emotion, he pulled the silk down a centimetre or two to uncover this delight fully. It was, he thought, extremely pretty, being perfectly round and shallow, much like a dimple, and most enticing. He pushed the wet tip of his tongue into it and heard Madeleine's little sigh as her fingers wound themselves into his hair.

Where her thighs met there was a delicate shadow to be seen, where her curls showed faintly through the thin silk. He pressed his mouth to it and drew from her a little exclamation of pleasurable surprise when she felt his hot breath touch her through the fine silk. He eased the knickers over her bottom and down her thighs until he had revealed the walnut-brown curls that adorned her mound. With eager hands he gripped her bare bottom firmly again while he kissed her curls and let the tip of his tongue flit lightly along the soft pink lips beneath the curls.

But thrilling as his actions were, Madeleine was a married woman of twenty-nine and was accustomed to be resting comfortably on her back when her husband paid his respects, not standing upright. She slipped out of Armand's loving grasp and, hobbled as she was by her knickers round her knees, took two tiny steps and sat on the side of his bed to remove them. Then, crossing her legs each way in turn, she took off her black frilled garters and rolled down her silk stockings.

Armand undressed himself quickly while Madeleine watched with interest, posing gracefully with her back propped against the headboard, one arm bent behind her head to display a soft and smooth-shaven little armpit, and one knee slightly raised. She observed his body carefully, his straight shoulders and the black curls on his chest, his narrow waist and long legs. Certainly she took careful note of that cherished part of him with which she was about to become most intimately acquainted.

He glanced down at it in admiration himself, knowing how women were fascinated by its firm uprightness. It was shivering with excitement, much as a finely-trained racehorse prances with short little steps as he comes up to the starting-line, ready for the moment when a flick of his rider's whip will send him hurtling down the course with flying hooves, flat-out to reach and jump the first fence.

Madeleine moved sideways a little when he got on to the bed and lay beside her, perhaps to make room for him, but more probably for the somewhat more interesting purpose of making her elegant breasts jiggle in a manner guaranteed to catch and hold his attention. Verlaine's words about breasts were in his mind – *proud and teasing* – as he put first his lips and then his wet tongue to their prominent russet tips.

On this never-to-be-forgotten first time with Madeleine, he had unwittingly become so stupendously aroused by seeing and caressing her in her luxurious silk underwear, that he knew the time between penetrating her and releasing his essence would be very short. It was therefore greatly to be desired that Madeleine should be at least equally aroused before he slipped his imperious friend into her. He had read somewhere, though he was unable to recollect where, that the average length of time from a man's insertion to his emission is – three minutes!

The same review had also informed him that the average time from being transfixed to the instant of crisis for a woman is, on average – eight minutes! If this imbalance were true on ordinary occasions of love-making – though it was difficult to imagine why Nature permitted this inconvenience – then how much greater the disproportion on this unique occasion! There was not the least possibility that Armand could last for three whole minutes after making his grand entrance into Madeleine's warm burrow.

He played with the tips of her breasts until she was shaking from head to foot and her breath was rasping faintly in her throat, before he took her by the hips and eased her down from the head-board and laid her flat on her back.

'Armand . . . oh, Armand,' he was pleased to hear her murmur, recognising it as a sign of her high state of arousal.

The situation promised well, but to be certain that she would be ready to respond instantly and completely to his climactic episode when it arrived, he slid down the patterned satin bed cover and parted her legs with gentle hands. A moment later he was kissing her warm belly, close to her neat triangle of walnut-brown fleece. Her groin carried the delicate fragrance of the perfume she used, the Chanel he had recognised behind her ears and between her breasts. He was flattered – as what man would not be in his place – to think that Madeleine did not customarily dab perfume between her legs: she had done so that day especially for him, guessing that he would kiss her there.

To intensify her suspense he pressed slow and lingering kisses all the way up the satin-skinned insides of her thighs – to within a centimetre of her curls. He watched her bottom lift off the bed and her legs part wider in anticipation of his kiss on the plump pink lips visible between her curls – and he heard her swift intake of breath as he played his little deception on her: instead of doing what she expected, he held her by the thighs while he slowly trailed his wet tongue up her trembling belly to her dimple of a button. The tip of his tongue explored it for a moment, then he went back to just above her pretty little triangle of curls and licked up her belly again – and repeated the gesture until she was gasping continuously.

Giddy with desire though he was, he knew that he must make an expert judgement of the state of Madeleine's excitement – it would be self-defeating to take her just that fraction too far and precipitate her climax before he was inside her! He left her wet belly and flicked his tongue into her perfumed groin until her legs strained as wide apart as they could go, offering herself to him in total surrender. Now at last Armand boldly kissed the tender object of his desire and almost at once, under his insistent attentions, the soft petals of flesh parted to display her moist pink interior.

'Armand – I'm going to faint!' she gasped, her smooth belly distending and deflating to the rhythms of the overwhelming sensations that his tongue was giving her.

She is ready, he thought feverishly, observing her back and bottom squirm on the bed, her face flushed and her eyes very nearly closed, *Any more and she will do it without me!*

His fingers pressed slowly into the long vermilion slot his tongue had opened while he positioned himself between her legs. She moaned in delight to feel his stalk jerking against her as it probed for the soft entrance to Paradise. Though *jerking* seems an inadequate word to describe the condition of Armand's life-long companion – its head was as swollen and purple as if apoplexy was only an instant away, and it shook as if in a high fever. As soon as it touched the open folds of flesh between Madeleine's thighs it pushed itself deep into her warm wetness, dragging Armand bodily behind, until his belly was flat on hers.

'Ah, ah, ah!' she exclaimed in shrill delirium, her bottom writhing beneath him and her heels drumming on the backs of his thighs. Armand's hands were on her breasts, plucking at their hard buds to urge her to greater heights. He had hoped to remain unaffected by the turmoil of her belly for a little while – just long enough to bring her to the point where she was fully committed and unable to check her responses. But the voluptuous feel of her flesh was more than he could endure and he was moving quickly in her, knowing that in another second or two she would siphon his passion from him.

'Armand, Armand, je t'adore!' she gasped frantically.

All things considered, he had achieved his objective well – Madeleine was in the extremity of climactic arousal. Her back arched off the bed and her crisis arrived before he had been inside her for thirty seconds. The timing might be considered a little short of perfection, Armand thought wildly, but it would do well enough for their first time together. He could feel her belly rise and fall in rythmic waves to his rapid pumping and he passed beyond the bounds of conscious control. An incoherent cry of triumph burst from him as the pressure in his champagne bottle flicked out the cork and his frothing passion gushed into her.

After so ecstatic a celebration of the rites of love, the breathless participants lay hugging each other for a long time, gently content with the touch of their bodies together. But eventually Armand removed himself from his comfortable position above Madeleine and they turned to lie facing each other, holding hands and exchanging calm little kisses. For her an important barrier had been passed – she had allowed a man other than her husband the freedom of her body! This was the moment when regret and self-recrimination might have seized her and turned delight into cold and bitter ashes.

But Armand had played with her so very skilfully that he had guided her up the mountain-side of sensation to a higher pinnacle of pleasure than she had attained before. Her climax had been prodigious – devastating almost – and she could recall nothing approaching it with her husband. In consequence, there were no second thoughts about what she had done – far from it – she was certain that the step she had taken was exactly the right thing to do. She lay very much at her ease, exchanging kisses and murmured endearments with Armand.

It was the most natural thing in the world to take in her hand the instrument that had given her so much pleasure. After its magnificent performance it had relaxed completely and lay soft and warm in her hand, wet with the dew of her own arousal and the torrent it had released.

'So small and helpless,' she whispered, 'yet a little while ago it was strong and masterful.'

Madeleine's experience of male appendages could hardly be described as extensive. Indeed, Armand's was only the third she had held in her hand in the whole of her twenty-nine years. The one she knew best, of course, was that of Pierre-Louis, since it had pleasured her very satisfactorily throughout their marriage until recently. Before she knew Pierre-Louis there had been a boyfriend who relieved her of her virginity when she was eighteen and his was the first stiff appurtenance she had seen or handled. But though her knowledge had been necessarily restricted by her modest way of life, her admiration for these interesting parts was boundless.

At this distance in time she no longer remembered much about her first boyfriend's personal equipment, except that it had introduced her in dramatic fashion to the greatest pleasure in life. Of her husband's implement she was very fond and she had never stopped encouraging him to insert it into her, night after night. Armand's, which had brought her to so fantastic an apex of delight, she regarded as very superior. And needless to say, it responded to her affectionate touch by rearing itself to its full height in her hand.

'The dear chubby thing,' she murmured, her fingers moving up and down its length, 'I believe it wants to do something nice to me again.'

'You may rely on that,' Armand replied. 'Before you leave here it will do very nice things to you several times over. But first I must play with you a little . . .'

His fingers were down between her slender thighs, caressing her with an expert touch. To Armand, a woman's wet little pouch – any woman's, young, middle-aged, blonde, brunette, red-haired or raven-black, capacious, tight, pretty or plain – was utterly irresistible. Merely to touch it brought on a compulsive desire to play with it most thoroughly, to explore to the limit its capacity for sensation, in short, to induce a climax in it. In some strange way he did not understand, Armand never felt that he truly possessed a woman, no matter how many times he penetrated her with his ever-ready spindle, until he had brought her to a full climax with his fingers.

This was the psychological basis of his teasing games in public places with Dominique – and with many another woman. Without doubt, Dr Freud and his coterie of Viennese professors who attribute complicated and secret reasons to everything we do – including the unquenchable desire men and women have to pleasure themselves with each other – would have been interested in an opportunity to interview Armand and explore this little quirk of his. His women friends accepted it without a second thought as no more unusual than other men's little ways in bed.

And beautiful Madeleine with the walnut-brown curls between her legs sighed in delight as his fingers played over her slippery button, believing he was preparing her for another triumphant entry. She turned on to her back and spread her legs widely apart. But still he did not mount her and, under his delicate attentions, her pleasure became so intense that her head rolled from side to side on the soft pillow, her hair charmingly dishevelled. And then her fingernails scrabbled at the bed beneath her.

'Yes – I'm ready, Armand!' she gasped.

'Oh, yes,' he agreed. 'You are certainly ready, *chérie* – magnificently ready. But make haste slowly, as they say – take a little time to enjoy the sensations you are feeling.'

'Armand – I must have you now!' she exclaimed urgently.

'And so you shall, dearest Madeleine, you shall have me inside you many, many times,' he answered, making not the least attempt to lie on her belly and satisfy her desires in the way she was expecting. His fingers fluttered between the long wet lips under her brown curls.

41

'Ah, ah,' she exclaimed, staring up at his smiling face incredulously as her shuddering legs strained outwards to the limit and spasms shook her belly.

'But what are you doing to me?' she gasped in wide-eyed surprise as his intentions became apparent to her. 'Ah, you are shameless!'

He paid no attention to her words, or her little cries, her gasps and moans. His fingers maintained their tender caress and she passed beyond words and made gurgling sounds as she twitched and squirmed, frantic for release from the overwhelming stimulation.

At the first delicious throb of her climax he exclaimed, 'Now Madeleine! Now, now, now!' Her shriek was piercing and her muscles tensed so rigidly that her body was lifted off the bed – bottom, back and shoulders – until she was balanced on her head and heels. For five endless seconds she remained locked in a rigid curve, her cry shrilling in Armand's ears, then she collapsed weakly and lay gasping and shuddering, her legs slowly drawing together until she was still again. Her beautiful brown eyes opened slowly and she stared up into Armand's face.

'Why did you do that to me?' she asked curiously.

'To amuse you in a different sort of way,' he said, less than truthfully, for it had been his own gratification that had been the motive.

'No one's done that to me since before I was married,' she said, reaching up to stroke his cheek. 'You made me feel like a seventeen-year-old girl again.'

'And did you enjoy it?' he enquired, knowing the answer.

'You took me by surprise – I didn't realise how far you were going until it was too late. But yes, it felt very nice.'

He helped her to sit up beside him, their backs propped comfortably on the big pillows against the bedhead. His arm was round her shoulders to hold her close to his side and his legs were spread apart on the bed. His apparatus lay up along his belly, fully displayed, hard and strong, for her admiration and affectionate attentions. But now that Madeleine's desires had been soothed for the time being, she was in no hurry, and there were matters she wanted to discuss with him. In particular, he learned, she had the utmost disdain for the disgraceful behaviour of his friend Vincent Moreau.

'His blatant unfaithfulness to Brigitte is atrocious,' said Madeleine. 'I'm sure you know where he goes when he disappears for half a day at a time.'

'He makes himself disappear?' Armand asked with a smile. 'I didn't know that. Did Brigitte tell you so?'

'She is heart-broken, the poor child. You men boast to each other about your conquests – you must know where he goes.'

'I assure you that I do not,' Armand said with a shrug.

'Perhaps he goes behind your back to visit your blonde friend with the fat bosom,' Madeleine suggested, a trace of spite in her voice. 'He made his interest in her very obvious the other evening. His hand was practically up her clothes the whole time they were dancing together!'

'Perhaps he visits Dominique,' Armand agreed, secretly amused but careful not to show it. 'She has many friends, though I would be extremely surprised to learn that Vincent was one of them. He'd had a glass of champagne too many the other evening – there was no more to it than that – and in consequence he allowed himself to become over-familiar with the women he danced with. You danced with him, Madeleine – surely you do not expect me to believe that he didn't try to stroke your bottom?'

'I soon put a stop to his impudence, I can assure you,' she retorted, her cheeks blushing a faint pink, 'but your blonde friend seemed to welcome his advances! At least, she made no effort to discourage him, though she must have known that his wife was watching.'

'I doubt if Dominique gives any thought to the wives of her men-friends,' said Armand, struggling not to show his amusement that Madeleine was so evidently put out by a meaningless incident on the dance-floor. 'And when Vincent was sober the next morning, he probably didn't remember giving her bottom a squeeze, any more than the others he patted.'

Including yours he almost added, but stopped himself in time, realising the remark would be offensive.

'There was only one woman he danced with that evening whose bottom he did not attempt to stroke – not to mention even more impertinent familiarities,' said Madeleine, her voice heated, 'and that was his wife! Brigitte alone had the right to expect he would behave towards her with affection, and she was disappointed. Promise me that you will find out who his mistress is, the next time that you see him. If you keep the conversation casual enough he will tell you without realising that he is giving himself away.'

The blush on her cheeks had deepened and an odd tone of determination made itself apparent in her voice. Armand looked at her curiously.

'But, dear Madeleine, it is no business of mine if Vincent has a little friend he visits. Why should I want to find out? What possible good would it do if I found out his girlfriend's name and address and told you so that you could pass it on to Brigitte? Surely you don't expect her to go and tear the other woman's hair out?'

Instead of answering his question, Madeleine closed her eyes and leaned back weakly against the pillows, her face suddenly pale. At last Armand understood that there were depths in their conversation about Vincent Moreau that it would be disagreeable to explore any further. Evidently, the true subject of Madeleine's castigation was not merely Vincent – it was marital unfaithfulness in general, a topic in which Armand had no interest whatsoever. Once or twice in the past the subject had been raised by married women who had admitted him to their intimate favours, their motive being to convince him of his incredible good fortune in being so adored that they had made the supreme gesture of deceiving their husbands for him.

It goes without saying that Armand had believed not

44

a word of these admittedly tender but nevertheless wholly preposterous avowals of affection. Until now, the numerous young married women who had succumbed to his charms had, to his certain knowledge, had other lovers before him. They could fairly be said to have established for themselves a regular routine of deceiving their husbands for their own pleasure. The delights these ladies offered to Armand were not precisely brand-new, so to speak. Naturally, they were no worse for that – on the contrary, Armand held the firm belief that, up to the age of forty, most women improved with experience of love. After that, in his view, they became over-anxious, or sometimes even cynical, as their charms faded.

To take a young girl to bed was delightful, of course, but for sustained rapture Armand's personal preference was for a wife of thirty, or thereabouts, who had already had at least two lovers. Not that Madeleine came into this category, for he was certain that he was her first adventure since her marriage to Pierre-Louis. But in Armand's mind she was so exceptional that his ordinary rules had no application. What he must beware of was an attack of remorse on her part now that she had given herself to another man.

The answer to incipient tears and recrimination was simple enough, in Armand's experience, and he turned towards her to take her in his arms and kiss her face and closed eyelids.

'How beautiful you are, Madeleine,' he sighed expressing much emotion between his little kisses, 'I adore you madly! I am so happy to hold you in my arms at last. I shall make you the happiest woman in the world – I swear it!'

He was not telling deliberate falsehoods, of course, for no man whose member is standing upright and who has a naked woman in his arms has the slightest intellectual comprehension of true and false – his urgent need to penetrate the one with the other cancels all concept of right and wrong. Armand's words at that moment were nonsense, but they were the kind of nonsense that makes women feel wanted and cherished and drives away any melancholy fears that may be in their hearts. By means of the right little words and the right little kisses and the right little caresses, he was soon able to banish any remorse or doubt that Madeleine may have felt.

More than that, his words and his kisses and his caresses had excited her, as he meant they should. He had long ago learned that the feel of a sturdy male part between her legs is the surest consolation a woman can be offered and he felt sure that he had dispelled any gloomy after-thoughts when she put her hand down between his legs and took hold of him. His own hand was between her smooth-skinned thighs, playing delicately over the little bud swollen with desire inside her warm and slippery niche.

'So soon, so soon?' he murmured. 'My beautiful Madeleine!'

Before he could ease her down on her back and spread her long slender legs to prepare her for his loving penetration, Madeleine took charge of the proceedings. She freed herself from his encircling arm, pushed his legs down flat on the bed and knelt astride his thighs, her open portal only a hand-breadth from his twitching peg. He stared in wide-eyed delight as she grasped it and guided it towards herself.

'You think that this is too soon?' she whispered, a tender smile on her face. 'For me it has been too long since you made love to me, Armand – it must be almost an hour. I don't count what you did to me with your fingers.'

Armand was half-sitting on the bed, his back resting comfortably against the pillows and the head-board. He took Madeleine's elegant little breasts in his hands while he stared down between his belly and hers to see his hard shaft slide up into her as she pressed down to impale herself on it.

'There – all the way,' she murmured, her soft belly touching his. 'Now say if it is too soon.'

'It is never too soon for me,' he gasped, his hands

fondling her breasts in delight. 'You are so adorable that I want to feel myself inside you all the time.'

'Good,' she replied softly, 'because I mean you to be,'

Truth to tell, to observe himself embedded in Madeleine's walnut-brown nest elated Armand so very highly that he dare not move his body for fear of bringing on an immediate emission. Madeleine stared at his face and smiled curiously – she had recognised his plight and was amused and at the same time touched by it.

'You really *do* adore me, Armand,' she acknowledged, a gleam of what at that moment could only be triumph in her velvet-brown eyes.

Kneeling over him, her thighs widely splayed to accept him deep inside her belly, she started to slide herself up and down slowly. Armand cried out in delight, feeling his crisis approaching and he stared up into her face, so near his own. Her red-rouged mouth parted in a smile that showed her pretty white teeth and the gleam in her eyes, under half-closed lids, was beatific. So much so that her expression alone almost did for Armand – his body shook at the surge of his emotions and the movement very nearly betrayed him into release. His hands squeezed her breasts hard and he knew that he had only a very few moments left before his torrent of desire broke down the frail dam that held it in check.

As for Madeleine, the pleasure she was experiencing as she rode gently up and down on Armand's swollen limb was more profound even than the annihilating satisfaction she had enjoyed earlier, when he had lain on her belly. Her present pleasure was beyond the purely physical – there was that, of course – but it was a marvellously primitive and overpowering sense of revenge that accounted for her ecstatic state of mind. In spite of her agitation during their conversation about Vincent, Armand had failed to guess the secret that had brought her to his bed – her painful awareness that her own husband had a mistress.

For the eight years of their marriage she had cared for Pierre-Louis, she had cherished him, supported him,

47

deferred to him, admired him, and encouraged him to make love to her night after night. But it seemed that however much she had done for him, it was not enough. It had been twelve months at least since Pierre-Louis had wanted her for more than a single brief climax before falling asleep. And in the last few months, since finding out by chance his secret, she had made excuses to refuse him even that.

There was a brief wordless cry from Armand as he lunged hard upwards and delivered himself of an ecstatic outburst in her belly. Madeleine cried out too, a little squeal of rapture and of triumph and brought her mouth down to suck the breath from Armand's open mouth as her body shook furiously in spasms of delight. This was real revenge on Pierre-Louis for his infidelities – not merely to let another man make love to her, but to take immense pleasure in the act of giving herself.

Naturally, being who she was, she could have had her pick of twenty men, when she decided to avenge herself in this way on her husband. She had chosen Armand because she was sure that he would be very expert at arousing her and giving her satisfaction. That he was a cousin of Pierre-Louis somehow added to the rightness of her choice, she felt. And, gratifying as it had been to lie on her back and let him make love to her, it had been ten times better to straddle him and make use of him herself to bring on her crisis of passion.

Armand lay back limply against the pillows, breathing deeply as he returned to tranquillity. Madeleine's soft cheek was against his cheek, her pink-fleshed pomegranates were pressed to his chest and his arms lay loosely round her waist. In his heart there was a feeling of immeasurable joy that he had won so marvellous a mistress as Madeleine. Naturally, having a good conceit of himself, he was certain that he deserved her – and while their secret love-affair lasted all his devotion would be hers. She was going to discover that she was loved beyond all sense and reason.

But, alas, if Armand had had the ability to see inside

48

her head at that moment and so learn *her* love-secret, his elation would have been swept away like dry leaves before a strong autumn wind. The exhilarating events of the past hour had taught him to adore her, body and soul, but Madeleine's feelings towards him were not equally intense. Of course, she retained the same mild affection she had always had for him as a friend of long standing. But he inspired no deeper sentiment. That he had proved to be so agreeable and effective an implement of revenge on her husband, she attributed not to any quality of his but to her own good sense in selecting him.

She eased herself off his softening stem and gave it a fond little pat. Armand would do very nicely until Pierre-Louis regained his senses and came back to her.

3

The View from an Upstairs Window

If a friend arrives very late in the evening, unannounced, dishevelled and with the general appearance of having drunk too much and slept too little, then evidently he has serious troubles. In short, Pierre-Louis had the look of a man nearing the end of his tether. He collapsed into one of Armand's armchairs and took the offered glass of cognac with an unsteady hand. He was wearing a dark blue suit that needed pressing and a shirt that looked none too fresh. He had arrived without hat, overcoat or gloves – proof enough, if any was required, of his distracted state of mind. He stared into his glass for a moment, heaved a deep sigh, and emptied it.

'You look absolutely terrible,' said Armand. 'Where on earth have you been? What have you been doing?'

Not that he was in any doubt about the answer. Earlier that evening, around six or a little later, he had been enjoying an aperitif in the Café de la Paix when Pierre-Louis came in, with a girl on his arm. Naturally, Armand was intrigued and raised his arm to attract his cousin's attention. But when Pierre-Louis spotted him, he blanched and shook his head slightly – a gesture that indicated very clearly his wish not to be recognised. Armand shrugged a little and set himself to observe closely this young person that his cousin intended to keep secret from him. There could be only one reason for that: she must be his girlfriend and he was ashamed to admit it.

Pierre-Louis took his girl to the most distant table he could find, but Armand ordered himself another drink and observed the couple surreptitiously. They seemed to be arguing with each other – at least, the unheard conversation was very animated, with much gesticulating and facial expressions that could best be described as vehement. Several times Pierre-Louis struck the table with his hand, to emphasise whatever point he was making. The girl shrugged frequently and, at the height of the exchange, made an impolite gesture with her hand that everyone understands perfectly well. Evidently she was not to be intimidated by anything that Pierre-Louis might say or do.

She was a girl most men would have found very attractive, Armand thought. He put her age at eighteen, or thereabouts, a girl with light brown hair that almost shaded into blonde. She had pulled off her impudent little Basque beret when she sat down and Armand could see that she wore her hair brushed straight back from her forehead, above a full-cheeked face. But her most striking characteristic was her air of well-being. Without going so far as to describe her as chubby, she was well-fleshed, her fair skin positively glowed with health. Armand's nature being what it was, he half-closed his eyes as he stared at her across the room and used his imagination to undress her.

Under her close-fitting honey-yellow frock, what would he be most likely to find? he asked himself in delight. In his experience, many young ladies of her age preferred to drape their smooth bodies in flimsy camiknickers, often in bright and stirring colours. Armand considered that sort of underwear to be deliciously convenient for his tantalising game in public places – open-legged garments were a positive invitation for a man's hand to penetrate their silk recesses and fondle the delightful secret they concealed.

And when, with eager but experienced fingers, he unfastened the pair of tiny mother-of-pearl buttons that closed, in pretended modestly, the narrow strip of transparent silk that passed between the wearer's thighs – ah then! From the waist down she was laid bare for him. First his hand and then his eyes would savour the furry delight Mademoiselle had to offer between her legs. And in another few moments the camiknickers would be off completely, to let him see and savour all. In his mind's eye Armand could see the plump breasts and rounded belly of Pierre-Louis' girl, her fleshy thighs and the soft oval cheeks of her bottom.

He could tell from her face that her whole body gleamed with the health and vitality of vigorous youth. She was an appetising mouthful to be tasted delicately on the tongue and then devoured whole – a soft and luscious fruit full of sweetness. Indeed, so enchanting was the vision that Armand conjured up in his fantasy that his ever-eager companion woke up and started to stretch himself inside Armand's trousers. The girl became aware of the intensity of his stare and turned on her chair to see who was looking at her. For a moment their eyes met across the room, then she turned back to her animated discussion with Pierre-Louis.

There was no doubt that she asked him if he knew the man who was staring at her, for Armand saw her gesture in his direction. And just as certainly, Pierre-Louis denied any acquaintance with him, for he shook his head firmly. Soon afterwards the two of them got up and left the café. They passed close by Armand's table on their way to the door and he noted that the coat his cousin had helped the girl into was an expensive one of vicuna with broad fur cuffs. Eighteen-year-old girls did not usually own coats of that quality – unless they had well-to-do friends like Pierre-Louis.

Armand looked up from the coat to take the opportunity of studying her smooth face, not to look for an indication of her personality, for he did not expect to find any strong traits of character in a girl so young. His principal interest was to ascertain the colour of her eyes. Pierre-Louis was staring with much unnecessary embarrassment into the distance, pretending that Armand was not there. In consequence he failed to notice his girl return the tiny smile Armand gave her.

Although the two smiles were no more than tiny movements of the lips, they conveyed more than an hour's conversation could have done. Armand's smile said to the girl, *Though the man you are with knows me well, he does not wish to introduce us — nevertheless, I find you very beautiful, Mademoiselle, and I would dearly love to kiss your hand and whisper to you certain sentiments that are in my heart concerning taking off your clothes and kissing other and even more delicious parts of you.*

And the smile she gave him said, *I don't know why he wants to keep us from meeting each other, Monsieur, yet I understand what you intend towards me, and if I were alone I might well be disposed to linger and hear more.*

In contrast to Pierre-Louis' arrangements, this was one of Armand's rare evenings alone. He left the Café de la Paix in another half hour to enjoy an excellent dinner and a bottle of wine in one of his favourite restaurants, followed by a pleasant stroll along the Boulevard des Italiens, observing the people, especially the young women. He had been so attracted to Pierre-Louis' companion that he could not get her out of his mind, and his state of continuing arousal made him vulnerable. During his stroll he was approached by several women with friendly propositions to accompany them and avail himself of their charms in return for a reasonable fee.

Armand was acquainted with the better establishments that provided young women for their clients, in particular the well-regarded *Chabanais* just off the rue Colbert, but only once had he made use of a street-girl. That was when he and Vincent Moreau, schoolboys of fifteen, had incited each other to the great adventure of having a woman for the first time. Together they had accosted a comfortable-looking redhead one afternoon outside the Gare de Lyon and gone with her to a frowsty hotel room, where each in turn looked on while the other performed his rite of initiation into adulthood.

Even so, if one of those who spoke to him on the Boulevard had resembled Pierre-Louis' little friend, Armand would have been tempted almost beyond endurance to go with her for a few francs. But needless to say, none of them could offer him a convincing counterfeit impression of the smooth succulence of the young woman in the vicuna coat. There were short girls and tall thin girls, dark-haired girls, ginger-haired girls, streaky-dyed blonde girls, girls of fifteen, of twenty-five, of thirty-five, and one huge-breasted old girl Armand would have sworn was a grandmother of fifty-five.

With a polite shake of his head and a courteous word or two, he declined their offers and strolled on alone. Autumn was drawing towards winter and the evening air was damp enough to cast pretty golden halos about the street-lamps. Perhaps it was the deception of the lamp-light acting upon Armand's romantic state of mind that made one of the lurking street-girls look like Pierre-Louis' friend for a few moments. She wore no hat and her hair was a light brown, though darker and coarser than that of the girl he had seen arguing with his cousin in the Cafe de la Paix – hers had been a light brown that shaded into blonde, and as fine as silk.

When the prowler saw Armand hesitate and give her a second glance, she smiled her professional smile at him and stepped back into a doorway. Momentarily intrigued, he halted and turned to face her, wondering whether it was her custom to conduct her business uncomfortably in shop doorways, and if so, what sort of clients she managed to attract. She was wearing a dark-blue raincoat, its buttons all unfastened but belted very tightly about her waist. As he stood staring, she undid the belt and grinned at him while she whipped up her long green jumper, to give him a brief foreview of the charms she was offering.

But alas, a closer inspection showed him that, though she was not much over twenty, her face was fat rather than girlishly chubby, and the skin of her cheeks and chin was blotched. She had hoisted her jumper to her thick and short neck to show him that she was naked under it, but the pair of breasts she was exposing as bait sagged like worn-out handbags and their elongated tips pointed away from each other, as if they were on bad terms. Thinking she had caught him, the girl told him her fee and assured him she had a room just round the corner. Armand smiled courteously and, feeling inexplicably sorry for her, gave her the price of a drink and walked on.

By ten-thirty he had returned to his apartment and was preparing for bed. He was in his dressing-gown and pyjamas and reading a magazine when Pierre-Louis arrived out of nowhere.

'I've been walking about for hours,' Pierre-Louis said in a miserable voice. 'I don't know what to do.'

'You expect me to believe that?' Armand exclaimed. 'You spent the evening with that marvellous girl I saw you with in the Café de la Paix and you didn't know what to do? Really, you must think I'm a complete fool!'

'No, I didn't mean it like that,' Pierre-Louis explained apologetically, 'but since Madeleine left me a month ago I have been utterly distraught – I think I'm losing my mind!'

'Then you must ask her to forgive you and come back to you.'

'Don't you think I've tried? She won't even talk to me,' said Pierre-Louis, hiding his pale face in his hands. 'I've been to her sister's home a dozen times to try to persuade her to come back to me. The first time I got as far as seeing Yvonne, who told me very rudely that Madeleine didn't want to see me. Since then I've been turned away from the door every time by the servants.'

'Madeleine left you because she found out that you were keeping a girlfriend,' Armand pointed out with a certain lack of sympathy for his cousin's suffering. 'I thought that she must be mistaken, but this evening you proved me wrong. She's very attractive, the girl you were with, but if you love Madeleine so much that you cannot live without her, then you will have to give up your little friend. Is that so very difficult?'

'Yes, impossibly difficult,' Pierre-Louis moaned. Nevertheless, he had recovered a little and was holding out his empty glass for more cognac.

'I can well believe that you enjoy making love to her,' said Armand, refilling both their glasses, 'but she is only a young girl, after all. Madeleine is a beautiful, charming and intelligent woman, the sort of wife any man would be proud to have. And if you will permit me to speak with total frankness, although naturally I shall never have the honour of making love to either lady, I cannot believe that your girlfriend is as exciting as your wife.'

It was a bare-faced lie, of course. For the past six weeks Armand had been making love to Madeleine very frequently – for two weeks before she had made up her mind to teach her husband a lesson by moving out of the family apartment, and for the month since then. At least fifty times he had undressed her and kissed and fondled her and plunged enthusiastically between her legs to sate his appetite – and hers. In consequence he knew from enjoyable personal experience that Madeleine was easily one of the most exciting women he had ever made love to. It was extremely hard to believe that Pierre-Louis' girlfriend could be the equal in bed of Madeleine, let alone surpass her.

His remarks brought in reply from Pierre-Louis a lengthy monologue of almost tearful self-justification. Much as he loved and adored and respected Madeleine, and so on and so on, he was obsessed to the point of imbecility by Suzette and was incapable of giving her up. Young as she was, she was cruel and greedy and although she pretended to be in love with him, he knew that she wanted him only for what she could get out of him. She had another lover, he was certain, a young man of her own age, and as soon as Pierre-Louis left her, Suzette slipped into bed with the young man and between bouts of love-making they laughed at Pierre-Louis for being such a fool.

'Have you any evidence of this?' Armand asked. 'Or is it merely that your guilty conscience is punishing you with jealous inventions?'

The answer to his question was confused and unsatisfactory, but as Pierre-Louis rambled on, Armand gathered that after the near-quarrel in the café, he had gone with Suzette to her apartment and they had attempted to reconcile their differences by making love. 'She's always ready for that, no matter what mood she's in,' Pierre-Louis declared bitterly. But it soon became apparent from his account of the evening that, although it was superbly exciting to lie between Suzette's thighs and plunge into her warm burrow, it was inadequate as a resolution of the deep-seated problems of their mutual insecurity.

In short, the convulsive release of their physical tension did nothing to end the dispute between them – it merely caused them to forget it for some moments. When they disengaged from their intimate connection and lay naked together, the argument that had its origin in Pierre-Louis' gnawing sexual jealousy flared up yet again. The pleasure they had given each other did not soften their hostility – the quarrel grew worse. Suzette wrenched herself away from Pierre-Louis' arms and knelt up on the bed, her plump breasts wobbling as she waved her arms furiously to give emphasis to her scornful words.

In another moment they were shouting abuse at each other at the top of their voices, and she aimed a futile smack at Pierre-Louis' face. At that, his temper snapped, and to restrain her and silence her contemptuous words, he started to beat her! He struck at her with his open hands, and she screamed and tried to protect herself with her arms, but after he had slapped her plump bare breasts only a few times, his despairing rage was transformed into a different passion – but one that manifested itself with equal violence.

Hardly knowing what he was doing, he forced Suzette down on her back and pried her legs apart with his knees, to expose the tender and delicate source of her power over him. And not content with this barbarous attempt to shame a beautiful young woman, he hurled spiteful taunts at her to the effect that she let anyone have her for the price of a dinner and was no better than a street-walker. And in a paroxysm of rage, to show how much he despised her, he spat on her writhing belly.

'But this is frightful!' Armand exclaimed in dismay. 'You must be insane! Are you telling me that you raped her – or that you murdered her?'

Though Pierre-Louis denied any such malefaction on his part, it was obvious from his chaotic tale that the dreadful insult of spitting on her had driven him right out of his senses. His recollection of what had happened next was hazy, but he thought he had hurled himself on Suzette and pinned her to the bed, shrieking and struggling.

'And then?' Armand asked when his cousin hesitated. Shamefaced, Pierre-Louis conceded that he had pierced Suzette so furiously that it could almost be said to amount to rape.

Not that Mademoiselle Suzette was the type of young woman who could be terrorised into submission by a ravenous male intruder between her thighs! At the instant when Pierre-Louis' muscles relaxed after he had discharged his passionate rage, she fought her way out from underneath him like a wild-cat. She used her fingernails, her elbows and her knees, to such effect that she drove him off the bed and backwards across the room, into the corner by the wardrobe, where he crouched naked with his hands clasped over his tender parts to protect them from her furious kicks.

Serious and perhaps permanent damage might have been inflicted upon Pierre-Louis by the infuriated girl had he not had the sense to grab her ankle as it bruised his thigh viciously. With a quick heave he flipped her leg up shoulder-high. She hopped twice on her other foot, lost her balance as he heaved higher still, and fell over on her back on the floor. The fall knocked the breath out of her and she lay gasping inaudible threats at him, her legs waving in the air and her curly-haired delight exposed involuntarily in the most humiliating way. Pierre-Louis stepped over her, seized an armful of his clothes and fled for his life.

'Then the *affaire* is finished,' said Armand. 'It is impossible that you can ever see her again after so savage a leave-taking. You should give thanks to

Heaven that you escaped so lightly, my friend. If matters had gone much further you might have faced a murderer's fate at the guillotine.'

'I suppose you are right,' Pierre-Louis agreed with a sigh, 'but I am still desperately in love with her. I stood outside your door for at least five minutes before I rang the bell – in two minds whether to come in and talk to you or go back and abase myself before Suzette in the hope that she will take me back and let me stay the night with her.'

'You'll get over it if you stay away from her,' said Armand, shrugging. 'In two weeks you will wonder what you ever saw in her. After all, she's only a pretty girl you've had for a month or two. Paris is full of young girls like her. Far more important, what are your intentions towards Madeleine now?'

Pierre-Louis embarked upon a lengthy and indirect reply to that simple question. He expected his wife to return to him, of course, but the thought of asking her forgiveness appeared to him absurd. Everyone knew that married men wandered off into little adventures with other women from time to time, he pointed out to Armand. As a matter of fact, everyone expected it, because that was how the world was arranged. It was a very well established fact that men were polygamous and, if society allowed them only one wife, then automatically they sought variety elsewhere. It was flying in the face of nature to think otherwise, or to demand that a man should remain faithful to the same woman for forty or fifty years!

'You have been married for eight years, not half a century,' said Armand. 'In any case, your argument is wasted on me – it is Madeleine you must convince.'

Pierre-Louis said that he knew Armand had taken Madeleine out to dinner a few times since she moved into her sister's apartment, and he was very grateful to him for his care. Armand was a true friend and he'd never forget his kindness. It would be too heart-rending to think of Madeleine sitting alone and moping every evening. And while Pierre-Louis went so far as to declare that he regarded his wife as above reproach and incapable of even the tiniest act of disloyalty, nevertheless, he felt constrained to admit in confidence that he would have been uneasy if she had gone out dancing with other men.

He mentioned Vincent Moreau as an example of what he meant – they had both known Vincent long enough to be aware that he was without scruples and would take advantage of any woman's loneliness to get her clothes off. How much better that Armand had been there to relieve Madeleine's boredom by taking her to restaurants of a good class occasionally and helping to keep her cheerful until the situation was resolved and she returned to her own home. To that Armand thought it wise to say nothing – the extent of the consolation he had furnished to Madeleine was a secret utterly unsuitable for the ears of her husband.

It emerged that the reason why Pierre-Louis had mentioned the few dinners he knew about was that he believed Armand, as a friend of both parties, to be the ideal person to mediate between them and help reconcile their differences. Armand thought the idea stupid, and said so. But Pierre-Louis argued his case so strenuously and with such persistence that Armand found himself – however reluctantly and however incredulously – telephoning Yvonne Hiver's number to try to talk to Madeleine on behalf of her husband.

'At this time of the night!' was Yvonne's astonished reaction when explained.

'Dear Yvonne, I know it is late,' said Armand, 'but Pierre-Louis has been here for an hour or more pouring out his anguish and I couldn't refuse.'

'You're as mad as he is,' said Yvonne. 'Come round if you must, but don't bring Pierre-Louis with you. I'll tell Madeleine to expect you – I don't think she's gone to bed yet.'

It was almost midnight when Armand arrived at the impressive Hiver apartment in the rue Saint-Didier and, to his surprise, Yvonne herself opened the door to him. She was dressed to stun male admirers, in a silver frock that was sleeveless and cut like a tunic, with a sash tied low on her hips. Though the frock was loose, it concealed nothing. Yvonne's breasts were clearly outlined and, when she moved, they swayed under the thin material. The sash dipped in front, where it was tied, and the knot drew the attention unerringly to its position – precisely where Yvonne's thighs met.

'Good, you're alone then,' she said as Armand kissed her hand. 'I refuse to have that idiot Pierre-Louis coming here to upset Madeleine.'

'I would not inflict him on either of you in his present state of mind,' said Armand.

'Go through to the salon and I'll tell her you're here,' said Yvonne, casually rearranging the sash over her loins in a way that gripped the imagination. 'I know it's no business of mine, but I don't understand why you allow yourself to be talked into coming here at this time of night by that lunatic husband of hers. But if Madeleine is prepared to listen to you, you can talk all night if you want to. The servants have gone to bed and a friend is calling in five minutes to take me dancing. Good-night, Armand.'

Yvonne was older than Madeleine and, while there was a strong family resemblance of face and figure, there were also striking differences. Instead of Madeleine's delicate aura of concealed sensuality, Yvonne radiated an open sexual invitation, as if she were a brightly-coloured flower in a park attracting honey-bees to itself. She had made no mention of her husband, Jean-Roger, in her plans for the night and it would have been indiscreet to enquire.

Like everyone else who knew the Hivers, Armand was well aware that Jean-Roger and Yvonne pursued their separate interests now that she had adequately fulfilled her marital obligations by presenting him with two sons. They lived together nominally in the fashionable apartment in the rue Saint-Didier, but Jean-Roger spent many nights elsewhere and he and his wife met mostly on formal occasions, when the company of both was required.

The salon into which Yvonne had directed Armand was large and had been designed to impress upon visitors that they were in the presence of good taste, sophistication and a great deal of money. One whole wall was a window, looking out on to the street below, and opposite, almost covering the wall on which it hung, a vast rectangular mirror etched with a graceful design of lilies reflected back the light to make the salon even more spacious. The other walls were pale pink, the curtains and the carpet were the same dark and dusty red-ochre as the tiled roofs of old palaces in Tuscany. A large square white fur rug lay in the centre of the floor.

It went without saying that the furniture had been made especially for the room in a style that was modernist and chic. It was upholstered in white satin. There were low armchairs that had no arms, long sofas that could each accommodate three or four people in comfort, and a chaise-longue shaped in a swan-neck curve. Facing each other on opposite sides of the square rug stood a pair of oblong occasional tables, made of shiny black ebony to contrast with the white fur. Armand found the room charming, yet it seemed to him that it was so graciously well-ordered that it was almost intimidating – only an admirer bold to the point of foolhardiness would dare attempt to kiss Yvonne into submission on one of her satin sofas and put a hand up her knickers.

He rose to his feet as Madeleine entered the salon and kissed her hand in adoration. She made a pretence of having already retired for the night before Armand telephoned, but it was evident to him that she had spent the time since then in grooming her shiny walnut-brown hair, making up her face and choosing garments that would make her exceptionally alluring. She was wearing a beautiful chiffon wrap-over negligee of forget-me-not blue and pale cream that clung to her slender figure in the most charming way. It tied above her left hip in a large bow and was full-length, so that only the tips of her blue satin slippers peeped from under it as she led him to one of the white sofas and sat down with him.

Armand's heart was beating furiously, for under Madeleine's soft negligee there would be, he was certain, a matching nightgown of chiffon so filmy that the buds of her breasts would show through. And, if he could persuade her to let him remove her negligee, he would be able to see how the nightgown shaped itself over her long thighs. He sighed to himself in delight as in his trousers his shameless pendant became interested, stirred and stiffened. At this moment Armand abandoned whatever good intentions he may have had in respect of Pierre-Louis and began to devise ways of turning the meeting to his own advantage.

Madeleine sat straight-backed, her hands folded in her lap, and looked at him calmly.

'I find this situation extraordinary,' she began. 'You do yourself no good in my eyes by acting as messenger for Pierre-Louis in the middle of the night. I suppose he's having a fit of drunken remorse – what has he sent you to say to me?'

'You have summed up the position very clearly,' he replied, taking her hand in his. 'He is afflicted by remorse, regret, self-pity and confusion. He wants you to return to him.'

'Does he indeed! I suppose he has given you solemn and sacred assurances that he has ended his affair with the slut and will never see her again?'

'No,' said Armand, truthfully enough.

'No?' Madeleine exclaimed. 'Then why are you here?'

'Though Pierre-Louis is my cousin and my friend, the plain truth is that I adore you to madness, Madeleine, and I must be candid with you,' he answered with much sincerity of feeling. 'What seems to have happened, as far as I can understand his incoherencies, is that he and his girlfriend have quarrelled and he is feeling miserable. He sees this as an opportunity to persuade you to return to him.'

'And if I agree, he will never see her again – is that what I am supposed to believe?'

'Let me be utterly frank, even at the risk of causing you distress,' said Armand, kissing the palm of her hand gently. 'In my opinion, he is infatuated. If the young lady telephoned him tomorrow and invited him to visit her, he would go instantly.'

'But this is ridiculous!' said Madeleine, her cheeks pink with anger. 'He expects me to return to him while he is besotted by a young girl?'

'If I have correctly understood his state of mind, he is clutching at the hope that if you are back with him he will be able to resist the temptation of seeing his girlfriend again.'

'I see – he wants me in his bed only in order to exhaust himself so that he can stay away from his slut – this is outrageous!'

'No doubt it is,' Armand agreed, 'but Pierre-Louis is serious about it. He wants you to return to him tonight. He is sitting outside in a taxi.'

'He's waiting outside in a taxi!' Madeleine exclaimed in exasperation. 'Has the man gone mad?'

She jumped up from the sofa and went quickly to the window, where curtains of watered silk were drawn across to shut out the autumnal chill and the dark. She paused with one hand raised and, before moving the curtain, turned to speak to Armand, a note of deliberation in her voice.

'I refuse to give him the satisfaction of seeing me at the window. Turn the light off.'

Armand went to the switch beside the door and put out the lights. Madeleine drew back one of the curtains a little, not in the middle where it met the other curtain, but at the side, by the window-frame and the wall. She opened only a narrow slit, just enough to look through.

'It's true!' she said, astonishment in her voice. 'There is a taxi waiting outside, down by the lamp-post. But why is it on the other side of the street?'

'We turned into the street from the far end and Pierre-Louis told the driver to park opposite. I suppose he wants to be able to look up at the apartment windows in the hope of seeing you.'

'Never!' she said firmly. 'Ah, if only I had something heavy to throw at him.'

While her face was pressed close to the glass, Armand moved across the salon in silence and stood close behind her, his hands resting lightly on her hips, while he looked out of the window over her shoulder.

'He was hoping that curiosity would make you do exactly what you are doing,' he said.

'Look out of the window at him, you mean? Is that what he said to you, the slimy worm? If I had a pistol I would shoot him dead from here!'

'He cherishes the hope that this display of silent devotion will induce you to take pity on him,' said Armand. 'It is his fondest wish that you will run down and get in the taxi with him and go home. He intends to stage a scene of reconciliation, reaching its tender conclusion in bed.'

'The animal! I'll never let him touch me again!' Madeleine said forcefully.

Standing behind her, Armand slid his hands further round her waist from where they had held her hips with gentle confidence. And at the same time he eased himself a little closer to her, until his loins were against her bottom.

'Be careful or he'll see you,' said Madeleine with an anxiety that did not accord with her fierce denunciation of Pierre-Louis a moment before.

'He can't see a thing,' Armand assured her. 'I'm hidden by the curtain. The most he could see is your face peeping out.'

His fingers were exploring above her hip the loose knot of the tie-sash that held her negligee together. It came undone easily, as well-designed garments always do at the appropriate moment, and the delicate chiffon creation fell open. Armand sighed gently and used both hands to stroke her smooth belly through her flimsy nightgown.

'No, you mustn't do that!' Madeleine exclaimed. 'Suppose someone came into the room and saw us standing like this?'

'Yvonne's gone out dancing,' he reminded her, 'and the servants are in bed. Not that it would be news to Yvonne that you and I are lovers.'

In the dark, everything is permitted, as the old saying has it. Armand unbuttoned his trousers and let his stiff part leap out, quivering joyfully in its sudden freedom. He laid it upright along the crease between the soft cheeks of Madeleine's bottom and pressed himself close to her, only a flimsy layer of chiffon between his hot flesh and her cool skin.

'Oh, Armand!' she breathed. 'What if one of Yvonne's little boys came in and found us?'

The sensations imparted to his rampant member by the feel of her bottom through the fine material was so engaging that Armand slid up and down slowly in near-ecstasy. His hands were inside the deep decolletage of her nightgown to clasp her bare breasts. It would not take a great deal to bring on his emission and soak her bottom through her pretty garment – and exquisite the sensations would be!

'Yvonne's children are fast asleep,' he said. 'Do you imagine their nanny lets them wander about the apartment in the middle of the night? No one will interrupt us, Madeleine.'

She was rubbing her bottom gently against him, helping his throbbing piston to glide up between her cheeks.

'It feels so hot,' she whispered.

'It burns with love for you – I must have you, Madeleine.'

He reached down to grasp a handful of her wispy nightgown and lift it until he could get his hands under the lace-trimmed hem.

Madeleine breathed out sharply as his fingers moved into the soft join of her thighs.

'Armand, no . . . !' she whispered, but he pressed himself against her taut round bottom to make her feel how distended was the shaft throbbing there.

'Move your feet apart just a little,' he murmured, his mouth close to her ear and the perfume of her hair in his nostrils.

'But this is madness!' she said.

For all that, her slippered feet moved far enough apart for him to stroke the treasure between her slender thighs.

'He's staring at us!' she exclaimed. 'Look, he's opened the taxi window!'

And she was right. A pale blob which could have only been Pierre-Louis' face was visible in the space where the glass of the taxi window had been two moments before. But a dim blur was all that it was – there was no possibility of seeing his expression. Armand kissed the back of Madeleine's neck while he pressed the tip of his middle finger gently up between her legs and into her.

'He can't see anything,' he assured her.

'What a pity,' she retorted. 'It would serve him right!'

Her agitation was evident. Perhaps the cause was a bitter pleasure at the thought of her husband's reaction if he knew what she was letting Armand do to her at the window. Or perhaps it was the result of the sensations that rippled through her belly from the caress of his fingers.

'What am I saying?' she rebuked herself. 'Of course he mustn't find out about us – it would give him the excuse he wants for running after his slut! He'll get no justification from me. You must stop this at once!'

Armand was breathing warmly into her ear, amused by her indecision and the way her emotions were swinging backwards and forwards like a pendulum. *Yes*, she was aroused and wanted him to continue what he was doing to her, and *No*, she was reluctant to let him go any further because her husband was sitting outside in a taxi.

Despite her unfounded anxieties about being seen, and despite her half-hearted protests, the hidden bud under Armand's fingertip was swollen and wet. She put her hands behind her back, between Armand's belly and her bottom, to feel the stiffness jutting out of his open trousers and he heard her little sigh.

'But this is inexcusable behaviour on your part,' she

said tenderly. 'Pierre-Louis trusted you to argue his case for him – is this how you go about it? Are you his proxy? Am I to take it that it is my husband making love to me through you?'

'By no means,' Armand objected. 'It is I who am making love to you, dearest Madeleine – and what you are holding in your hand is mine and no one else's.'

'Then you admit that you are here to betray the trust that Pierre-Louis placed in the friendship between you? Not to mention that he is your cousin! Have you no shame?'

'None at all, *chérie*,' he answered softly, his fingers fluttering inside her wet opening.

'And if he finds out that you deceived him by forcing me to submit to you, how will you excuse yourself then?'

'Am I forcing you, Madeleine?' he murmured, his lips against her ear. 'You love this kind of compulsion as much as I do. If I had my way, I would force you to submit to me every morning and every afternoon and every evening and every night.'

Armand was prepared to play with Madeleine until she slithered right over the edge into ecstasy, if that was what was needed to persuade her to let him have her. But in the event, as might well be anticipated between two people who had made love to each other many times before, no such course was necessary.

'Come on, then,' she murmured, 'we can lie on the sofa.'

'There is no need of a sofa,' he said. 'Let's stay where we are – here by the window.'

'But . . . we can't do that!' Madeleine gasped, her voice shocked as the implication of his words struck here. 'Not here, with Pierre-Louis watching us!'

'You said only a moment ago that you don't care if he sees us,' Armand reminded her.

'But that was different! You were only touching me, we weren't doing anything serious,' she replied, with that often charming and sometimes infuriating lack of logic that distinguishes pretty women.

Armand chuckled in amusement. 'Pierre-Louis is not watching you,' he said. 'It is you who are watching him. That's not the same thing at all.'

Before she could continue with any more of these protestations that he knew were meaningless and not to be taken seriously, Armand slipped the wide-sleeved negligee off her shoulders. It rustled down between them until it lay on the floor and he could feel the warmth of her smooth body through the gossamer chiffon of her nightgown.

'But this is impossible!' she exclaimed. 'Things like this only happen in dreams, not in real life.'

Armand put his hands on her hips and arranged her gently for what he proposed to do. She took up the position as readily and naturally as if she'd made love like that a hundred times before, although he was as certain as anyone could be in these matters that Pierre-Louis had never been enterprising enough to do it with her in this way. And yet, as if by some inborn female instinct, she arranged herself so that she leaned forward, her naked rump thrust out towards Armand.

Enough light came through the window from the street-lamps to let him see that her parted feet in their pretty blue satin slippers were firmly planted half a metre out from the wall, and her hands were joined on the window-frame to support her. She bowed her head and rested her cheek on the back of her hands in an attitude of submission – though she had ensured that she could continue to look out of the window, through the narrow space by the wall, where she held aside the curtain.

'Unreal things happen far more often in real life than in dreams,' said Armand, his curiosity aroused. 'Do you often have dreams of making love?'

'Oh, yes,' she said breathlessly.

'And am I in them? Do you dream that I am doing delicious things to you?'

'I'm sure you'd like to know,' she replied.

'Will you tell me of your dreams?' he asked eagerly, his hand down between the cheeks of her bare bottom caressing the split mound thrust towards him by her position. 'If this reminds you of them, they must be enormously interesting – I am bursting to hear!'

'Not now,' she murmured, 'not now, Armand.'

'But sometime?' he persisted.

'Perhaps . . .' she whispered, almost as if she were reluctant to share the intimate secrets of her dreams with him.

At that moment it was irrelevant, as Armand prepared to make the very most of this extraordinary occasion. He unfastened his trousers completely and let them slide down his legs to his ankles, then gathered Madeleine's fragile nightgown up round her waist with one hand while he took his rearing pintle in the other. His hand trembled uncontrollably as he guided it between her splayed thighs and up towards her *petit palais*.

'Oh, *you*!' she exclaimed a little breathlessly when she felt his key being inserted in her keyhole. 'Don't you ever think of anything else when we're together?'

'Afterwards, yes,' he breathed and, with a strong push he went deep into her.

'Ah, you will split me open with your great strong thing!' she gasped.

As soon as he was firmly embedded in her warmth, Armand slipped off his jacket and pulled the front of his shirt right up to his chest, in order to enjoy the pleasure of having his bare belly against her bottom.

'This is insane!' Madeleine moaned.

Whether it was that or not, it was unimaginably enjoyable. Armand could hear the swiftly rising excitement in her voice as she moaned his name over and over again, while her bottom bumped insistently against him, as if to teach him what to do. His arms were round her and his hands up under her nightgown to clasp her soft little pomegranates and play with them. Now, when all was ready, he began to rock against her bare cheeks.

'Is Pierre-Louis still staring up at the window?' he asked, his lips nuzzling against her neck.

'I don't know . . .' she sighed, 'I think so . . . I'm sure he must be wondering what we're doing all this time.'

'He's praying that I have been so persuasive on his behalf that you have agreed to go back with him tonight,' Armand murmured. 'He's hoping you'll let him do what I'm doing to you – surely you understand that's why he's waiting down there.'

'Then he can wait out there all night and freeze!' she exclaimed fiercely, her bottom ramming back hard to hasten the onset of Armand's crisis and so spite her husband.

'Oh, Madeleine,' he sighed, 'it feels so enchanting that I can't hold out any longer!'

'Good!' she gasped, swinging her bottom faster. 'Do it now – I want you to!'

Nature took its course and Madeleine got her wish almost instantly. Armand was driven so deep into her that she gave a little squeal of surprise, his hands crushed her breasts fiercely and he fountained his elixir into her quaking belly.

'Yes – that's it!' she exulted, glaring down wild-eyed at the taxi in the street below. 'More, Armand – more!'

His savage plunging brought on her own critical moments in a headlong rush. She wailed ecstatically, her body shaking so hard in her frenzy of triumph that her senses almost left her. She would have fallen to the floor, except that Armand felt her beginning to sag away from him and saved her. He wrapped his arms tightly round her waist and held her suspended while he jolted his offering into her. By then her knees had buckled beneath her and she hung in his arms, spasms shaking her furiously while her long paroxysm progressed to its conclusion. Her hands had fallen away from the window, but her forehead was still pressed hard to the glass.

When it was all over at last, Armand heard her draw in a long deep breath. The burden was lifted from his supporting arms as she got her feet under her again and straightened her legs to take her weight. Armand continued to hold her tightly.

'Darling Madeleine . . .' he murmured. 'I hardly know what to say after that! I adore you to madness!'

'It is you who are superb,' she replied softly. 'So much the worse for Pierre-Louis!'

'I'd forgotten all about him,' said Armand. 'Is he still waiting down there?'

'Oh yes, he's still there – and I think he's starting to become impatient,' she answered, a malicious little chuckle in her voice. 'He put his head right out of the taxi and stared up at us at the very moment that you made me hear the golden trumpets and enter into Heaven.'

'What a charming and poetic way to describe it! I shall remember your words the next time that we make love.'

'And that will be soon, I promise you,' she said, pulling herself off his wet spike, 'but for now, I think you'd better go down and tell my stupid husband that he's wasting his time out there. Make sure he goes away – I don't want the household disturbed by a madman trying to beat the door down in the middle of the night.'

Armand pulled his trousers up from his ankles, tucked in his shirt and fastened his buttons. He groped about on the floor in the dark until he found his jacket and put it on. In the heat of the encounter Madeleine's frilly negligee, lying discarded on the floor, had somehow found its way under his feet. He retrieved it, hoping he had not done it any harm and helped her into it, his hands roaming over her breasts, through her filmy nightgown.

'When shall I see you again?' he murmured, his lips against her soft neck. 'I cannot live without you.'

'Whenever you wish,' she replied casually, moving to the side, away from him, while she closed her negligee by tying the sash at her hip.

She went with him to the apartment door and put her arms round his neck to kiss him good night. The

72

electric light was on in the entrance hall and Armand stared into her velvet brown eyes and stroked her face with his fingertips. He thought he understood why she had consented to let him make love to her almost within sight of her husband – evidently she took a certain malicious pleasure in humiliating Pierre-Louis in her mind in this way.

But in this, as in much else, Armand naively underestimated the complexities and contradictions of the female heart. How could he, a mere man, guess that in sating herself with so full and bizarre a vengeance, she had remembered that it was Pierre-Louis she loved, not Armand? It was in her mind to return to Pierre-Louis and resume the role of loving wife – when she had reasonable assurance that his love-affair was finished. While Armand was revelling in the secret knowledge that he had enjoyed Madeleine right under her husband's nose, she was hugging to her heart the secret that before very long she would be lying on her back with Pierre-Louis between her legs.

But not immediately, of course: not until he had tired of his unsatisfactory love-affair and come back to plead with her himself. She was pleased to learn that he was quarrelling with the slut who had entrapped him – it was to be hoped that he was suffering sleepless nights and bleak days. From her long and intimate knowledge of him, Madeleine guessed he would soon be at her feet – sending Armand was an indication that she would not be kept waiting very much longer.

Though no more than five minutes had elapsed since the marvellously cataclysmic episode at the window, Armand had her back against the apartment door and was pressing close, his lips on hers in a hot kiss and his hand inside her negligee to fondle her breasts.

'Oh Madeleine, *je t'adore, je t'adore*,' he murmured, and she could feel his ramrod against her thigh. In another moment or two he would have her night-clothes up round her waist again!

'*Au revoir*, dearest Armand,' she said softly, sliding sideways from between him and the door. 'You have exhausted me with your marvellous love-making. Telephone me in the morning, but not before eleven-thirty.'

Before Armand had collected his wits to reply, she had the door open and he was on his way out, his hopes disappointed and his congested part fluttering in his trousers.

4

Under the Bridges of Paris

Knowing that Madeleine was estranged from her husband and had been living with her sister for over a month, Marie-Therese Brissard was tactful enough not to embarrass either of them in the matter of her party. And since it was Madeleine who was her friend, she sent no invitation to Pierre-Louis and suggested to Madeleine that she should be accompanied by Armand Budin instead. Whether this seemingly innocent proposal signified that Marie-Therese was aware that Madeleine and Armand were lovers, who can say? The intimate liaison they had formed was supposed to be a secret, known only to very few of Madeleine's closest friends. But the natural exhilaration that accompanies the secrets of love makes it impossible for them to remain confidential for long.

There were a great many people present in the Brissard salon that evening, for Marie-Therese and Maurice had a considerable reputation as hosts. And left to his own devices while Madeleine was chatting to her hostess, who should Armand spy at the other end of the long room – to his discomfort – than Dominique Delaval in a blue frock: Dominique, who had been his dearest friend before he had discarded her for Madeleine. If Marie-Therese had known of that love-affair, she had made no effort at all to spare Armand and Dominique any embarrassment!

Of course, Armand kept well clear of Dominique. He plunged into lively conversation with everyone around him, charmed every woman and amused every man with his wit. The truth was that he felt guilty and a little ashamed of the less than courteous way he had behaved towards Dominique – one smile of promise from Madeleine and he had terminated his *affaire* with blonde Dominique abruptly and without explanation or excuse. There are those who say that this is the kindest way of all – a sharp stab of the knife to the heart rather than the lingering agony of protracted farewells.

But Dominique was not to be ignored in this way. By stages, pausing several times to greet friends and exchange a few words with them, she made her way round the perimeter of the Brissard salon until she stood alongside Armand. And since even then he appeared to be unaware of her presence at his elbow, she tapped his arm and said, with a smile as enigmatic as that of Mona Lisa herself, '*Bon soir*, Armand'. He turned towards her, an answering smile on his handsome face, as he kissed her hand with as much charm as if he were truly pleased to see her.

For a woman scorned, she exhibited not the least anger or embarrassment as she joined in the conversation of the little group around Armand. To be truthful, she looked ravishingly beautiful. The style of her pale hyacinth-blue frock proclaimed it to be the work of a master – it was of softest satin, the neckline scalloped and cut so deeply that most of her generous bosom was exposed. Her bare arms were adorned at the wrist with a diamond bracelet each, evidence that though Dominique no longer had a husband, she did not lack generous admirers.

Few women agree with the theory of the quick and fatal stab ending to a love-affair. In general they prefer to be told – which means that they demand to be told – the reasons why their lover is about to depart forever. Dominique was of the majority who regard it as their right to know, especially when the circumstances were as unusual as those surrounding her desertion by Armand. At the time she had found it inexplicable; after an evening of dancing together, he had accompanied her to her apartment and made love to her five or six times with enormous enthusiasm, before leaving silently in the early morning while she was still asleep.

Since that day she had heard not one word from him, and her telephone calls to his apartment were unanswered. Naturally, being a young woman of some experience with lovers, it was not difficult for her to guess the reason. And tranquil though her outward demeanour might be, in Dominique's mind was a steel-bound determination to get her own back on Armand. It was not that she was in love with him – he was, after all, only one of the half-dozen men who entertained her and took her shopping and were granted access to her personal charms. Perhaps he had been her favourite of them all, but that aside, as a matter of principle he must be paid back for the way he had behaved.

From her little evening-bag she took a cigarette and waited for Armand to light it for her. He flicked on a gold lighter – a birthday present to him from an earlier mistress – and Dominique took hold of his wrist, as if to steady it, while she bent over the tiny flame. If anyone had taken the trouble to observe this action, it would have been obvious that she was bending forward much lower than was strictly necessary, low enough in fact for Armand to be able to glance down the loose and scalloped front of her frock, if he had been so inclined. And as Dominique had guessed, the habit of a lifetime drew his eyes to her bosom.

From the closeness of their former friendship, Armand had good reason to know that it was Dominique's custom to support her enchanting though unfashionably large breasts in all-embracing white or pink brassières. To a man who took great delight in fondling women's breasts at every possible – and even impossible – opportunity, these useful garments were inconvenient and frustrating. In glancing down her frock he expected to see no more than two domes of white satin. Judge then his surprise and delight to observe a pair of bare and bouncy pale-skinned globes with prominent crimson tips!

Unknown to Armand, she had recently discovered in

the rue Cambon a veritable genius of a corsetiere, who had introduced her to the elegance of a type of brassière of his own devising, or so he claimed. Needless to say Monsieur Lecroq's creations were expensive because they had to be made and hand-sewn to fit each client individually, for, as he never tired of informing the visitors to his boutique as he handled and measured their soft delights, in his expert professional opinion the breasts of every lady were uniquely her own in their roundness and their size and their positioning on the body.

The ingenious little garments that came from his work-room had no shoulder-straps and fastened closely round the body, with curved platforms of reinforced satin to provide firm and yet discreet support to over-sized breasts while leaving them entirely uncovered. As a result of Lecroq's skills, and several fittings and adjustments, the sight that met Armand's gaze down the front of Dominique's frock was so enthralling that he stood with his hand held out and the little flame of the gold lighter still burning for seconds after she stood upright again and blew out a long plume of light blue smoke.

She smiled knowingly at the expression she saw on his face as he stood like a fool with his lighter. It was an expression with which she had become familiar during their time together – a wordless statement of admiration and desire. And being a sharp-witted woman, Dominique instantly seized the initiative thus presented to her. She looked at the glowing end of her cigarette, declared that it was not properly alight and bent over Armand's hand again. She stayed in that position for some moments, to give him ample oppor-tunity to feast his eyes on her uncovered treasures, her fingertips caressing his hand under guise of holding it steady – caressing it slowly to and fro as if it were some other part of him!

When she released him from the spell she had cast over him, there was a faint pinkness to Armand's cheeks that betrayed his exalted state of mind. By unspoken agreement, he and she moved imperceptibly away from the little group of people they had been part of, until they could speak to each other without the inconvenience of being overheard. Now that he knew that Dominique's succulent melons were bare inside her frock and slip, Armand couldn't take his eyes away from them – he stared at the bodice of her frock as if he was trying to discern her buds through the satin, as indeed he was.

While they were conversing in meaningless trivialities, Dominique stimulated his exaltation with deliberate shrugs and twisting movements of her shoulders to make her loose breasts roll a little under her frock. And the delicate flush on Armand's cheeks grew darker and more intense as something that hung inside his underwear rose to the occasion. But though it was an immensely exciting game they were playing together, Armand was secretly terrified that Madeleine would notice him standing alone with Dominique and leap to the inevitable conclusion. That would be disagreeable in the extreme.

He had been very pleasantly surprised that Dominique had uttered not one word of reproach. Indeed, she was behaving towards him with all the casual affection of an old and trusted friend. For a woman, so very enlightened an attitude was remarkable, he thought, but then, he had always known Dominique to be a remarkable woman! It goes without saying that in this Armand was deceiving himself. Dominique's emotions operated on the same primitively instinctive level as those of every other woman whose lover has deserted her for another – as in due course Armand was to find out, to his regret!

But for now she was enchanting. She put her head close to his for a moment, so that the sensuous perfume she wore drove him almost dizzy with delight, and in a confidential whisper she said that there was something of great importance to them both about which she needed to consult him.

'Of course, but not here,' he replied, taking her bait like the least suspicious fish in a river.

'Out in the hall?' she suggested, raising her eyebrows in question.

But when they slipped separately out of the salon, there was no privacy in the entrance hall. One of the maids was stationed there to assist those arriving and those departing with their coats and hats, and other servants passed through constantly with trays, bottles, clean glasses and the other requisites of a reception. Armand shrugged in disappointment, but Dominique had suggested the hall only as the first step in removing him from the crowded salon. She waited for a moment when they were not observed, took his hand and led him quickly away from the entrance hall and the salon, towards the rear of the Brissards' very large apartment.

Armand had no idea of where they were going, and nor did Dominique. But the location was of no importance, as long as they found somewhere to be alone for a few minutes while she said what she had to say to him. After some minutes of searching, she found a place she thought perfect – a maid's narrow bedroom right at the back of the apartment, with a window that faced a wall no more than two metres away. The servants were all fully occupied in attendance on the guests, there was no risk that the occupant of the dismal little room would return to it for hours yet.

Dominique switched on the single electric light that hung in the centre of the ceiling. The glow was far from bright, and as soon as the door was shut, Armand took her into his arms and rained hot kisses on her face.

'Ah, so that's it, is it?' she exclaimed, pushing him away from her. 'Almost two months from you without a word – you have deliberately avoided me all that time! And when we meet by chance, you expect that everything will be as it was once between us!'

'But I thought . . .' he stammered, astounded by her change of temper towards him.

'No, Armand, you never think. You met someone else and left me without a word,' she said with so

80

much conviction in her voice that it should have been a warning to him. 'You never use your brain, my dear – you simply do what *this* suggests!' and the diamond bracelets glittered on her wrists as she reached forward and downward with both hands, and before Armand had time to prevent her, she snatched open his trouser-buttons, from waist-band to groin.

'Dominique, for Heaven's sake,' he exclaimed, grabbing at her wrists and appalled by the thought that Madeleine might come looking for him and find him indecently exposed in this way with another woman.

Dominique had no such qualms, she jerked the front of his silk shirt out of the way with one hand while, with the other, she took hold of his appendage and pulled it out through the slit of his underwear for her scrutiny.

'As I suspected – limp and soft,' she declared. 'It's obvious that you've been giving it a lot of use recently, though not with me. Who has been having the benefit of it, Armand, tell me! Is it Madeleine Beauvais? Everyone knows that she's left her husband. Was it for you she left him?'

He managed to pull her hand away from him, but that was by no means the end of the matter – Dominique understood how to get her way with him. Before he could tuck his equipment back into his trousers, she fell to one knee and engulfed him in her hot mouth. Not for nothing had she and Armand been the most intimate of friends for almost a year before he abandoned her for Madeleine – in that time she had come to appreciate his extreme susceptibility to female charms and knew how simple it was to arouse him. Half a dozen laps of her tongue and his stem was stiff in her mouth.

Armand stared wide-eyed down the length of his body to his gaping trousers, where his dearest part was rearing itself upwards from a nest of curly black hair and Dominique's blonde head was bobbing up and down on it. Her eyes were closed and her face was calm under her blonde fringe, and the sight was so arousing that Armand was lost. She heard his little sigh, interpreted it correctly, and raised her scarlet-painted mouth from its task to look up at him. Her dark blue eyes stared boldly up at his face while she grasped his solid hilt tightly in her fingers and massaged it.

'But Dominique . . . we can't do it here!' Armand sighed.

There was sincere regret in his voice. It had taken only a few seconds expert work for Dominique to make him forget his fear of discovery and the consequences. She wasted no words on answering him – she stood up quickly and raised the hem of her hyacinth-blue frock to her waist. Armand stared down in fascination at the creamy expanse of her bare thighs between her stocking-tops and the lace-frilled eau-de-nil silk knickers she wore. He murmured her name, as if to himself, when she pulled aside the loose leg of her knickers and bared the light brown fur that adorned her plump mound.

'That's more like it,' she said with approval, taking hold of the long peg she had made wet and slippery with her tongue. 'As stiff as a broom-handle and nearly as thick! That's very creditable, my dear. She hasn't drained you completely yet.'

'Dominique, if anyone sees us!' he gasped, his fears returning now that the psychological moment was here.

He was in so advanced a condition of arousal that the irony of the situation was lost on him – he was repeating almost exactly the little objections that Madeleine had raised when she stood at the window of Yvonne's salon and he had pulled up her nightgown to fondle her sleek and naked body. In her case the objections were fictitious, for it had been improbable in the extreme that anyone would interrupt them in Yvonne's salon. But here, during a party, standing with Dominique beside an iron bedstead in a maid's room of the Brissard apartment, his male magnificence fully exposed and erect, the danger was high.

But as all the world knows, when a man's cherished part stands upright, then all his powers of reason, logic and intelligence flow down immediately into it, which is to say that he is capable of any stupidity. Armand's pride was fluttering in Dominique's hand, and the sensations were so very delicious that he was prepared to risk all: his friends, his reputation; he was even prepared to risk losing Madeleine herself. And Dominique knew it and was counting on it.

He tried to turn her round and lay her on the hard bed, but she had no time for that. With a firm grip on his handle, she dragged him towards her and directed him upwards between her bare thighs until, hardly knowing in his delirium of delight what he was doing, he drove deep into her.

'Yes!' she cried in triumph, as he gripped her by the waist and pumped in and out of her with hard thrusts.

Her hands were inside his open trousers and, in her urgency, she ripped off the waist-band button that held his striped silk underpants closed. She forced her hands into the sagging garment to reach round him and clutch his bare bottom fiercely. Armand groaned in pleasurable pain as she sank her nails into the flesh with the cruel strength of a lioness tearing its hapless prey with its claws.

'What are you doing!' he moaned, his loins slamming against her in an uncontrollable paroxysm of desire.

Dominique threw her blonde head back, her mouth wide open and gasped, 'Now, Armand!' Almost at once she felt his spout gush his release into her. 'Oh, yes!' she sighed, as her own crisis overwhelmed her.

But there was to be no shared and tender after-glow of passion. Almost before his embedded part had ceased to jerk, Dominique pulled herself away from him, leaving him unsupported on legs that were trembling. It had all happened so quickly that Armand couldn't believe that it was over, that his instantly-inflated balloon had swollen past its limit and burst already. He took a shaky step towards the bed, and sat on it, staring wide-eyed at Dominique's pale blue frock sliding down over her hips to cover her to the knees – like the descent of a theatre-curtain when the performance ends!

Alas, there were no curtain-calls, no cries of *Encore*,

no bouquets of flowers for the performers of the little comedy that had just been played. Armand sat speechless on the bed, his wet limb exposed, and glared at Dominique in an accusing manner. His emotions were impossibly confused at that moment – in his mind Dominique had lured him into this dark little room and tricked him into making love to her, she had trapped him into taking an absurd risk, and for what? The pleasure she had given him had lasted no longer than a snow-flake falling on to the Seine! But there was worse to come.

'You remember how you raped me on the staircase, Armand? I thought it only polite to return the compliment,' said Dominique, a distinct note of spite in her voice. 'Stay there just like that – with your trousers down. I'll send your new girlfriend in to see what you've been up to.'

And with a flounce of her skirt, she was gone, leaving him alone and feeling utterly foolish in the uncomfortable little room. Then panic gripped him as his vivid imagination presented him with a scene of Madeleine flinging open the door and glaring at him in jealous fury. With fingers that were twitching, he stuffed his wilting shaft into his crumpled underwear and got to his feet to do up his trousers, the paramount thought in his mind that he must hide away that which, in other circumstances, he was more than happy to show to Madeleine.

It was then that he made the unwelcome discovery that Dominique's brutal assault on him had torn off two of his trouser buttons, as well as the mother-of-pearl one from his under-shorts. He fastened those that remained and examined the result in the mirror that stood on an old-fashioned dressing-table by the wall, but the light in the room was poor and he was not at all confident that the condition of his trousers would pass wholly unnoticed when he returned to the salon. And another thought struck him – if the maid who occupied this room came across a couple of men's trouser-buttons on the floor, questions would surely be asked!

There was nothing for it but to get down on his hands and knees and search in the dim light for the missing buttons. One had rolled under the narrow bed and was soon retrieved, and the mother of pearl button lay on the bed itself, where the impetus of Dominique's savage jerk had flung it. But the other trouser-button was nowhere to be seen. He scrabbled about under the dressing-table and the dark corners of the room, listening fearfully for footsteps outside that would herald the arrival of Madeleine. And after five minutes of futile search, he gave up and fled from the little room.

Needless to say, Dominique said nothing to Madeleine and never had the least intention of doing so. It was an empty threat on the spur of the moment, to take advantage of the bad conscience she had seen revealed on Armand's face when he collapsed on to the bed after his bolt was shot. As a threat it was highly effective – she succeeded in giving him a very bad quarter of an hour. And by the time Armand reached the salon, Dominique had said her farewells to the Brissards and gone, dragging her bewildered escort along behind her.

The simple truth was that Armand was mortified by the episode with Dominique and the urgent necessity to keep it secret from Madeleine. His vexation lasted for the rest of the evening and was so apparent that, when he and Madeleine left the Brissards', she requested that he take her directly to her sister's apartment. Their earlier intention had been to go on to a nightclub with Yvonne and her current escort, to dance a little and enjoy themselves. When Yvonne heard of the change of plan, she shrugged and departed in her admirer's gleaming new motor-car, in no way put out.

Armand took Madeleine by taxi to the rue Saint-Didier, and though he would have gone up to the apartment with her, she stopped him at the street-door.

'Good night, Armand,' she said firmly. 'You may telephone me tomorrow if you are in a better mood.'

Very calmly she presented her cheek to him for a polite but perfunctory kiss, and left him standing on the pavement, feeling foolish – and not for the first time that evening. On the assumption that she would invite him up for a drink and perhaps just a tiny embrace, he had paid off the taxi before getting out of it. By now it had driven off; he saw the red twinkle of its rear-lights in the distance, turning into the Avenue Kleber. The autumn evening was cold and melancholy and the air felt thick with unshed drizzle.

Armand crossed the street to stand on the opposite pavement and look up at the curtained windows of the Hiver apartment on the first floor. It was only a week ago that he had stood behind those curtains in the dark with Madeleine, feeling her naked little breasts under her nightgown! Ah, what an entrancing evening that had been – the delicious sensation of enjoying her elegant body while she stood at the window staring down at Pierre-Louis. The situation had induced a fantastic crisis in him – and in her – for without his arms round her she would have fallen to the floor.

At the memory, the faithful companion dangling between Armand's thighs threw off the lethargy that had overtaken it and raised its head. Without their retaining button, Armand's striped silk underpants hung in a tangle inside the legs of his trousers, so that, when his eager friend came to attention, there was nothing to stop its head butting against the incomplete fastenings where Dominique had torn buttons away. And, with an infallible instinct to penetrate into whatever convenient gap was nearby, it thrust itself boldly through this slit to rub against the black satin lining of his overcoat.

My poor friend, Armand silently addressed his thwarted part, *the beautiful Madeleine has deserted us, you and I. The pleasure you demand is not available to us this evening. She is up there in the salon behind the window, and we are out here on the pavement sharing the miserable secret of whose hot receptacle you spat in earlier. I am far too dejected to contemplate a visit to the Chabanais or Maison Junot or any other establishment where young women make themselves available. There is nothing for it but to go home and to bed.*

After so vexing an experience, Armand's astonishment may be imagined when, the very next morning while he was drinking his coffee and skimming through the newspaper, Madame Cottier interrupted to announce Madame Delaval! Madame Cottier was the middle-aged widow who came in each morning to look after Armand's simple domestic requirements. She brought his newspaper from the nearest kiosk and fresh bread rolls from the baker, made his coffee, cleaned the apartment, washed and ironed his shirts and, in general, made herself utterly indispensable to his bachelor way of life.

Before Armand had time to tell her indignantly to send the unwelcome visitor away, Dominique pushed her way past her and into the sitting-room where he was comfortably settled in dressing-gown and pyjamas in an arm-chair, with a small table at his side for his coffee and croissants.

'*Bonjour*, Armand,' she said cheerfully. 'Forgive me for calling on you so early, but I was passing and it seemed a good opportunity to tell you something you will be pleased to hear.'

She was wearing a most elegant full-length chinchilla fur coat, of a subtle shade of grey, and a little cloche hat of a darker grey. Her cheeks were slightly flushed and, when she pulled off her black suede gloves, she rubbed her hands briskly together to warm them. Madame Cottier withdrew to continue with her work and Dominique sat herself in an armchair opposite Armand. He made a pretence of returning her greeting by half-rising to his feet, making no attempt to touch her hand, and sank back into his chair, glaring suspiciously.

Not for a moment did he believe that she was passing by on the way to somewhere else. It was only a little after nine o'clock – much too early for Dominique to be up and about and going anywhere. She was here for some devious purpose, he was sure, but her next words took him by surprise.

87

'I've come to apologise to you most sincerely, Armand,' she said. 'I behaved disgracefully yesterday. There's no excuse at all. I'd had no more than two glasses of champagne. What must you think of me?'

She shrugged her shoulders in a rueful little gesture that expressed her dismay in the most charming manner in the world. Armand could never resist an appeal to his good nature by a pretty woman and he accepted her apology graciously.

'Good, then we're friends again,' said Dominique, standing up as if to leave now that she and he were reconciled.

But as he now discovered, it was not her intention to leave, at least, not immediately. She pulled loose the knot of the pink silk scarf round her throat and tugged the ends out of her coat to expose the smooth skin of her neck and chest. Her only jewellery was a small gold cross on a chain round her neck. And as Armand stared, half-wondering and half-guessing what was to come next, she opened her fur coat completely and slipped it back on her shoulders – and with a broad smile let him see that she had no clothes. But her beautiful body was not entirely naked – around her waist was a suspender-belt of white lace and satin to support her grey silk stockings.

'Oh, Dominique, why are you doing this to me?' Armand asked with a long sigh.

'I thought it would be nice to remind you of what you are missing,' she answered, holding her coat wide open. 'Why was it you found me unattractive so suddenly, after you made love to me six times in one night? Am I ugly now?'

Armand stared at her bare breasts – big, round and with prominent dark-red buds. He remembered vividly how enjoyable they were to the hands, in the days when he and she regularly made love to each other. He looked down to the sensuous curve of her belly, cut across by the white suspender belt, and he remembered all too well the joys of lying on that soft belly. His glance fell lower, to the fleece of blondish-brown curls that covered the tender peach he had split so often and with such delight. And he sighed again.

Dominique's red lips were curved in a smile as she watched the easily recognised expressions flickering across Armand's rapt face. She advanced towards his armchair and sank to her knees before him. Without another word she undid the belt of his dressing-gown, wrenched open the buttons of his scarlet silk pyjama jacket and dragged the trousers down, baring him from throat to knees with one snatch of her hand. His sturdy friend was already at full-stretch and it twitched in gratitude as she stroked it, much like the humorous response of a dog that sits up and wags its tail when its owner pats its head.

'Come into the bedroom,' Armand whispered. 'I want to see you lying on your back with your legs open and your fur coat spread under you . . .'

'There's no time for that,' she murmured, her hand moving up and down with great skill and rapidity. 'Lie back in the chair, but don't you dare close your eyes. Look at me!'

As if for a moment he – or any other man fortunate enough to be in his position – would close his eyes or turn away from the delicious spectacle of Dominique's fleshy melons bouncing up and down to the fast rhythm of her tightly clasped hand, and the little gold cross joggling from side to side between them! He reached out to squeeze her plump beauties and she moved in closer between his thighs to put them within his grasp.

'Dominique, Dominique . . .' he gasped, '*Je t'adore, chérie!*'

His adored *chérie* was so pleased with the effect she was having on him that her hand moved even faster, and at once she was rewarded by such a show of affectionate tail-wagging that she almost laughed aloud at the simplicity of men, especially handsome and vain young men like Armand. He was staring down enraptured at the little blondish fleece between her legs as he waited for the incredible moment when she would straddle his lap with her bare thighs and impale herself on him. And as if she had read his thought, an instant later he was ensconced in that soft niche and she was bouncing up and down on his lap, so fast that he knew it would be no more than seconds before he jetted his desire into her.

Or so he fondly imagined – but that was not what Dominique had in mind. It was not to gratify Armand that she had left her warm bed hours before her usual time to take a taxi-ride naked in a fur coat to his apartment, it was to continue the lesson she had decided to teach him – a lesson that would put him in his place. He would find the beginning pleasant enough – as he had in the Brissard apartment last night – but the end would be a very different story.

'Dominique,' he gasped, feeling his belly clench in readiness for what was about to happen.

'Yes, Armand,' she said calmly, 'this is it.'

She had very deliberately hurried him along faster and further than he realised; it was too late now for him to prevent what she had intended from the first. His dark brown eyes widened at the first familiar throb in his belly, and Dominique's mocking blue eyes beneath her blonde fringe and little cloche hat stared directly into his as she suddenly and unexpectedly straightened her legs and stood up! The movement lifted her completely off him and deprived him of his warm berth at the very moment that he discharged his vital cargo.

'*No!*' Armand gasped in dismay, staring aghast at his mindless traitor of a tail as it betrayed him by bounding in glee and spraying his passion over his own bare belly, all the way up to the dark hair on his chest.

Even before his climactic spasms ended, Dominique stepped back from him, an unfathomable smile on her face while she tied her silk scarf round her neck and surveyed the results of what she had done to him. Armand looked up at her uncomprehendingly, while she fastened her fur coat to conceal her smooth-skinned naked body from him.

'I really must run along or I shall be late,' she said,

as casually as if she had dropped in for a cup of coffee. 'Are you expecting Madeleine this afternoon? She's welcome to what's left. Don't forget to give her my regards. *Au revoir*, Armand.'

And with a graceful little wave of her hand, she turned on her heel and was gone, leaving him dumbfounded. She left the sitting-room door half-open on purpose, and Armand could hear voices and a little laugh from the entrance hall, where Madame Cottier was seeing his visitor out. With the perspiration of near-panic shining on his forehead, he flicked the cream silk handkerchief from the breast-pocket of his dressing-gown and dried himself hastily, afraid that Madame Cottier might come into the room before he had time to rearrange his pyjamas decently. Once again Dominique had succeeded in putting him in an abjectly embarrassing situation!

Her parting shot had not been far from the truth, and that too was upsetting. Over his second cup of coffee, only a minute or two before Dominique arrived in his sitting-room, he had decided to telephone Madeleine at the socially acceptable hour of eleven o'clock to apologise for his ill-humour the previous evening. And when she had forgiven him, he would invite her to lunch, and afterwards bring her back to his apartment. Madame Cottier would be long gone by then and it was his intention to give Madeleine exquisite reassurance in bed that he still adored her more than any other woman in the entire world.

The fact was, he admitted to himself, that Dominique had outmanoeuvred him – and his nerves were jangled rather than soothed by the deceptive climax she had inflicted upon him. With that secret gnawing at him, he knew himself to be in no fit condition to talk to Madeleine, without grave risk of a repetition of last evening's debacle. He decided that the most sensible course was to postpone his telephone call until after lunch – by then he hoped that the disagreeable feeling of defeat that pervaded him would have abated. Perhaps Madeleine would consent to dine with him that evening. And afterwards – who could say?

But when he made his telephone call, a servant informed him that Madame Beauvais was not at home. To have missed another opportunity to put things right with her so annoyed him that he immediately telephoned Dominique to give her a piece of his mind. *She* was in, though she irritated him further by sounding amused when she recognised his voice.

'But why are you telephoning me, Armand? Did Madeleine not visit you after all – or has she already left because you were unable to meet her expectations?'

'Dominique, this nonsense must stop!' he said. 'We must reach an understanding to respect each other's privacy.'

'But I respect your privacy very much,' she answered, her laughter only just suppressed. 'Surely that was apparent this morning when I went down on my knees to lavish esteem upon it.'

'This is no laughing matter,' he said testily. 'Meet me in half an hour from now and we will settle things between us, once and for all.'

'Aha!' Dominique exclaimed. 'Are you inviting me to visit you for the second time today? I'll be there. Would you like me to wear my chinchilla coat again?'

'Not here!' he said in alarm.

'Then you would prefer to come to me? So much the better – I shall expect you in half an hour. I went shopping for underwear after I left you this morning and I found knickers made of crepe de chine so fine that they are completely transparent – imagine that! I shall put them on while I'm waiting for you.'

'No, no, no!' said Armand, infuriated by her refusal to take him seriously. 'I do not trust you – we shall meet and talk in a public place.'

'As you wish,' she said, chuckling at his alarm. 'I will meet you in front of Notre-Dame. You couldn't ask for a more public place than that. We shall be surrounded by foreign tourists – that should make you feel safe from me.'

'In half an hour, then,' said Armand, still suspicious.

It was much too late in the year for foreign tourists, of course, and the intermittent rain had driven away even the most hardy of indigenous sightseers. Armand walked across the bridge to the Ile de la Cité, the big collar of his camelhair overcoat turned up almost to his hat-brim to keep the cold and damp wind off his neck. Over the parapet he saw the Seine, grey and dirty, carrying along broken pieces of timber, water-logged newspapers and other less identifiable rubbish. It had been stupid of him to allow Dominique to choose their meeting-place, he reflected.

She kept him waiting in the open no more than ten minutes, and she arrived dressed to dramatic perfection for the day – in a shiny black mackintosh and a matching hat pulled well down over her ears. The coat was belted tightly round her waist to emphasise the full curves of her breasts and bottom. She offered Armand her hand and he kissed the back of her soft black leather glove. She smiled and offered him her cheek and he paused before touching his lips to it. At that she laughed and offered him her mouth to kiss, but he took a half-step back and reminded her that they were here to talk.

'Then talk Armand,' she said cheerfully, 'I am listening.'

'The rain will start again in another minute – we'll find a café where we can be comfortable,' he said.

But Dominique would have none of it. It was he who had insisted on the discomfort of a public place for their meeting, rather than her apartment or his – very well then, the talking would take place in the open air, or not at all. And so it came about that Armand found himself strolling with her along the gleaming rain-wet cobbles of the square and down the side of the cathedral. They crossed over the bridge to the other island – the Ile St-Louis – and went down to the embankment promenade by the river's edge.

'Why have you decided to persecute me, Dominique?' he asked her. 'I admit that I ought to have arranged our parting in a less abrupt manner – I'm sorry about that and I hope you'll forgive me for my discourtesy. But we were never in love with each other, and you will surely not claim that I was the only man on terms of intimacy with you. So why are you doing this?'

'I find it extraordinary to hear you complaining because I let you make love to me yesterday at the Brissards' party. Or are you protesting because I dropped in on you this morning and gave you a little reminder of past pleasures?'

'But that is the point exactly!' said Armand. 'All that is over between us.'

'Heavens, how times have changed!' she retorted. 'Not long ago you would have been beside yourself with delight if I dropped in naked to treat you to an unexpected little thrill at breakfast-time.'

The Quai was almost deserted – the inclemency of the weather had driven away even the derelicts usually to be found down there under the bridges with their bottles of cheap wine. There was so much moisture in the air that the old and derelict buildings across the river on the Left Bank were barely visible through a shroud of haze. Only a solitary fisherman sat huddled in a waterproof, his legs dangling over the stone edge, staring with the insane patience of the obsessed at his float bobbing on the sullen grey water.

Armand and Dominique walked on, wrangling with each other, until suddenly the rain descended again, this time not just a heavy shower but a miserable downpour that seemed set to last. Armand dragged Dominique at a trot along the Quai towards the next bridge, to shelter under it.

'You admit that you never loved me,' she accused him, 'and now you hate me!'

They were safely out of the rain under the bridge and she turned to face him.

'Why?' she asked. 'What have I done to deserve your hate?'

'I don't hate you, Dominique, please don't think that,' he said, putting his hands on her arms. 'I regard you as one of my dearest friends, truly I do. But – how can I explain . . .'

'There's no need to,' she said, 'I understand you better than you understand yourself. You are unbelievably fickle, Armand – that is the terrible flaw in your character.'

'I know it,' he confessed, 'but what can I do?'

Dominique leaned her back against the grey stonework of the bridge and he moved closer to keep the wind off her. He was half a head taller than she was and she rose on tip-toe, her face turned up to kiss him.

'You are impossible,' she murmured. 'Peace between us?'

'Do you mean it?' he asked, and for reply she kissed him again. Her lips were cold but the tongue that touched the tip of his tongue was warm. The kiss was lingering and pleasurable – it lasted long enough for her to have time to unbutton his overcoat and, with a gloved hand, to feel his soft bulge through his trousers. Accepting the challenge, Armand glanced quickly left and right: they were alone under the bridge, with a curtain of rain cutting off the view both ways.

'I warn you, my dear Dominique, I am not here to be your victim,' he told her as he took her wrists and raised her arms until her hands were on his shoulders, well out of harm's way.

'Then what will you do, Armand?'

'I shall retaliate.'

'I forbid it!' she exclaimed, her blue eyes shining.

He undid the tight belt round her waist, unbuttoned her shiny wet mackintosh and opened it, to find that she was wearing a high-necked woollen jumper with a bold pattern of black and white diamonds, and a black skirt. His hand was up the skirt in a moment, and the silk chemise beneath it, and he felt between her bare thighs, above her stocking-tops.

'Your hands are cold!' she gasped. 'Stop it, Armand!'

His hand was indeed cold, for he had left his apartment in a state of irritation and confusion after his conversation with her on the telephone, and he had overlooked his gloves. Dominique's warm thighs clamped his hand tightly between them, to prevent it reaching further and touching the centre of her delight with icy finger-tips.

'I warned you that I would retaliate,' he said.

He pressed his lips to her lips – and she opened them a little so that this time it was his tongue that found hers. The kiss endured longer than the last, and was certainly as pleasurable – perhaps even more so, for after some seconds Dominique relaxed the grip of her thighs. Armand's hand, warmed a little by the clasp of her bare flesh, continued its short, exciting journey upwards and found the embroidered edge of her knickers. He wondered whether they were the totally transparent creation she had mentioned when she taunted him on the telephone.

'Oh, yes,' she said when he asked her. 'I told you I'd put them on specially for you, Armand. They are made of rose-pink silk so thin and fine that everything shows through.'

Perhaps she was telling the truth, and perhaps not. It was of no consequence at that moment – Armand's hand was up inside her underwear and the source of her most intimate pleasures was clasped in his palm. He pressed her head back against the stonework with his mouth on hers in another long kiss and his eyes were closed to give his fervid imagination full play – in his imagination he glimpsed Dominique's fleece of blondish curls through silk as fine as gossamer.

The image was so arousing that he licked slowly with the tip of his tongue around her red-painted lips – and in his fantasy it was not her mouth that his tongue was touching but the other lips under those blondish curls of hers. Dominique sensed how excited he was becoming and whispered, 'Armand, Armand, Armand.' He slipped his tongue inside her hot mouth, making believe that it was the opening he was clasping full-handed inside her embroidered – and perhaps transparent – silk knickers.

Dominique fluttered her tongue against his tongue

and moved her feet apart when she felt his fingers easing themselves into the secret alcove between her thighs. She understood very well the fascination that playing with it had for Armand, and it was for this that she had been waiting. She congratulated herself that her plan to repossess him had succeeded even more quickly than she had foreseen. It had required no more than two little assaults – last night and this morning – to provoke him into what he in his innocence thought of as reprisals. In effect, by putting his hand between her legs he had surrendered to her, though he did not know that yet.

He was deeply engrossed in his erotic reverie, his fingers teasing Dominique towards a delicious climax, and he paid no attention when her hands moved away from his shoulders. Nor did he object when she unbuttoned his trousers, slipped off a glove and insinuated her hand into his underwear – perhaps to balance his inside hers – and took hold of his staunchly upright part. She handled it with such tenderness and delicacy of feeling that Armand was hardly aware of her touch, only of an increase in the pleasure he was already experiencing from his skilful manipulation of her.

'Oh, Armand,' she sighed, 'I would have given anything in the world if only things could have stayed as they were between us! You are a very special person, my dear – no one has ever given me half the pleasure that you do – I've adored you for it since the first time!'

It need hardly be said that he was enraptured by her little compliment, for Dominique's experience of male pride was sufficient for her to know how she could achieve her purpose.

'Do you like me at all, Armand?' she asked, as plaintively as the tremors of passion shaking her body would permit.

'But I adore you,' he murmured, so highly aroused that he hardly knew what he was saying – and cared even less in the heat of the moment how his words could be interpreted.

'Then I give myself you, body and soul!' she gasped,

as her crucial moment arrived and she rubbed herself against his fingers in ecstatic convulsions.

'Dominique!' he exclaimed feverishly.

Truth to tell, his pleasure was so intense in having brought her to so evidently satisfactory a conclusion that he was almost beside himself. All this time her hand in his trousers had been holding the head of his throbbing projection between thumb and finger. When her spasms shook her she tugged until she had it out of his open trousers and into the loose leg of her knickers. She was hardly aware of what she was doing, but the result was dramatic in the extreme – Armand gasped and sank deep into her with a ferocious lunge, and instantly released a veritable flood of passion.

When they came to their senses again she buttoned his trousers for him and waited for him to speak first. He was silent for a long time, his cheek resting against hers, as if in deep thought, though in truth he was experiencing emotions of gratitude for the pleasure she had given him.

'Dear Dominique,' he said at last, 'it seems to me that I have allowed myself to behave abominably towards you. We have enjoyed each other so much – how could I ever be fool enough to lose sight of that, I ask myself? When I think of the distress I have caused you, I am desolated. Can you truly forgive me?'

'Come home with me,' she murmured, her lips against his cheek. 'I will let you adore me in my new transparent underwear to prove that I have forgiven you.'

Her loving words affected him so much that he slid his hand back up her skirt to clench the fleshy mound between her legs.

'Let's go and find a taxi.' he said. 'But I give you fair warning – adoring you will not be enough for me. I shall insist on doing more to you than that, much more. And if your new frillies are ruined by what I may do to them, I shall buy you another half-dozen sets.'

With arms about each other's waists, they climbed the wet steps up to the bridge, ignoring the rain on their faces. Armand was pleased to have made his peace with Dominique – her lasciviousness was entrancing and matched his own – and she had always been content to go along with whatever little games he devised. As for Madeleine, beautiful and desirable though she was, it must not be overlooked that she was the wife of Pierre-Louis, to whom as a cousin a certain respect was due.

To be fair, it must be admitted that Madeleine had never denied Armand access to her charms in certain interesting and slightly out-of-the-ordinary ways from time to time. She had been persuaded to get down on her hands and knees naked on his sitting-room carpet one afternoon, for instance, and there had been that delicious episode at the window in her night-gown. But, during eight years of marriage to Pierre-Louis, she had become accustomed to a certain style of horizontal love-making in bed, and that was what she preferred. Never in a life-time would it occur to Madeleine to arrive at a rendezvous naked in a fur-coat!

It was most fortunate that Dominique had reappeared in his life at exactly the most propitious moment, Armand thought, ready to forgive and forget and continue their intimate friendship as if nothing had happened. Of course, he did not propose to break with Madeleine, for he truly adored her. But there would be a gradual lengthening of the time between their meetings and love-making. He had no doubt of his ability to keep her satisfied, even though Dominique had returned to him – for this was the mistaken manner in which he described to himself the events of the past twenty-four hours.

As for Dominique, the set smile on her rain-wet face meant nothing – for she understood Armand too well to deceive herself that she had regained control of his affections. At most she had led him back by the bridle, so to speak, and harnessed him alongside the other half-dozen stallions that drew her carriage. And there she might be able to keep him for a while – with an occasional flick of the whip on his imagination when he became restive. He was, after all, a generous man and an amusing companion, and always ready to think of new ways to gratify her desires. At the taxi rank, she hugged him round the waist and smiled at him.

'It's not a long ride to my apartment, Armand,' she said, 'but if I open my mackintosh in the taxi and let you put your hand up my skirt, are you clever enough to give me another little thrill before we get there?'

'You may be sure of it,' he murmured, although now that she had relieved him of his urgent desire under the bridge he was having second thoughts about the resumption of their liaison on any basis other than the most casual.

It was as well that he had no suspicion of the calculations going on in Dominique's blonde head of how she might benefit financially from him before his failing interest in her vanished completely.

5

Love Has Its Price

In one of the many celebrated cafés of the Boulevard du Montparnasse, Armand rose to his feet as he saw Suzette Chenet come in from the street. She was wearing her expensive vicuna coat with the dark fur cuffs and a scarlet and grey silk scarf tied round her head, peasant-style, in place of a hat. She looked round the crowded cafe, saw Armand and made her way towards him.

'*Bonsoir, Monsieur,*' she said, holding out her gloved hand. 'I recognise you now.'

Evidently she was expecting her hand to be shaken, but that was not Armand's way. He took it as delicately as if it were the most priceless and fragile *objet-d'art* in the collection of a connoisseur, and kissed it with exquisite courtesy. She smiled briefly and then resumed her serious expression, though it was easy enough to see that this cost her an effort, the habitual expression of her pretty face being a cheerful smile. At Armand's invitation she sat down, pulled off her colourful head-scarf and brushed her hair back from her forehead – hair with the texture of finely-spun silk, he thought, looking at it closely, and of a shade of light brown that was almost blonde.

As is well known, first impressions, whether good or bad, are often permanent. When Armand had first caught sight of Suzette with his cousin Pierre-Louis only six or seven days before, the impression she had made on him was favourable in the extreme. Her face and figure held a delicious chubbiness – sadly unfashionable in this era of tall, thin women devoid of bosoms and bottoms under their close fitting clothes. But in an eighteen-year-old like Suzette, this well-fleshed, clear-skinned, healthy glow gave her an air of devastating eroticism.

She pulled off her grey gloves and looked Armand straight in the eye across the little table. 'So Pierre-Louis does not have the courage to come here and look me in the face,' she said. 'He sends you in his place, Monsieur. After the atrocities he committed I suppose it is hardly surprising.'

'He is totally desolated, believe me,' Armand responded. 'What may I order for you? He is overcome with shame and grief and abases himself on the ground before your feet. In his bitter remorse he feels himself unworthy to even speak to you.'

Hearing this preposterous exaggeration, Suzette could not prevent herself from bursting out in laughter. But in a moment she made herself look solemn again. Now that he was close to her, Armand could determine the question he had not been able to resolve satisfactorily when he had seen her before – the colour of her eyes. They were a rare and delightful hazel. He wondered what she was wearing under her beautiful coat. When he saw her with Pierre-Louis she had been wearing a honey-yellow frock that fitted closely enough to display her plump breasts to great advantage. He recalled very well undressing her in his imagination on that occasion.

In response to his question she decided to have a little glass of liqueur – as a protection against the cold, naturally – and eventually settled upon Benedictine. Armand ordered it, and another glass of Armagnac for himself. At his suggestion she removed her beautiful winter coat and he saw that she was dressed very simply in a cream satin blouse and a skirt with a chequered pattern of grey and bright red similar to that of her head-scarf. He smiled at her in secret pleasure, and she smiled back briefly, forgetting that she was here to play the role of one who has been wronged.

She could have no suspicion that in his highly-developed though monomaniacal imagination Armand was removing her clothes – and not for the first time. In his mind's eye he had undone the buttons of her blouse and was kissing her plump breasts. He stood up to take her coat and stared down into her lap – and his fantasy he made her skirt disappear, to reveal her well-rounded thighs and her frilly-edged knickers. Vivid red, he said to himself, that's the colour I would like them to be – and of shiny satin!

But though men may deceive themselves that their innermost thoughts are a secret from everyone else, it was not in the least impossible for Suzette to guess what was in his mind. Young as she was, she had the same infallible intuition that every woman is born with. That being so, it required no great feat of intellect to interpret correctly Armand's interest in her blouse and skirt – or rather, in the exciting charms they concealed. She smiled a little, as if to herself, and crossed her legs under the table, not from alarmed modesty or to protect herself from his prying eyes, but to advise Armand that more was required than a few admiring looks and words.

'Pierre-Louis abases himself at my feet, does he?' she asked. 'I would dearly love to see him grovel in front of me, and in a public place! The Place de la Concorde at midday would be a good choice – I should have insisted on that as part of the settlement.'

'Your wish to hurt and humiliate him is as strong as that, Mademoiselle?' said Armand. 'He must have treated you abominably badly to arouse such intense feelings. What can I say – I assure you that I had no idea of his deficiencies.

'Deficiencies! You have no idea of the physical atrocities he inflicted on me.'

She pronounced *atrocities* with such emphasis that it was evident she enjoyed using the word to describe her misfortunes.

'But this is terrible,' said Armand, his voice sincere and full of sympathy. 'Can you bring yourself to tell me of it, or is the memory of it too distressing?'

'He raped me!' she said dramatically. 'He beat me and spat on me. Can you believe that of your cousin, or do you think I am lying to you from malice? He threw me to the floor with all his strength – I fully expected to be trampled to death.'

'Good god!' Armand exclaimed and, seeing her eyes bright with tears of shame and rage at the memory, he reached across the small table and took her hand to comfort her. 'Horse-whipping is too good for him. But he will make what amends he can, and I am here as proof of that. Difficult though it may be, I urge you to put this dreadful memory behind you and take up your life anew, full of the hope and confidence of youth and beauty that should naturally inspire you.'

'You are very understanding,' Suzette sighed, letting her warm hand rest lightly in his.

It was necessary to bear in mind that she had been Pierre-Louis' mistress for almost a year before the regrettable incident that terminated their intimate friendship. And while it was undoubtedly true that Pierre-Louis was by nature rather too impulsive and given to ill-considered actions, to accuse him of attempted murder seemed a little over-dramatic. Setting Suzette's account of the unfortunate events alongside that of Pierre-Louis, Armand concluded that, for her own ends, she had considerably over-stated the extent and degree of her sufferings. For his part, and to mini-mise his culpability, Pierre-Louis had exaggerated the provocation and played down the outcome of his loss of temper.

'I find it impossible to imagine how anyone – even a madman – could find it in his heart to abuse so very delightful and charming a person,' he told her. 'If I may speak frankly for a moment, in my cousin's place the only impulse in my mind would have been to enfold you tenderly in my arms and shower gentle kisses on your lips.'

'Ah, I see that you and he have very different natures,' she murmured. 'So much the worse for me that I became acquainted with the wrong cousin! Have you brought the money?'

'Of course,' and Armand took from his inside jacket-pocket a thick sealed envelope of blackmail money and showed it to her.

'It is not enough, you understand,' said Suzette sadly, 'nothing would be enough to compensate me for my sufferings at his hands. But as a small token of apology on his part . . .'

'But our way of thinking is so similar!' Armand exclaimed. 'You have repeated exactly what I said to Pierre-Louis when he asked for my advice. I told him that there was not enough money in the whole of France to recompense the beautiful and innocent victim of his brutal ferocity.'

'Did you?' Suzette breathed, carried away for a moment by the evident strength of his feeling.

'That being understood between us, you and I,' he continued, squeezing her hand gently, 'I bring you this inadequate and yet significant token of Pierre-Louis' sincere repentance.'

He handed the envelope to her and she weighed it in her hand for a moment, as if estimating the value of its contents. He expected that she would prise open the flap, but instead, she tore off one end of the envelope and riffled a pink-painted thumbnail across the edges of the thick wad of bank notes it contained. Armand was watching her pretty face in secret delight, observing the moment of greed and the moment of satisfaction in her expression. His mind was firmly set on the course that had suggested itself to him when she first came into the café and he had seen her in the doorway – to have her.

'In return for your gracious acceptance of this token of his shame,' he said, gesturing at the envelope in her hands, 'Pierre-Louis will deny himself the pleasure of ever seeing you again. All suggestions of interesting the authorities in the most distressing affair are to be dismissed and never again mentioned. And even though you signify your forgiveness of his vile actions by this acceptance of what I bring on his behalf, you will continue to punish him by never making contact with him again. Are we agreed on that?'

'Completely,' she answered, with a smile at the pleasantly euphemistic manner in which he had set out the hard terms she had forced on Pierre-Louis under threat of reporting him to the police for rape and assault.

To be precise, a strong desire to enjoy Suzette had formed itself in Armand's mind – if that is the location within the human organism where such desires arise – the very first time he had seen her in the Café de la Paix. He recalled vividly what he had said to Pierre-Louis later that evening, when they were discussing the possibility of Madeleine returning to her husband; *Naturally I shall never have the honour of making love to either lady, but I cannot believe that your girlfriend is as exciting as your wife.* It was not true, of course, for by that evening Armand had made love to Madeleine many times. And now it seemed that the opportunity was almost within his grasp to sample Suzette's charms also – and so put himself in the same position as Pierre-Louis to make the comparison.

He signalled to the waiter, ordered more drinks and set out to ingratiate himself with Suzette, to the full extent of his considerable ability. The extent of his success may be judged by the fact that, less than an hour later, he had the honour of escorting her to the nearby rue de Varenne, where she lived. Naturally, if his desires had not so entirely occupied his attention, it might have occurred to him that a young lady capable of extracting a large sum of money with such ease and efficiency from his cousin might be formulating plans for him also – and that his success owed perhaps as much, if not more, to her intentions than to his own undoubted charm.

The apartment to which she took him was in an unusually well-maintained building with an inner courtyard – and it was on the expensive first-floor, not up under the roof. And when he entered, there was a further surprise for Armand in the way the apartment was decorated and furnished – if Pierre-Louis had been keeping his little girlfriend in this style, it must have cost him a small fortune! The pay-off in the envelope, though originally far too much in Armand's opinion, now took on the appearance of a good bargain.

While she went to fetch a bottle of cognac, Armand instantly seized the opportunity to look at the pictures hanging in the sitting-room. At first glance he had taken them to be prints, but closer inspection revealed that they were original works by contemporary artists of fine reputation. And, a point he noted with interest, all the pictures were of women, including the recumbent nude by the well-known Cubist Juan Gris. It was a modernist caricature in bilious green of a deformed creature with bulky square breasts and hips and a daub of purple where real women had a little fleece of brown or blonde curls.

It may be, thought Armand, that the artist's vision had been original and vital – the perception of a world other than the real world of men and women – but the resulting picture was merely ridiculous to a person with Armand's overwhelming love for women's voluptuous curves and the texture of their flesh. Nevertheless, he knew the picture had cost a lot and that fact was impressive. More interesting to him, if for no better reason than that it displayed a somewhat less distorted figure, was a pen-and-ink drawing by Georges Rouault of a naked whore putting on her stockings. She had the hard face and ungainly breasts and body of all Rouault's prostitutes – a typical statement of his despair and anger – but at least she was recognisably a woman, undesirable or not.

The undoubted *chef-d'oeuvre* of the little collection – in Armand's view, at least – was a painting by Pierre Bonnard that hung over a sofa on the wall facing the window. It was a view over Paris through an uncurtained top-floor window, a landscape of roofs and streets in gentle sunlight. Looking out through the window, her back to the viewer, stood a naked woman – naked, that is, except for her red shoes. The solid flesh of her bottom and thighs indicated the opulence of her figure; if she turned round, Armand knew instinctively, she would display full round breasts and a well-shaped domed belly.

But, without any question at all, it was the unknown woman's position at a window that gripped Armand's interest with such force that reminiscent little tremors of delight were sent flickering through him. The picture recalled for him the night when Madeleine stood at her sister's window, her slender and elegant body covered only by a flimsy nightgown through which Armand's fingers traced the smooth flesh of her breasts. In the dark he had lifted up the fine chiffon to bare her bottom and had pressed his belly against it while he penetrated her.

The image affected Armand so strongly that in three strong jerks his noble friend rose stiffly to attention. Suzette, coming back into the room with a bottle in one hand and two glasses in the other, saw him staring at the Bonnard painting and recognised the expression on his face. She glanced downwards automatically and saw the unmistakable swelling in the trousers of his dark blue suit.

'Ah, I see you are a connoisseur of modern art,' she said with a mocking little smile. 'Everyone admires that picture, but not with such fervent appreciation as yours.'

As soon as she was close to him, Armand put his arms round her waist and kissed her. She stood with her arms held out awkwardly to the sides, encumbered with cognac and glasses, and giggled.

'Very well, then,' she said, when the kiss ended. 'Just this once – as the case is so desperate. But don't think I make a habit of taking pity on strangers.'

She led him into a bedroom decorated in ivory and primrose yellow, set down the glasses and bottle and turned to face him, putting her hands on his shoulders. Without a word he undid the buttons of her cream satin blouse, precisely as an hour before in the café he had done in his imagination. But in the fantasy her chubby breasts had spilled out at once into his eager hands, whereas here in her pretty bedroom they were still hidden from his eyes by a chemise of rose-pink crepe-de-chine. He felt them through the thin chemise, his fingertips finding their buds and teasing them to a firmness that showed in two delicious little peaks.

While he was occupying himself with this exciting task, Suzette unfastened the waistband of her bright red and grey skirt and let it slip over her hips and down her legs. It was then that Armand saw that what he had taken to be a chemise was in fact camiknickers, cut sleekly to her body to shape her roundness, and with an embroidered rose, crimson and life-size, on the pale pink silk over her left hip. Once more he was amazed that so young a girl could afford such quality and opulence. If Pierre-Louis represented her sole source of income, then he had spent a great deal of his money on her.

Not that there was the time for crassly materialist speculation on the price of furnishings and clothes at that moment. Suzette stripped off her stylish camiknickers and bent over to remove her silk stockings, deliberately turning away so that her soft round rump was thrust towards him. At once Armand stepped forward to fondle the satin-skinned cheeks presented to him, and she giggled when his fingers found the fleshy apricot between her legs and stroked it. Before he could prolong this exploration of her charms, she had thrown back the quilted counterpane and was stretched out on the ivory sheet.

Armand devoured her hungrily with his eyes while he ripped off his clothes. She lay on her side, facing him, propped up on an elbow, her eyes bright and greedy for pleasure. Her legs were stretched out to their full length and crossed at the ankle, and the colour of the sparse little patch of curls where her thighs joined was just different enough from the brown-blonde shade of her hair to be strangely arousing. She held her soft thighs closed, so that they resembled a large replica of the lips she concealed between them.

Not for Suzette the pleasures of long and tender love-making, thought Armand, as he threw himself on the bed and grasped at her breasts. She was not a Madeleine, to be wooed by repeated kisses and caresses to a gentle penetration and slow ride to the peak of sensation. Nor was she a Dominique to tease with perverse fingers to multiple climaxes before a relentless impaling on his iron-hard implement. At least this was Armand's view of the delights of the beautiful eighteen-year-old body that confronted him, gleaming with all the vitality of youth and health.

From the first moment he had set eyes on her, all his male desire had screamed to him that Suzette was like a ripe and luscious fruit – a peach, an apricot or a nectarine – full of sweetness to be devoured whole. She was of the same mind, it soon appeared: she rolled over on her back the instant that he touched her, took hold of his jerking stiffness and pulled him towards her, her legs parting wide to offer herself to him with unbounded generosity. Armand was so aroused by her touch that it was as if in a delirium that he slid over her and felt her warm bare belly against his own.

Her hand lay down between their bodies, holding him and guiding him quickly into her soft enclosure, as wet and ready for him as if he had played with her for half an hour, he realised as he pierced her with a long thrust. His hands were kneading her plump breasts while he slid backwards and forwards with the strength and inexorability of a giant piston on an express train racing down the track. She was moaning with delight and jerking under him, her head upturned on the satin pillow to thrust her little chin towards the ceiling and her mouth open to show her sharp little teeth.

She lay spread-eagled in hot desire on the satin sheet, her legs as wide open as they would go, her hot belly heaving under Armand's belly as he plunged and plunged into her. Her fingers were digging hard into the flesh of his shoulders and her head lifted abruptly up from the pillow to cup her open mouth over his and force her wet and flickering tongue into his mouth. In his feverish excitement Armand had the sensation that her belly had opened even wider, to let him plummet to her very depths, and a moment later, in a crescendo of small whimpering cries, her back arched briefly off the bed, lifting his weight on her.

Then she collapsed underneath him, her head rolling from side to side on the pillow, while Armand drove on pitilessly. She was squirming beneath him, moaning a little, then she clutched at his shoulders again and her hot and open mouth covered his and sucked at it. Armand had let go of her breasts to slide his hands under her and grasp her by the fleshy cheeks of her rump. She began to swing her hips upwards to meet his strokes, crying out wordlessly in urgent need of release from the excruciating pleasure that held her tightly in its grip.

Armand gasped as he sensed his culminating moment rushing towards him – it was moving so fast and its impetus was so enormous that nothing could stop it now. He rammed fast and deep into Suzette's slippery warmth, his belly smacking against hers brutally, unable to hear her ecstatic cries for the deafening roar in his ears of the mighty locomotive that was roaring towards him with its powerful pistons flashing in and out of the cylinders to accelerate it along the gleaming steel rails.

This titanic force had been compact enough to fit inside his belly at the moment when he first became aware of it, but as it came rushing on, it grew and grew in size until it was bigger than he was, much bigger; bigger even than the bed he and the girl lay on, bigger than the whole world, bigger than the universe itself. It was moving faster than the speed of light when it hit him. The impact destroyed him utterly, hurling him in shattered atoms into outer darkness. He thought he heard himself cry out, but that was impossible, since he no longer existed.

When at last he came to himself again, Suzette was lying limp and still under him, her belly stuck clammily to his with their mingled sweat. As he eased himself off her, she opened her hazel eyes and smiled at him.

'That was incredible,' she said. 'I'm stupefied.'

Armand poured two little glasses of cognac from the bottle on the bedside table and arranged the satin pillows behind him, propping himself in a comfortable half-sitting position. Suzette twisted herself round until she lay facing him, her back towards his feet, an arm over his belly to support her, or as a sort of proprietary claim. Her position ensured that her plump red-tipped breasts were fully displayed to him, perhaps by chance, but more probably by design. Her shapely legs lay one on top of the other and bent at the knee, so that her heels touched her rump and only the merely glimpse showed of the apricot curls between her thighs.

She took one of the glasses from Armand and sipped a little cognac. Naturally, now that she had admitted him to terms of intimacy she wanted to know all about him: was he married, where did he live, what did he live on, how did he pass his days? She asked these things and more in the most flattering manner, so that it was a pleasure for Armand to tell her. And when she had the information she wanted, she told him a little about herself – that she was born in Ivry-sur-Seine, that her father worked for the railways and beat her when he had drunk too much. She left home after her mother died and had been living in Paris for almost a year.

None of which did anything to explain how she came to be living in circumstances that were more than comfortable. Armand approached the question with great tact by asking about the pictures in the sitting-room – why she had chosen them – and it came as no surprise to learn that they were not Suzette's at all. Nor was the apartment, she told him – it belonged to a woman friend who had invited her to stay until she could find a suitable place of her own. Armand asked the name of the friend, being interested in a woman who bought pictures by artists of high standing.

Her friend's name was Fernande Quibon, said Suzette, but she hadn't bought the pictures herself, they were given to her by an admirer as an investment in the way that other men often gave their women friends diamonds by way of an investment for the future that provided pleasure in the meantime.

'But would not Mademoiselle Quibon prefer to be given diamonds?' Armand asked, amused by the story.

'*Madame* Quibon,' Suzette corrected him. 'Her husband died bravely fighting the Boche at Verdun and they gave him the Croix de Guerre after he was buried. Fernande already has enough jewellery. Her gentleman-friend makes her presents of pictures because that is his business. He is the owner of a gallery on the rue de Rivoli.'

Armand knew the gallery, and whenever he had occasion to pass it he looked in to see what new work was on exhibition. He had himself bought pictures there, though his taste was for a more traditional style than Cubism, Dadaism, Fauvism, Futurism, Synthesism, Vorticism, Surrealism or any of the other fashionable *isms* of the day. The identity of Madame Quibon's generous admirer was known to him: the gallery in question was owned by Marc Leblanc, an elderly man of great charm and distinction and with a prodigious knowledge of art. That he had a mistress at his age – he was certainly nearer seventy than sixty – was a matter for congratulation, in Armand's view.

Now that Suzette had ascertained to her complete satisfaction that, in addition to proving himself a vigorous lover, Armand was possessed of a sufficient income to look after her at least as well as Pierre-Louis had and perhaps better, having no wife with expensive tastes to maintain, the obvious conclusion was that he would make a useful replacement for his cousin. Suzette made a start by suggesting that he took her to dinner and then somewhere chic to dance, and he agreed readily. By then he had regained his breath, so to speak, and he fondled the rolypoly breasts that were displayed so temptingly near to him.

'How can it be true,' he asked softly, 'that my cousin struck these enchanting breasts with his fist? Evidently

113

he was suffering from a form of temporary insanity – there is no other possible explanation.'

'But it is true,' said Suzette. 'There were bruises as big as your hand for days afterwards. Even though they have faded you can see faint blue marks if you look closely.'

Armand needed no second invitation to examine her treasures – and nor would any other man lying naked with her on her soft bed. He sat up more fully and cradled her in his arms, so that he could bring his face very close to the plump objects of his desire, and with minute attention he scanned their flawless skin for any last trace of vanishing bruises inflicted by Pierre-Louis. Needless to say, there were none and never had been, but that was of no significance. In the process of his scrutiny Armand became so enraptured that he put the wet tip of his tongue to the nearest red-brown bud. And when it stood proudly, he turned his attention to the other one.

'It's marvellous to be treated with so much courtesy after the brutalities of a certain person,' Suzette sighed.

'And here – on this elegant little belly – it was here that he had the criminal audacity to spit?' Armand exclaimed, kneading her flesh gently, with a hand that shook a little.

'It landed just here,' she said, taking his hand and guiding it until his fingers were touching a spot to the right of her belly-button and just above her apricot-coloured little fleece.

'The man should be locked up in a hospital for incurably insane psychopaths!' Armand gasped, his fingers finding their way down from the site of the insult to her curls.

Given the intimate circumstances, he fully expected that she was going to open her legs and let him caress the juicy split peach between them. And that was what he wanted – to use his skilful fingers to steer her up to the very apex of sensation, and then tip her over into climactic release. Then he would know that he had really had her! But Suzette rolled away from him, until

114

she lay face down on the bed, her breasts flattened against the soft mattress and her face above his swollen pride. She took it in her hand and tested its strength with a little squeeze or two.

'Very impressive,' she said, 'but after the devastation you made me endure, I am much too exhausted to let you do it a second time. I see that *you* have no need to beat women with your fists – you beat them into submission with this!'

'But you must permit me to make honourable amends for the cruelty of a member of my family whom I despise for his insane actions,' he murmured, his hand groping at the plump cheeks of her bottom. 'I give you my word that I will make love to you so gently that you will be enchanted.'

Thus reassured – if a young lady of her experience needed any reassurance – she pressed a brief kiss to the red-purple head of his twitching member and turned over on her back to demonstrate that she was offering herself to him in implicit trust. Utterly charmed by the gesture, Armand took her in his arms and rained gentle kisses on her, from her forehead right down to her toes, missing no part of her in between. She sighed luxuriously, parted her legs a little, and let him do as he wished to her. And so matters took their natural course, until at last, after a thousand repeated caresses, Armand mounted her soft belly and sheathed himself in her wet warmth.

He was sighing continuously in delight as he began a stately to and fro rhythm. But after no more than half a dozen long thrusts, Suzette's hands clutched at his shoulders and her thighs slid apart on the satin sheet to their very limit. Her fingernails dug into his flesh and she gasped, 'Harder, Armand, harder!'

And so what had begun with elaborate delicacy was transformed by Suzette's sharp urging into another violent devastation. Armand stabbed and stabbed furiously into her hot slipperiness, as if attempting to plunder all her succulence in a desperate act of piracy.

And Suzette, his willing victim to the death, clawed

at his back and squirmed under him as if she were in the throes of a seizure. She was crying out loudly in her delirium, kissing him frantically and sobbing his name again and again. Her widely stretched legs kicked off the bed to thrash around his legs, her hard little heels drumming against him. Then her sweating thighs locked round him and with all her strength she was trying to drag him deeper into her belly. Armand's whole body was shaking as he felt the moment of truth arriving. There was just time to gasp out her name before his loins jerked sharply and ecstasy overwhelmed him – and her.

'*Ouf!*' she said, when she could speak again. 'You do things to me I never expected. You drive me crazy.'

Armand rolled off her hot body and lay facing her.

'There is something about you which makes me act like a wild man from the jungle,' he said, surprised by his own actions. 'I don't know what it is, Suzette, but we shall surely kill each other with love if we go on like this.'

'And does the thought of that frighten you?' she asked, her fingers tracing the droplets of perspiration in the dark curls on his chest.

'Not in the least!'

'Good – then Fernande will find us dead together on this bed one day,' she said with a grin. 'I shall be on my back with my legs wide apart and you will be lying on top of me, with your truncheon still in me, and we shall both have died at the same moment – carried off in a flash by the intensity of our climax.'

Armand laughed, but his exertions had made him hungry and he reminded her that she had promised to go to dinner and dancing with him.

'Yes, but not tonight,' was her unexpected reply, as if she were a Josephine refusing the advances of her Emperor. What emerged was that she wanted him to take her to lunch the next day, so that she could get his opinion on whether some sets of very elegant underwear she had seen in a shop would suit her, now that she had Pierre-Louis' parting gift to spend.

Only eighteen, and yet she knows the ways of the world, Armand thought with amusement. *Evidently her friend Madame Quibon is a good teacher.* He knew that Suzette had not the least intention of spending her own money – that was to be his privilege. He smiled and shrugged his shoulders and told her that he would be delighted to call for her the next morning at eleven. And if, in one of the exclusive shops he knew they would visit, he by chance encountered Dominique with one of her other admirers, then so much the better – she had been slightly demanding since their reunion and to see him with another woman would remind her that, adorable though she was, she was not his sole interest in life.

Half an hour after Armand had gone, Suzette was soaking herself luxuriously in the bath, enjoying the relaxation of hot water and the foam of an expensive bath essence which filled the air with the delicate spring-time scent of wild flowers growing beneath the tall trees of a forest. She turned her head when she heard a door opening and closing as someone entered the apartment, and then Fernande's voice called her name.

'I'm here,' she called back lazily. There was a pause of a minute or two, and then her friend came into the bathroom.

Fernande Quibon was a lithe and slender woman of middle height, very elegant of appearance and in her movements, her face still smooth, her figure chic and her hair raven black, even though she would never see thirty-five again. She had taken off her hat and outdoor coat on entering the apartment and presented herself in the doorway of the bathroom wearing a half-sleeved Paquin frock of lime-green taffeta printed with a design of pale orange circles that interlaced. But in contrast to the brightness of her clothes, her mouth was set in a grimace of darkest disapproval.

'So you brought him here!' she said accusingly. 'Don't bother to deny it – I've been into your room and seen the bottle and glasses by your bed. Why did you bring him here – answer me that?'

117

'Why not?' Suzette replied casually. 'He brought me the money from Pierre-Louis. I thought that was worth a drink.'

'In your bedroom?' Fernande demanded.

Suzette shrugged her bare shoulders prettily. As she lay in the scented water, her chubby breasts half-rose above the surface like a pair of unimaginably enticing pink mountain-islands set in the tropical South Seas, each with its rounded crimson peak. The movement of her shoulders shook the islands, as if the sea-bed quaked, and sent ever-widening ripples outwards. Fernande stared in fascination and the harsh set of her face softened.

'Well, what's done is done,' she said with a sigh. 'I'll help you wash off the savage smell of the male.' She closed the bathroom door behind her and advanced into the room.

'There's no need,' said Suzette. 'I've finished – I was just climbing out of the bath when I heard you call. Don't come too close, that frock will be ruined if it gets splashed.'

'Stay there for a moment,' said Fernande, her face dreamy with delight. 'I insist on helping you.'

In a second she had stripped off her pretty taffeta frock and draped it over the washbasin on the other side of the room. Off came her chemise and, in brassière and knickers of white lace, she sank to her silk-stockinged knees beside the bath and reached for the oval cake of soap.

'The traces of the vile brute are about you as surely as if you were a virgin martyr ravaged by wild animals in a Roman arena,' she murmured, and Suzette giggled.

'Do not laugh!' Fernande admonished her. 'I always wash after shaking hands with a man – even with gloves on.'

'But you are the one who was married, not me,' said Suzette. 'Did your husband wear gloves in bed when he touched you?'

'I was only a child, hardly older than you, when my family married me off,' Fernande sighed. 'What could

I know of the senseless desires of men? Night after night I lay paralysed with terror while he had his way with me. Sit up, darling.'

Suzette grinned and sat up in the hot and scented water. Fernande took off her many rings of diamonds, emeralds, rubies and mere gold, and dropped them in the soap-dish as if they were worthless imitations, rather than the valuable souvenirs of past associations with members of the despicable race of men. She rubbed the soap to a creamy lather between her palms and gave herself the task of washing Suzette's breasts, her hands encircling their fleshy fullness with great tenderness.

'You have such beautiful breasts, Suzette,' she sighed. 'Why do you let men handle them? You know that men are rough and uncaring primitives – hairy brutes without the least sensitivity in their nature. You must refuse to submit to their animal appetites or they will maul these tender breasts completely out of shape and make them slack and loose. If you keep going with men, before you are thirty these superb globes will be like half-deflated balloons that hang to your elbows, and by the time you are my age they will be long empty pouches dangling on your belly!'

Suzette giggled in disbelief, her hazel eyes half closed with pleasure, while Fernande's sensitive fingertips caressed her plump red buds until they were firm and pointed boldly upwards.

'So delicate, so delicate,' Fernande murmured. 'Listen to me when I tell you that there is no man in the whole wide world capable of appreciating the beauty of breasts like yours.'

'But surely Monsieur Leblanc handles yours when you go to visit him, Fernande? Yet I see no evidence of sagging yet.'

'No, I let him look at them all he wants, but not touch them,' Fernande whispered.

The hot water had given to Suzette's round breasts, and to all her smooth young flesh from neck to toes, a pink glow that could fairly be described as enchanting.

119

No, it was more than enchanting, it was positively alluring. Fernande kissed her friend's wet shoulders, tasting the scent of the bath-essence on them, as she played with her and sighed in pleasure.

'Have you got rid of the man-smell for me yet?' Suzette asked, her voice teasing. 'Or is it so deeply ingrained in my skin that I must soak myself in disinfectant?'

'From these two beauties, yes, it is gone, thank Heaven!' Fernande replied. 'But as for the rest . . . I can hardly bring myself to think of what this beast of a man has done to you, my poor child. But we must have courage. Kneel and let me ascertain the worst.'

She put her bare arms around Suzette's wet and slippery body and assisted her, in a manner that was more of a loving embrace than anything else, to rise up out of the water, fold her legs back underneath and position herself on her knees. With hands that were trembling slightly with the force of her emotions, Fernande took the soap and rubbed it gently over Suzette's round belly, and then, with her bare palm, she massaged around her dear friend's deep-set little belly-button. Her hand moved in a slow and circular motion, the circles increasing in size, until Suzette was white with scented lather from her breasts down to her groin.

After a while, the continuing movement caused one of the straps of Fernande's brassière to slip off her shoulder. The soft lace cup collapsed at once to half-expose a small and admirably firm and pointed breast for a woman of thirty-seven. Seeing it pop out as if it were demanding attention, Suzette turned slightly, her knees well apart down under the bath-water, until she could reach up to her friend's brassière and tug the lace cup all the way down, to bare the whole breast. She took its small pink tip between forefinger and thumb and rolled it gently.

'Ah, you will distract me from washing you properly if you do that.' Fernande exclaimed.

'They are so different, yours and mine,' said Suzette, ignoring the complaint. 'Though I am almost twenty years younger than you, mine are round and fat and have big reddish-brown tips, and yours are as pointed as pears and have little pink tips that hardly show until I make them stand up.'

Fernande moaned softly and her open hand slipped down the curve of Suzette's belly to the curls plastered wetly against the soft mound between her thighs and clasped it.

'Suzette,' she sighed, 'in spite of all I have told you since you came to live with me, you still do not understand how very special you are, *chérie* – or you would never for one moment allow a man's filthy and defiling hand anywhere near this precious *bijou*.'

Her lather-slippery fingers opened the pouting lips between Suzette's smooth thighs and inserted themselves tenderly.

'Now what are you doing!' Suzette exclaimed in mock astonishment. 'It is one thing to help me bath myself, but this – this is inexcusable.'

'I am trying yet again to make you understand why your darling *bijou* is so very special,' Fernande breathed.

'But I understand that already', said Suzette, slyly. 'You have told me a thousand times – and I believe you. It is because my *jou-jou* is so special that it demands to be admired – and surely handsome young men were put on this earth by the Good Lord for that very purpose.'

'No, you are wrong,' Fernande exclaimed in agitation. 'Men are stupid and cruel and unfeeling. They will abuse your treasure, violate it, ruin it, destroy it. Of course the dear morsel demands constant admiration, *chérie* – and I am here to kiss it for you until it has had enough and wishes to rest.'

'The man who brought me the money from Pierre-Louis – Armand is his name – he was no ferocious brute who wanted to ruin me,' Suzette tantalised her friend. 'He is very handsome and his manners are beautiful. He was so tender when he undressed me and made love to me that it was like a marvellous dream.'

She was not telling the truth, of course, for her

encounter with Armand had been strenuous and fiercely exciting. But she knew well enough that Fernande was by temperament incapable of understanding the excitement of rough love-making.

'Not another word, I don't want to hear about him!' Fernande exclaimed, her gently moving fingers sending little spasms of pleasure through Suzette's belly. 'Perhaps this one did not beat you and brutalise you as the last one did, but he is a man, all the same – and therefore he will violate you spiritually, if not bodily.'

'I think it is you, dearest Fernande, who understands how to ravish me spiritually,' Suzette sighed, plucking at the swollen little pink bud between her fingers until her friend whimpered in pleasure.

'You know that my only desire is to protect you, not ravish you,' she murmured. 'And as for this Armand you brought here today, handsome or not, I know that he was after what they all want – to poke his ugly stiff thing into your darling *jou-jou*. Oh, Suzette, how could you let him abuse you like that? The very thought of it makes me almost faint with shame and horror.'

'And when Monsieur Leblanc does it to you – do you faint with shame then?' Suzette asked with a smile. 'Or do you open your legs and ask him for another valuable painting?'

'He has never done *that* to me!' Fernande exclaimed. 'You know that.'

'I know what you tell me,' said Suzette. 'You strip naked and sit on a chair and have a conversation with him while he sits across the other side of the room and admires your body. But I don't believe you.'

'But I swear it's true!' Fernande exclaimed. 'Sometimes I let him caress me a little, but never between my legs.'

Whether Leblanc was allowed to feel her or not, her own caresses between Suzette's legs were producing the result she intended.

'Fernande!' Suzette gasped, her belly clenching in the throes of ecstasy. 'Ravish me!'

Fernande was leaning against Suzette's wet shoulder,

both her hands playing between her plump thighs – one in front and the other behind. '*Chérie, chérie . . .*' she moaned softly as she heard Suzette's climactic little wail and felt her loins shaken by passion between her two hands.

'See – this clumsy man could not even satisfy you – admit it, you were waiting for me to come home!' Fernande exclaimed joyfully as her hands registered her friend's little spasms.

'Darling Fernande, no one loves me like you,' Suzette gasped, knowing well enough what was expected of her.

Guided and supported by the hands that were ravishing her so exquisitely, she allowed herself to sink slowly backwards in the water until she lay on her back, her smooth and rounded knees up and well apart, and willingly surrendered herself to the ecstatic thrills coursing through her. In another moment Fernande slid her slender body over the edge of the bathtub as sleekly as a seal, sending little waves of scented water overflowing on to the floor, and lay closely entwined with the trembling girl.

Fernande's expensive lace underwear clung wetly to her body, the brassière off both shoulders, so that her pear-shaped little breasts were bare. Wide-eyed in helpless delight at the sensations that shook her, Suzette turned tremulously to lie facing Fernande, sending more water spilling over on to the floor. Her mouth opened to receive a long kiss and her hands pawed delicately at Fernande's bared breasts. 'Ah!' she moaned through the kiss, while Fernande's fingers fluttered between her thighs to wring the last shudder of pleasure from her.

Her eyes opened at last and stared into Fernande's, so close to her own; a long quizzical look with the merest touch of calculation in it. Fernande raised a knee out of the water and hooked her leg over Suzette's hip, so opening her thighs wide, as if in invitation.

'Ah, you make demands on me – as if you were a man!' said Suzette, smiling faintly.

'No, never! You must never say such things,' Fernande exclaimed, her eyes brilliant with desire. 'I adore you too far too much to make demands, you know that.'

'Then what?'

'I am at your mercy, *ma chérie*,' she answered humbly.

Suzette smiled again and slid her hand very slowly down inside the lace knickers that clung wetly to Fernande's belly, tormenting her by making her wait for the intimate touch for which she was longing with all her heart. Her fingertips roamed lightly over the sodden curls, prolonging the torture until Fernande was squirming in delightful frustration. When at last she caressed the tender *jou-jou* between Fernande's thighs, she elicited a long gasping moan.

'Yes, you may well groan,' said Suzette. 'It was you who insisted on feeling me and making me excited when I was so calm and relaxed, and now you must take the consequences, my dear. Do not deceive yourself that I am going to let you off with one quick little climax in the bath! This is only a foretaste – afterwards I am going to dry you and drag you into bed, and then, dear Fernande, I shall roll you on your back and spread your legs wide – and make love to you until you faint away.'

'*Je t'adore*, Suzette, *je t'adore*,' Fernande sighed, her body shaking with passion.

6

Madame Hiver at Home

In the elegance of Yvonne Hiver's salon, with its huge Lalique mirror etched in a graceful pattern of lilies, the furniture designed to order and upholstered in white satin, the four life-size busts of delicate Limoges porcelain on plinths of pink marble in the corners – even among all this, the most elegant work of art was Yvonne herself. She was reclining on her modernistic chaise-longue, leaning one arm casually on its swan's-neck curve, her long legs slanting out and crossed at the ankle, a pose that displayed very well her narrow pointed feet in soft indoor shoes of glossy white patent leather.

It was half past eleven in the morning and Yvonne was dressed to receive visitors in luxurious lounging pyjamas of white chiffon. The soft cuffs and draped collar of the close-fitting jacket were delicately scalloped, and the cut of the trousers subtly displayed the excellence of her legs. A large letter Y was embroidered boldly on the pocket that lay exactly over her pointed left breast, to draw attention to it. She smiled and stretched out a languid hand to Armand – a thin, long-fingered hand that seemed almost too frail for the weight of the large ruby and diamond ring it bore.

Ah, what a composition of shades of white for an artist, he thought, as he bowed over her hand and kissed it: Yvonne on her satin chaise-longue, her slender body hardly concealed in thin chiffon, with cleverly thought-out touches of colour; her mouth painted a shiny strawberry-red, her necklace jade green and, most effective of all, the glossy dark brown of her hair. She wore it in a bob, parted on the left to slant across her forehead towards her right eyebrow, and hanging sleek, straight and shiny to her earlobes. As early in the day as it was, her personal maid had evidently spent much time and effort on Yvonne's hair to achieve that perfection.

One could go further into semi-abstract speculation, thought Armand, as they exchanged greetings and he was invited to take a seat on one of the white satin armchairs that was so modern in design that it had no arms. Indeed, the entire setting of the salon was devised to impress the visitor with the mysterious depths of Yvonne's soul – or failing that, her personality – and to lead him into fascinated speculation on these mysteries. There was the obvious symbolism of so much white – a claim to tender and youthful purity that invited erotic fantasies of perversely debauching that seeming innocence. But the appearance of untouched purity was itself piquantly contradicted by the high-fashion lounging pyjamas and the self-conscious sophistication of Yvonne's pose on the chaise-longue.

All in all, there could be little question that she was a lady of intricate, concealed and perhaps dangerous motives, Armand considered – unlike her sister Madeleine, who was candid and generous of heart. Madeleine he adored, respected and admired – and took to bed with eager devotion – but Yvonne's expensively contrived desirability both aroused and repelled him at the same time. Indeed, his nature being what it was, it was impossible for him not to be drawn to Yvonne by the awareness that the only barrier between her slender and marvellously groomed and perfumed body and his avid eyes, the touch of his hands and lips, was a flimsy garment of chiffon.

On second thoughts, he concluded that there must be more than that. The little peaks of her breasts could be seen pushing at the chiffon, but there was no hint of their shade of red or pink or russet through it – evidence enough that she was wearing a chemise under her lounging pyjamas. And if a chemise, then it was logical to assume that she was wearing knickers to match. If the unthinkable happened and she let slip her self-awareness for a moment and permitted her long jacket to ride up high enough to show the join of her thighs, there would be no dark shadow of curls through the chiffon of her trousers.

These conclusions in regard to Yvonne's silk underwear were of immediate interest to Armand's ever-enthusiastic friend, and it reminded him of its presence by little tremors of eagerness. But, if he were completely honest with himself – a rare occurrence, as with most men – the very suavity of Yvonne's calculated sensuality made him a little afraid. He wondered what happened to her lovers when they could no longer command her interest – an event of unpleasing frequency for a woman so demanding, to be sure. The straightforward dismissal of a lover whom she had sucked dry – body, purse and soul – was hardly Yvonne's style.

Nevertheless, it was Yvonne and not Madeleine he had come to see – indeed, it was because he knew that Madeleine was out for the day to visit friends who lived at Versailles that he had come to Yvonne's apartment. But not to present himself to her in the role of an admirer and aspirant for her favours. The reason was more complicated and did him far less credit. The truth was that for two months his incandescent love-affair with Madeleine had been the central point and pivot of his life, but he had acquired certain other emotional interests that he wished to pursue and enjoy to the full.

For Armand, as for the pleasure-loving Duke of Mantua in Verdi's opera, it was truly a question of *This one or that one* as he surveyed the pretty ladies at his disposal. Madeleine, Dominique, Suzette – each of them with her own distinctively different style of love-making! Why should he – unattached, unmarried, independent, handsome – why should he be compelled to restrict himself to the delights of only one of these exquisite friends? The mere suggestion was against reason!

Not that he wanted to lose Madeleine, it must be

understood – to bare her soft little breasts and hold them in his hands while he kissed them was too thrilling an experience for any man in his senses to risk losing, and to lie on her soft belly and slide gently in and out of her warm niche was an experience little short of divine. But – and even in Paradise itself there are buts – Armand's wish at present was to scale down somewhat the intensity of his encounters with Madeleine, in order to leave him energy and time enough for his other loves.

How to bring that about without raising damaging suspicions that he had other intimate women friends was not particularly clear to him at first, but sustained thought at last produced a course of action: Madeleine should return to the home and husband she had deserted, while remaining his mistress. Her opportunities to visit his apartment would then be restricted, and her husband's legitimate attentions to her would reduce her natural appetites to a manageable level.

Naturally, no one but a madman would suggest outright to his mistress – whether it was over an excellent dinner in a favourite restaurant or perhaps in bed together between tender bouts of love – that she should return to live with her husband. It was necessary to approach the question with more delicacy and certainly by a much more roundabout route. It was in Armand's mind to plant the thought of a reconciliation between Madeleine and Pierre-Louis in Yvonne's thoughts and leave her, in her own way, to raise the matter with her sister. But to his amazement, when after a quarter of an hour's conversation on nothing much, he touched very lightly on the question, Yvonne reacted sharply.

'Do stop trying to involve yourself in the private problems of others,' she said. 'It is a sort of vanity, to believe you are more intelligent than the people concerned and understand them well enough to be able to suggest solutions to their personal difficulties.'

'But in addition to family ties, both Pierre-Louis and Madeleine are my dear friends!' he exclaimed. 'Surely there can be no question of vanity in the wish to promote their happiness?'

Yvonne's dark brown eyes regarded him with all the warmth of a judge sentencing a criminal to a lifetime in prison.

'I am well aware that Pierre-Louis is a cousin of yours and Madeleine is your mistress,' she said at last. 'If you have now decided that her best course is to return to her husband, then I assume that you have tired of her.'

'Certainly not!' Armand said with great indignation. 'I adore her beyond all reason.'

'And your adoration is untroubled by the prospect of Madeleine in bed with another man – even if he *is* her husband?'

'You are cruel, Yvonne. The thought of my dearest Madeleine in the arms of another gives me atrocious suffering, I am lacerated to my very soul! But setting that aside for a moment – by a superhuman effort of self-control, believe me – and assessing the situation rationally, it is evident that her future is more assured if she returns to Pierre-Louis.'

'I take it that you have no intention of offering her marriage, if she were to obtain a divorce from him?'

Armand turned his hands outwards in a little gesture that acknowledged his shortcomings and apologised for them. 'Greatly as I love Madeleine, marriage would be a mistake,' he said. 'As a lover I am enchanting; as a husband I would be a domestic disaster. No, the best course, though it pains me beyond belief to admit it, is that Madeleine is reconciled to her husband.'

'And for you the matter is as simple as that?' Yvonne asked, her thinly-plucked eyebrows arching on her forehead.

'As you and I know, she left him when she discovered that he had a little girlfriend. Well, he has parted from her – I know that for certain. Thus there is no further obstacle to a tender reconciliation between him and Madeleine.'

Yvonne stared at him, her long thin fingers playing with the beads of green jade round her neck. She crossed her ankles the other way and the movement caused her breasts to roll a little under the flimsy white chiffon jacket.

'Since you have planned the future of Madeleine and Pierre-Louis comprehensively,' she said, 'no doubt you will be pleased to hear that he came here last evening to plead with her to go back to him.'

'He was sober, I hope.'

'Sober and sincere.'

'And what happened – don't keep me in suspense, Yvonne.'

'I think that Madeleine was favourably impressed by his manner, and by his solemn assurance that he had to rid of his girlfriend.'

'But did she agree to return to him?'

'That's a very big step,' said Yvonne, her casual tone at odds with what she was saying, 'and one which requires a certain amount of thought first. What can I tell you? Madeleine is thinking it over.'

'Then there is hope?' Armand asked. 'What do you think?'

'What I think is – that you are prying into matters between a married couple that do not concern you. Perhaps Madeleine turned to you for an afternoon's amusement to distract herself momentarily from her suffering at the collapse of her marriage, but that gives you no privileged position to enquire into private affairs that are none of your business. After all, she is my sister, and I shall respect her confidence.'

'A thousand, thousand pardons,' Armand said hastily, putting on his most charming smile. 'My sincere desire to see this unhappy episode brought to a satisfactory conclusion may have made me seem over-eager. Forgive me, Yvonne.'

He was rewarded with the controlled little smile that had devastated the tranquillity of more men than he could imagine, and she leaned forward to rest her fingers lightly on his sleeve as if taking him into her confidence – a gesture she knew to be charming.

'We have known each other for some years, Armand,'

she said softly, 'and therefore I feel I can speak frankly with you. Madeleine has not finally made up her mind whether to return to Pierre-Louis, but it is my belief that she will – and soon.'

'I am delighted to hear it,' he said, touching the back of her hand on his sleeve for a moment with his fingertips.

'And my reason for believing that she will return to him is that she allowed him to stay with her last night.'

'What!' Armand exclaimed. 'Here? He made love to her?'

'It is not for me to guess what happens between a woman and her husband when they share a bed after a long separation from each other,' said Yvonne, with totally uncharacteristic primness, 'but I saw her this morning before she left for Versailles and there was a gleam in her eye that suggested to me that the events of the night had been to her satisfaction.'

Yvonne's account of these marital developments aroused fierce jealousy in Armand's heart – so fierce that he forgot completely that his purpose in visiting her was to obtain her support for a reconciliation between Madeleine and her husband. Far from being pleased by the news of a promising *rapprochement* between them, his ever-active imagination inflamed itself with visions of his beloved Madeleine and Pierre-Louis naked in bed together. All too clearly in his mind's eye he could see Pierre-Louis fondling her breasts and kissing their delicate red-brown buds.

'Are you feeling unwell?' Yvonne enquired. 'Your face is suddenly pale.'

But Armand's feverish imagination insisted on worse yet – an image of Pierre-Louis parting Madeleine's slender thighs with his brutal hand, to press kisses on the walnut-brown curls between them. And the ultimate horror – Pierre-Louis stretched out on Madeleine's smooth belly to plunge his hateful rigidity into her!

'Shall I have a glass of water brought for you?' Yvonne asked solicitously – or with the semblance of solicitude – for she had been able to guess what his sentiments were and found the inappropriateness of his suffering greatly amusing.

'No, thank you,' said Armand, struggling to regain control of himself. 'It was no more than a moment's dizziness. I was out very late last night and perhaps drank a glass of champagne too much. It's gone now.'

'Ah, we all have too many late nights for our own good,' she said with a knowing little smile, 'but one cannot sit at home and turn into a pumpkin. Come and sit here by me and tell me where you were last night – dancing at *Les Acacias*, perhaps?'

Armand moved obligingly from his chair to sit beside her on the chaise-longue, his mind still in a turmoil, though his face was composed and his hands no longer clenched into fists to beat Pierre-Louis to pulp for sleeping with his own wife. He stared at Yvonne with hardly-concealed dislike – as ready as any despot of the past to blame the messenger for the ill-tidings of the message itself. He had no appetite for small-talk about nightclubs and dancing.

'To me it is extraordinary that you permitted Pierre-Louis to stay here with Madeleine last night,' he said in a tone of accusation. 'I remember very well that you told me not long ago that you refused to let him come here to upset her – that was the night he begged me to come here and plead with her to go back to him.'

'Times change,' Yvonne retorted, obviously displeased with his tone. 'Yesterday he did not upset Madeleine – he gave her pleasure. And who can say, perhaps he was able to give her love as well as pleasure. I must tell you that I find your attitude difficult to understand. It is as if you begrudged Madeleine her happiness! And apart from that, your attitude is far from flattering to me, in fact, I find it insulting for you to sit here along with me and have nothing on your mind but the domestic affairs of Madeleine and Pierre-Louis.'

'Ah, a thousand pardons,' said Armand, taken aback by the sudden realisation that he was creating an

132

extremely poor impression. 'It would be better if I left you for now?'

Yvonne turned a little towards him on the white chaise-longue and placed her hand lightly on his thigh.

'No, I will not permit you to leave in a bad humour,' she said with an enchanting little smile. 'Of course, I understand what you must feel when you hear that your love-affair with my sister has reached its conclusion – she is a very attractive woman and I am sure you are devoted to her. And it is not at all difficult to understand what she sees in you: you're extremely good-looking and exceptionally charming – when you are in a good mood.'

Being vain, he was also highly susceptible to flattery, and it was on this that Yvonne was counting. Her hand moved a mere fraction of a centimetre on his thigh, but he could feel the warmth of her palm through the fine wool of his trousers.

'For me almond-brown eyes and curly black hair are a devastating combination in a man,' she said, with a little sigh, 'but looks are not everything, as we all know to our cost. A book may have a superlative binding of expensive leather and gold blocking and be so tedious that the reader falls asleep before the end of the first page. Apart from being a handsome man, Armand my dear, are you a good *lover*?'

'I have the honour to inform you that no lady of my acquaintance has ever yet complained,' he answered with a smile of pride.

With his head cocked a little to one side he watched Yvonne's hand on his thigh – it lay still no longer, but in a very assured way was moving slowly up towards the join of his legs, where his rapacious companion was stiffening fast.

'Oh yes, I've no doubt that my sister is pleased enough with you,' said Yvonne dismissively, 'but, after all, she is such an innocent that the only person she is able to compare you with is her husband. I imagine that Pierre-Louis is no more than an average performer in bed.'

133

She turned her lean pyjama-clad body a little more towards him, her bent knees close together, and tucked her feet back out of the way. The expression on her face was tranquil, though the pink tip of her tongue showed between her slightly parted lips as she raised her left arm across her body and put her fingertips to the jacket of her lounging pyjamas, opposite the monogrammed pocket. As casually as if she were doing no more than pat her glossy brown hair, she stroked her breast through the flimsy chiffon with an upward flick of her wrist.

'From the look on your face I infer that you would like to caress me like this,' she said calmly. 'Perhaps you even have ambitions to put your hand inside my pyjamas!'

His apprehensions about Yvonne forgotten as his greedy portion bounded inside his trousers, Armand assured her that he would be enchanted to be permitted to embrace her and kiss her breasts. But when he reached for her, she fended him off with her free hand and told him to sit still.

'But . . .' he stammered.

'Try to remain articulate,' she admonished him. 'Tongue-tied men are extremely boring.'

'It is not a question of being at a loss for words, Yvonne,' he answered, 'but of not completely understanding your intention. You are a fascinating woman, as you well know, and I am on fire to take you in my arms.'

'Of course you are,' she agreed with serene self-regard, her fingers trailing over her breast in a way that heated Armand's blood to near boiling-point, 'but what of that? I am under no obligation to submit to your desires.'

'Only the natural obligation you owe to yourself to enjoy to the full the pleasures for which you are so perfectly made,' he countered, smiling as he fell in with her mood.

'Perhaps,' she said, 'but I understand my worth, Armand. I am not a foolish woman who allows herself to be used casually by any man who has an itch he needs to relieve. I am very beautiful, and highly desirable. I know what marvellous joys I can offer a man – what have you to offer me?'

By way of reply Armand reached down with both hands to unbutton his trousers from waist-band to groin. He neither hurried over what he was doing nor lingered over it – he pulled his trousers wide open and tucked the front of his pale blue silk shirt up out of the way.

'You are very direct!' Yvonne exclaimed, her poise slightly shaken at last. 'I expected you to tell me of your skill and experience in love-making – not to expose yourself!'

Armand eased his stiff appendage out through the slit of his underwear and let it stand proudly for her scrutiny.

'There are occasions when words are not adequate to express the intensity of one's feelings,' he told her.

'Evidently,' she answered and glanced up from his lap to his eyes, her eyebrows arching in contained amusement.

'As you confess so openly, you are very beautiful and very desirable,' he said, 'and the proof of that is here in my hand. This never lies – it reveals its approval or disapproval with total frankness.'

'It has a certain look of promise,' Yvonne admitted, almost as if she were assessing the quality of fruit on a market-stall before deciding whether to purchase it or not. 'The size is acceptable and it looks strong enough – at the moment. And that passionate shade of dark red that is almost purple never fails to enthral me!'

Needless to say, Armand agreed with every word of her verdict during this examination of his credentials. He sat with his thighs parted and his legs stretched out, suffused by pride at her words of praise. Here was a woman of true discernment, he thought, perhaps even more so than her sister Madeleine!

'But alas,' Yvonne continued, a hint of disdain creeping into her voice, 'all the world knows this part of a man to be undiscriminating to the point of crudeness at the instant it attains its distended condition. Beauty and refinement have no significance or value to it – let it catch sight of even a fat middle-aged kitchen-maid bending over and it will be up her skirt and into the unattractive slot between her legs without a moment's hesitation.'

'If that has been your experience of men, I regret that those with whom you are acquainted are unworthy of you,' said Armand, though if the truth were told, he knew that she had spoken no more than the plain truth.

'Ah, then you regard yourself as worthy of me, do you? You are different from other men, more discerning, is that it?'

'In short, and without wishing to sound boastful, yes,' said Armand, smiling as he watched her long fingers stray across into his lap to touch his fleshy stanchion. 'Since I first became old enough to adore women, I have insisted on having only the best as my intimate friends. Other men may pursue lesser delights – I feel that I owe it to myself to consort only with women blessed with beauty and refinement, to use your very apt words.'

'Then it seems we have much in common, you and I,' she murmured, a faint smile on her strawberry-red lips. 'But this search for the best, it can at times be exhausting and even disappointing – do you not find it so? The partner who seems at first to be exquisitely in tune with one's own innermost longings then proves unsuitable in some way or inadequate in strength of mind or body. These are the moments of near despair in endless search for the perfection of love.'

She had hold of him firmly now and seemed to be assessing his strength and solidity for the purpose she had in mind.

'What you say is very true,' he said. 'We are like artists pursuing an ideal that is unattainable, but it is our destiny and, however many disappointments we meet, we never for a moment consider abandoning the quest.'

'How well you put it,' Yvonne sighed. 'I begin to believe that there is a possibility that you may prove to be worthy of me. At the very least you have earned an opportunity to show me the extent of your understanding.'

She let go of him to lift her white chiffon jacket over her head – for the buttons were mere adornment and did not open. Beneath it she was wearing a thin chemise of milk-white silk that dipped down deeply into the valley between her breasts and had narrow ribbon straps over her thin and elegant shoulders. As Armand watched in breathless delight, she pulled the chemise out of her pyjama trousers and over her sleek head, so that she was naked to the waist. He gazed in rapture at her pale-skinned breasts, made even more pointed by unusually prominent buds of an enticing shade of russet-red.

'We shall not be interrupted here?' he asked.

'Of course not – the servants are trained never to disturb me when I receive a friend *tête-à-tête*,' she told him. 'Nanny has taken the children into the Bois and Madeleine is out for the day, as you know.'

She made no mention whatsoever of her husband Jean-Roger, who stayed in the apartment only occasionally. From her silence on the subject it seemed reasonable to assume that she was not that day expecting one of his visits of marital obligation.

'Well?' she asked, Armand's failure to compliment her on her desirability putting a faint note of petulance in her voice. 'I hope you do not imagine that I disrobe for every man who comes here to visit me!'

Armand was delighted beyond words that here – in her own salon – he had brought Yvonne to the point where she had stripped to the waist for him. And she had so far forgotten her normal chilly reserve as to find it acceptable for him to sit there on her white satin furniture with his trousers gaping wide open and his stiff pointer fully exposed to her stare. He was conceited enough to hope this was the first time Yvonne had been persuaded to such intimacy outside her bedroom.

He was also highly amused at her annoyance at his failure to fall on his knees at her feet and beg for the privilege of kissing her uncovered breasts. But he was determined to play her at her own game by preserving his composure – outwardly, at least, for his excitable friend was shaking in a silent demand of its natural rights.

'You have the most delectable breasts in the whole world,' he said, with a charming smile. 'And the delicate opalescence of your skin contrasts exquisitely with the green of your jade beads. I am so privileged beyond anything I have deserved that I am overwhelmed by your generosity.'

'Really?' she said, still disappointed that his response to her uncovering of her charms was only words, 'but *this* isn't overwhelmed, I see,' and for the first time she clasped his sturdy adjunct full-handed and stroked it with fast and nervous little twitches of her wrist.

'Dear Yvonne, you have put me in an impossible position,' Armand murmured, struggling to maintain his appearance of insouciance in spite of the ripples of pleasure she was sending through him. 'Only a moment or two ago you informed me that the part of a man you are holding makes no distinction between a refined and beautiful lady and her fat kitchen-maid – that it will enter the unattractive one as readily as the delicious one. If I were bold enough to confess that it is my dearest wish to put mine inside you, it may seem to you that any willing woman, even your kitchen-maid, would be acceptable to me in my present condition, and then you would be mortally offended.'

'But of course not!' she exclaimed. 'Since I know it to be the sight of *my* breasts that has brought you to this stage of high arousal, it follows that I am the one you want to make love to! You need have no anxiety on that account.'

The logic of her statement was too complicated for Armand to follow, but he agreed readily that it was the sight of her pretty breasts that was responsible for his longing for her and her alone with all his heart.

'Naturally, I am aware of the devastating effect my breasts have on men,' she said calmly, continuing to stroke him. 'It is because I bared them for you that we see this purple-headed part of you at its best. You are so excited by what I have shown you that it is at its full length and thickness – and as stiff as a broom-handle.'

'You see it not yet at its *very* best, but approaching it, Yvonne,' he replied, little spasms of delight running through his belly. 'The best of all is when a climax overwhelms it and makes it leap and spurt out its joy. But that is less a sight to enjoy with your beautiful brown eyes than a delight to experience by another means.'

'Ah, you are conceited enough to think yourself worthy of being admitted to my most intimate friendship, are you?' she asked, and the wet tip of her tongue slid slowly along her red-rouged lips.

'Only you can decide who is worthy of that,' he said, the effort to retain his apparent unconcern so difficult now that he knew that very soon it would become impossible and he would be pleading with Yvonne.

'I haven't made up my mind about you, Armand,' she said, and it seemed to him that her breathing was a little irregular and that her cheeks had a faint tinge of pink.

That being so, he reached out to fondle her breasts and roll their prominent points between his fingers, and she made no move to stop him, not even when he leaned over her and touched the tip of his tongue to them. When he heard her sighing, he put his hand between her legs and gently rubbed her through the thin chiffon. Soon she was shivering with pleasure and he started to slide his hand down inside her pyjamas – but she whispered, 'Wait a moment, Armand.'

He sat up while she undid two buttons on the waistband at her hip, and with bated breath he watched her hook her long thin thumbs into the milk-white knickers she wore under the pyjamas, and exhaled in a long sigh of delight as she pushed both garments down her smooth-shaven legs to her ankles. At once he was off the chaise-longue and on one knee on the carpet, to take off her soft shoes and then ease pyjamas and knickers over her feet and discard them.

Her knees were still close together, so that Armand saw only a small tuft of dark-brown curls on her belly, above where her legs met. He put a hand on each of her knees and parted them firmly, opening her up to his gaze. The curls were profuse, more so than Madeleine's, he noted, and beneath them were long loose lips of dark pink that made him gasp in desire. She let him stare between her legs for some time before she raised a bare and high-arched little foot and, with her scarlet-nailed toes, rubbed gently at the pompoms below his twitching peg.

'Oh look – I see that letting you take my knickers off has made it grow even stronger!' she murmured, 'surely it can't get any bigger.'

'But it can,' Armand breathed. 'When I put it inside you – then you will feel its full strength and it will be ecstasy.'

His words excited her further. Her eyelids drooped lazily, her mouth was half-open, and she was breathing rapidly. Armand took hold of her raised ankle and lifted her foot high enough to press a kiss on each of the toes. When he released her, she clasped his throbbing spike between the soles of both bare feet and rubbed up and down slowly.

'Put it inside me?' she asked, her thin-plucked eyebrows rising in surprise. 'I've said nothing at all about that! I haven't made up my mind yet about you, Armand. What leads you to suppose you are to have the privilege of pushing that very ordinary-looking thing into *me*?'

'Ordinary!' he exclaimed in astonishment. 'A moment ago you told me you found it enthralling.'

She shrugged her thin shoulders and her breasts jiggled.

'Perhaps I spoke a few words out of politeness,' she said, 'but surely you cannot be so naive as to believe everything that is said. Please bear in mind that I've seen a good few of these male playthings and so I know what I'm talking about. To be fair to you, yours is somewhat larger than the average, but that means nothing.'

'What you say reminds me of my uncle Henri,' Armand said softly, shuddering with pleasure at the massage her feet were giving him, 'I think you may have met him. He is a great connoisseur of wine. Blindfold him and let him sip only a spoonful from an unlabelled bottle and he will tell you the region, the vineyard, the year – and he is never wrong. But alas, the years of devoted wine-tasting necessary to make him so renowned an expert have ruined his appreciation – his attention is so closely focused on identifying what he tastes and comparing it with every other vintage he has ever drunk that he no longer enjoys wine at all.'

'I do believe your plaything has grown even bigger,' said Yvonne, paying no attention to his little parable. 'You promised me that you are a marvellous lover, so naturally I want to see what it is you are hoping to put into me. I'm used to the very best – so don't think you can deceive me. If against my better judgement I take the risk of allowing you to proceed, I fully expect you to keep your promise.'

'Very willingly,' he murmured. 'You will not regret it.'

He took her ankles in his hands and drew them apart, so that he could wiggle himself nearer to her on his knees, close enough for his impatient part to jerk itself boldly against her warm belly. He moved his hands up her legs to her splayed thighs and would have transfixed her as she sat upright on the chaise-longue, but she laid a hand over her dark-brown curls to bar his way.

'Certainly not like that,' she said severely. 'You are not making a good start, Armand. I like to lie on my back and enjoy the sensation of a man's body on top of me. Perhaps you regard me as old-fashioned in my respect for tradition – I am told that girls today think nothing of forcing a man flat on a bed while they squat over him – but I don't like that sort of thing. I feel that I am most completely a woman when a strong man has me beneath him, so that he is between my legs and I am at his mercy.'

She turned and lay full-length on the white satin chaise-longue, her hands joined under her head as if in complete surrender, but with her long slender legs pressed together. Armand got to his feet and took off the jacket of his blue-striped suit and his bow-tie, to make himself comfortable for the pleasant exertions to come. Yvonne smiled up at him, but it was not the adoring smile of a woman whose lover is about to mount her and carry her to the heights of ecstasy – it was the smile of polite encouragement a woman gives to a shop-assistant fitting her for a pair of shoes!

The moment she saw that he was ready for her – his straining projection in his hand, its red-purple head bared for action – Yvonne spread her legs with deliberate slowness. The effect was extremely arousing, as she intended it to be: Armand stood motionless and hardly breathing while he watched her thighs moving apart on the white satin. Little by little all was revealed to him: first her dark-brown fleece, then the tender hollows of her groin where the curls grew less thickly, and at last her fleshy groove. He sighed in delight, and still her legs continued to slide apart, centimetre by centimetre!

He was astounded by Yvonne's agility in the posture of love – her legs were stretched wider apart than he would have believed possible for anyone but a young Can-Can dancer from the *Folies Bergères* or an acrobat trained for the circus. When she felt the backs of her knees against the edges of the chaise-longue, she let them bend downwards, until her bare feet were flat on the floor on either side of it. Armand knelt between her thighs, excited almost to the point of delirium by the sight of the long pink lips pulled so widely open by the position of her legs that her secret bud, swollen and moist, was fully visible.

There was no more discussion of whether or not he was worthy to be allowed to penetrate that greedy maw.

'Put it in me,' she murmured, 'that's what you came here for today!' She was wrong, of course – the thought of making love to her had been far from his mind when he came to visit her that morning – but her inordinate self-esteem required her to believe that the prime aim in the life of every handsome young man was to worship her beauty by mounting her. Not that Armand was in any mood at that moment to dispute her mistaken belief – he was on top in a flash, and guided himself into her with an eager hand.

'Oh!' Yvonne exclaimed as he thrust home to the hilt, but whether she was expressing surprise, dismay or pleasure, he was unable to decide. She had insisted earlier that she preferred to lie on her back with a man's weight on her, so that she felt herself to be at his mercy, but what happened next was totally different. Now that she had enticed him in by opening herself impossibly wide, her feet came up off the floor and her slender legs closed over his back like a steel trap, so that it was Armand who was the helpless one.

She was moving underneath him, thrusting her hot loins up against him with fast and nervous little strokes, in effect sliding herself along his embedded stem and back. At once he went into action, plunging in and out of her, but her legs clamped tighter round his waist and her arms were round his back to immobilise him. She held him with his belly tight to hers and his chest squashing her breasts and forcing their hard points against him. 'Lie still, Armand!' she exclaimed sharply.

Short of using violence to break her grip, there was nothing else he could do but lie still while she had her way with him from below. Not that it mattered – the outcome was the same as if he had been the active partner and she the passive. As his emotions rose in a throbbing crescendo towards their eventual summit, Armand stared down in wonder at the face below his. Yvonne's dark brown eyes were set in a glassy stare, her mouth was open in a fixed and distant smile – it was obvious that she knew neither where she was nor whom she was with.

Her climax came easily and quickly. The muscles of her face went into spasm, pulling her mouth so far back that her smile became a grimace that exposed all her teeth, her arms clutched him so tightly that the breath was squeezed out of him and her narrow back arched off the chaise-longue, forcing Armand to her uttermost depth – a sensation so thrilling that he fountained his desire into her instantly. But as quickly as her gratification had arrived, it faded, and she released the grip of her arms round Armand to take hold of his wrist and turn it to look at his watch. And while he still shook in the after-throes of ecstasy, she pushed him off her.

'I didn't realise what time it was!' she exclaimed, sliding out from under him with the agility of long experience.

Armand turned over on to his back on the chaise-longue, his wet stalk still hard, and stared in bewilderment as Yvonne stood with her back to him, showing him her taut little bottom, while she scrambled into her underwear.

'But I don't understand,' he said. 'Why the sudden hurry?'

'Because I am lunching at one o'clock with the Duchesse de Beaumarchais and some other friends – and I have fifteen minutes to repair the damage you have done and change my make-up and get dressed before I dash!'

'I regret I was unable to retain your interest for more than a few moments,' Armand replied in great displeasure, sitting up to button his trousers and knot his bow-tie.

'What? Don't be silly, Armand – it was quite enjoyable.'

'No more than that?' he asked, outraged by her off-hand attitude. 'Then I shall trouble you no more.'

He was halfway across the salon, shrugging himself into his jacket and quivering with indignation, when Yvonne caught up with him and threw her arms round his neck to halt his march towards the door. She had put on her knickers and chemise, but her lounging pyjamas were draped over her arm, so that the soft chiffon touched his cheek.

'You must not be so touchy, my dear, or we shall never become good friends,' she said. 'I am sorry that I must leave you so soon, when we are beginning to be acquainted, but my lunch appointment was made more than a week ago and it would be most discourteous to break it at this short notice. Surely you can understand that?'

She was standing close enough to him for the tips of her breasts to touch him through her thin chemise and for the deliciously warm smell of her body, mingled with her expensive perfume, to titillate his senses in a manner he found irresistible. He felt under her chemise and grasped a handful of the soft flesh of her belly in a way that was half desire and half exasperation. And soon his hand found its way down inside her knickers, to feel her thick curls and then to caress the wet lips between her thighs.

'No . . . I really must go,' she whispered, her mouth touching his cheek. 'You'll make me late . . .'

But his fingers were busy in the slipperiness of her warm *embouchure*, and her belly was squirming against him.

'No, you mustn't, you mustn't . . .' she sighed, her bare feet well apart on the carpet as an indication that he must.

And he did: standing on the white fur rug halfway across the salon to the door he *had* her, as with great gusto he described it to himself, as Yvonne had undoubtedly *had* him on the chaise-longue. That is to say, he teased her secret button with deft fingers while she leaned sighing against him, her cheek pressed to his and her brown eyes vague, until, far sooner than he expected, she uttered a little shriek and went limp. But for only a moment or two – and then she stepped away from him and was pulling on the trousers of her lounging pyjamas.

'I shall come to your apartment as soon as lunch is over,' she said, giving him a small smile that could be

145

taken for distant affection or for a polite dismissal. 'Wait for me – I shall be with you soon after three.'

But as he strolled towards the Avenue des Champs Elysées and a suitable restaurant, Armand was not at all pleased at how his morning had gone. Yvonne was a discontented woman who used men for casual gratification – there was no secret about that – and he had meant as little to her as a hundred others she had tried. A hundred? Perhaps a thousand – who could say? He had in part restored his self-esteem by the little victory of fingering her to a climax while he watched her face, but his sense of grievance persisted, and it was not merely a question of predatory Yvonne having him as unconcernedly as if she had smoked a cigarette.

The profoundly disturbing conclusion he reached was that he was a target for malcontent women. His suave good looks, his stylish clothes, his courteous manners, his ability to delight in bed – he feared that these qualities had perhaps less to do with his successes with pretty women than his susceptibility! Evidently, it took no more than one look at him for a woman to know that she could use him for whatever purpose she chose – all she need do was let him bare her breasts and kiss them!

Yvonne had used him to amuse herself for an hour before lunch – her sister Madeleine had used him to revenge herself on Pierre-Louis. It had taken him a long time to understand that, but the news that she had spent the night with her husband had enlightened Armand. And Suzette, she was looking for a replacement for Pierre-Louis as paymaster, and Dominique, she too used men for her own purposes, but she was so entertaining that she could be forgiven. And before her – all the women he had adored and who said they adored him!

It vexed Armand to think that he was accepted for his usefulness – like every other man, he wanted to be loved for himself alone. By the time that Yvonne arrived at his apartment in the middle of the afternoon, she had become a little elevated by the excellence of the food and wine at lunch and the importance of her friends. But Armand was in a very different mood: his unhappy reflections on how his natural predilections seemed to make him an easy prey for women had reduced him to a cynical frame of mind.

If that's how it is, so much the worse! he told himself. *I shall take from them, just as they take from me!* And in a curiously detached frame of mind, he kissed Yvonne's hand with impersonal courtesy, as if this were their first meeting for days, as if the events of the morning had never taken place, as if she had never stripped naked for him in her own salon, as if he had never enjoyed the delights of her slender body. He took her fur-collared coat and, without a word, led her straight into his bedroom.

For her lunch with the Duchesse Yvonne had put on a simple little frock of sage green velvet – from the hand of a master couturier – with close-fitting sleeves that ended in trailing points and the bodice cut to show off her fashionably slender figure. The sombre colour of the frock was relieved by a row of flat ivory buttons from neck to hem and, by way of further adornment, she wore a matching pair of brooches in the form of large butterflies. They were made of diamonds, with round green emeralds for eyes, and she had a butterfly pinned above each of her pointed breasts.

There was an expression of condescension in her eyes as she saw Armand remove his jacket, and her red-painted mouth opened to deliver some suitably cutting remark about Armand's lack of finesse in attempting such directness. But the remark was never made, and the expression on her face changed to indignation as he bent down to grasp her by the knees and flip her over on her back on the foot of the bed.

'What the devil do you think you're doing?' she exclaimed, her sang-froid vanishing as Armand forced himself in between her legs.

He ignored the tempting row of buttons down the front of her frock and turned it up casually to her waist to display her underwear. She had changed the white satin knickers of this morning's encounter for flimsy black ones.

'*Chérie* – you've put on your most exciting lace underwear for me!' Armand said, ignoring her outcry and feeling the smooth bare flesh of her thighs above the tops of her black silk stockings. 'But how very chic.'

To keep her lying on her back and helpless, he lifted her legs to the perpendicular and put an arm round them to clasp them against his chest. Yvonne abused and threatened him with great ferocity and struggled so hard to free herself that her little round hat came off and rolled away across the bed. Paying no attention to anything she said, Armand heaved her legs upwards to raise her lean bottom high enough to slip her pretty knickers from under her and pull them up her legs until he had them off completely.

He held her by the ankles and played with her by opening her legs slowly, revealing to his admiring gaze her dark brown thatch and long pink lips, and then concealing them as he slowly made her thighs press together again – and then he showed himself her naked charms once more by parting her legs.

'Not like this,' Yvonne protested in red-faced outrage. 'Stop it at once!'

'Ah, you are impatient to see the implement of your delight and mine,' said Armand, and held her legs tightly to his chest with one arm while he unbuttoned his trousers and let them slide down his legs to his ankles. His excitable friend sprang forward so boldly that it was nuzzling the tender backs of Yvonne's thighs.

'No!' she objected, but he took her ankles again and parted her legs to show her his jutting pride.

'This morning, on your chaise-longue, I was most impressed by the superb muscular flexibility you displayed when you opened your legs for me,' he told her, though she was not listening. 'I must see you do it again.'

Very slowly, and much against her will, for she fought him all the way, he separated her legs, wondering how far he could go without splitting her up the middle. Eventually his arms were out straight at shoulder-level, an ankle in each hand, and still Yvonne showed no sign of discomfort, though she was making her annoyance extremely obvious. The position pulled the thin lips between her thighs wide apart and, by bending his knees a little and leaning forward, Armand was able to present the purple head of his stem to her opening. One long push took him inside – and caused Yvonne to give voice to her protest in a shrill scream of anger.

'You told me this morning that you enjoy being help-less on your back,' he said, pushing deeper into her. 'Do you feel helpless enough, now, Yvonne?'

She tried to bend her legs to cover her vulnerability, but Armand used his strength to keep them stretched out straight.

'You have very beautiful legs,' he murmured, slowly moving them back towards each other. 'Long and mar-vellously shaped, with slender thighs and long calves and fine ankles. And the delicate tone of your skin gleaming through your silk stockings – ah, what per-fection!'

'Let me go,' she begged him, her rage beginning to disperse at his words of praise. 'Let me go and we can still be friends.'

'But of course we shall be friends!' Armand assured her at once. 'Has anyone ever made love to your legs, Yvonne? Or have I the honour of being the first?'

Though neither he nor she realised it, their encounter presented a comical spectacle – Armand with his trou-sers round his ankles, his uncovered bottom heaving back and forth as he slid his spike in her soft burrow with a jerky little motion, and Yvonne naked from waist to stocking-tops, the cheeks of her bare bottom against his belly, and her feet on either side of his head. From the waist up her private charms were modestly conce-aled by her close-fitting frock with the diamond brooches, though her arms were flung wide and her fists were clenched in silent protest at not having her own way.

Armand had declared his interest in making love to her legs – whatever that meant – but it proved to be the slinky touch of her stockings that was arousing him furiously. He turned his head to press his eager lips to the fine black silk and she felt the wetness of his tongue through it on her calf.

'You're mad!' she exclaimed. 'Let me go, you pervert!'

He moaned a little in delight and thrust hard and faster into her, setting her legs shaking to the rhythm of his pleasure. He pulled off her pointed black shoes and held her foot to his face, showering wet kisses on the soft sole through its fine silk covering. And as his arousal soared to frantic heights, his hot belly jammed harder against the naked flesh of her taut bottom and he plunged into her with greater force.

'Oh, Yvonne – I adore you!' he gasped.

'No!' she shrieked, seeing him on the brink of ecstasy, 'You're not to do it like this — I don't want you to!'

But he was far beyond hearing her protests, even if he had cared about them, and his body shook as he stabbed into her soft sheath in frenzy. His eyes were open but he saw nothing. He was in that condition when he no longer knew whose body he was about to explode into – Yvonne's, Madeleine's or any other woman's.

'Oh my god!' Yvonne exclaimed in distaste and, even as she spoke, she saw his eyes roll upwards and his body convulse as he delivered his rapture inside her, his mouth pressed in a hot kiss to the instep of her right foot.

'Oh my god!' she repeated – and this time it was a wail as the sheer momentum of Armand's climax flung her headlong into ecstasy that made her body buck and writhe on the bed.

When Armand was tranquil again, he took hold of her ankles and opened her legs to the full extent of his arms, to stare down at his long wet spindle, half embedded in her pink slit. Yvonne raised her head to look along her body to their joined parts, an expression of disapproval on her pretty face.

'That was quite enjoyable,' said Armand, using her words of that morning, a touch of disdain in his voice.

'You are an animal and a pervert,' she replied in a voice that would have frozen a river, and although she tried to pull her legs free from his grasp, she soon ceased to struggle when he refused to let go.

'I have made love to your right leg,' he said, 'and it was delicious. Before I let you go I shall give myself the pleasure of making love to your left leg also – it would be discourteous not to. But before then, there is something else I wish to do to you.'

He straightened his back, withdrawing his softening stalk, tucked her shins under his armpits and put his fingers into her, to caress her secret bud.

'No!' she said at once. 'You did that to me this morning.'

'And it was delightful,' he said, and by then he had both his thumbs between her wet petals and was making her shudder with sensation.

'I intend to observe your little thrill several times before I attend to your left leg,' he told her. 'Lie still and enjoy yourself, Yvonne, for you are in no position to deny me.'

7

Ecstasies of the Mind

It was about ten o'clock in the morning and watery autumn sunshine showed at the bedroom window when Armand woke up to a marvellous feeling of well-being. The pride of his life had woken earlier and was at full stretch inside his mauve silk pyjamas, but it was not that circumstance alone that produced the sense of euphoria. It was, Armand recollected as he rolled over on to his back and put his hands beneath his head in contemplation, that his arrangements for the evening promised to be utterly delightful. At seven-thirty he was taking his new girlfriend out to dinner – fair-haired Suzette Chenet, nineteen years old and delicately chubby of face and body.

After a superb dinner they would go on to a club to dance for an hour or two, and then – *ah, then, then, then*, he thought, his stiff pride attempting to make a tent of the bedsheet – he would bring her back here to his apartment, and *then* – well, making love to Suzette was unlike making love to any other woman he knew. Her girlishly plump body aroused him to a pitch of passion he had rarely experienced, and his frenzy raised her to the same peak, so that they were perfectly matched. With Suzette, the act of love resembled the mating of two Bengali tigers.

The strange thing about this was that Armand was not usually attracted to girls as young as Suzette. As partners in love he tended to choose women of his own age – which was thirty – or even a few years older. His taste was not for unripe girls but for well-seasoned women, so to speak, well-groomed, well-matured, well-experienced – and preferably married. Such women brought to love-making a wealth of skill, acquired over fifteen years or more with a variety of men. They knew what they wanted from a lover, they were not coy and did not pretend to be, and they were not surprised by pleasant little deviations.

But what could one say? Every rule, if rule it was, has its exceptions. Suzette was the exception to the norm for Armand – for him she radiated a youthful sensuality that he was unable to resist. The hours of the evening and night they were going to pass together would be a banquet of unimaginable delight. By the time they finally fell asleep together in this very bed he lay in now, they would have loved each other to a complete standstill – he had not the least doubt of that. And when they woke up in each other's arms in this same bed at midday, it was possible that they might be too exhausted to make love once more before she left!

With this in mind, Armand closed his mind firmly to the eager twitchings of the staunch companion between his legs and got up for breakfast. Madame Cottier had been bustling about for well over an hour. She made his coffee and, when she brought it to the sitting-room with delicious-smelling fresh-baked croissants, he told her that he expected to have a lady staying with him that night. Madame Cottier nodded imperturbably and said she would put the new dove-grey satin sheets on the bed to please his guest. Then she enquired about breakfast arrangements for the next day.

'I am taking the young lady to a nightclub,' he said. 'We shall be dancing until very late. I doubt if we shall wake up much before midday.'

'Ah, yes,' said Madame Cottier, her head tilted to one side and her arms folded over her bosom,' I have heard that these nightclubs can be *very* tiring. It is to be hoped that you and the lady don't overdo it, Monsieur Armand. I shall be here and ready to serve *café complet* for two in the bedroom when you ask for it – even if it's the middle of the afternoon.'

With the pleasant exertions of the evening in his

thoughts, Armand gave himself a lazy morning, doing no more than chat to a few of his friends on the telephone. He went out for a light but sustaining lunch and a half-bottle of excellent red Bordeaux in a little restaurant he patronised nearby, and by half past two he was strolling back in his apartment, his plan to enjoy a siesta for an hour or two and so build up his energies, in order to do justice to Suzette.

Judge then his surprise when, the instant he put his key in the lock of the apartment door, Madame Cottier pulled it open and informed him that he had a visitor. A slight sinking feeling made itself apparent in the pit of his stomach: if his visitor was one of the three beautiful women he currently adored – passionate Madeleine, or that excitingly arrogant sister of hers, Yvonne, or deliciously perverse Dominique – it would be almost impossible not to be drawn into an afternoon of love that would deplete his resources for the evening.

'Who is it?' he asked, not sure which of the three he was most apprehensive of at that moment.

'Madame Quibon,' said Madame Cottier, astonishing him completely. 'I'll be off now you're back – everything is ready for this evening.'

Though Armand had never met her, he knew Fernande Quibon to be the older friend in whose elegant apartment Suzette lived. He also knew her to be the mistress of Marc Leblanc, the art expert. He could think of no reason in the world why she should call on him – unless she brought news of Suzette that was too important to convey by telephone! With his mind full of images of disaster – an accident on the street, a crash on the Metro, the collision of taxis – he rushed into his sitting-room without a moment's pause to take off his coat and hat.

But all such thoughts fled the moment he saw Madame Quibon sitting calmly on one of his armchairs, flicking idly through a copy of *La Vie Parisienne* she had found lying on top of the bookcase. As she looked up from the frivolous little magazine and he caught sight of the classic beauty of her face and the cold brown eyes that seemed to weigh him up in a glance, he hurried to excuse himself and take off his hat.

'I regret to have kept you waiting,' he said. 'Had I known that you were coming . . .' and he let the sentence trail off.

She gave him her hand to kiss, and he noted that she had short strong fingers and that each of the three between thumb and little finger was adorned by a large and expensive ring – one with a solitaire diamond, one with a square-cut emerald surrounded by small diamonds, and the third with two matching rubies.

He removed his overcoat and sat down facing her. Before him he saw a slender woman in her middle thirties, possessed of a cold and somewhat daunting beauty, her hair raven-black, and her dark brown eyes as lustrous and hard as precious stones. She was dressed with great elegance in a tailored jacket and skirt of black georgette that, to Armand's eye, had the look of Chanel about it.

'I found out only an hour ago that you have arranged to meet Suzette this evening,' she began, making it clear that she favoured the direct approach. 'I came here at once, for it is not a matter I wish to discuss on the telephone.'

'How fortunate that I returned immediately after lunch,' said Armand, his voice sarcastic now he understood that her visit was not a friendly one.

'It was obvious that you would be at home this afternoon, hoarding your strength for the exertions you plan for this evening,' said Fernande, matching his sarcasm.

'Then since we are speaking so openly,' said Armand, 'perhaps you will be so good as to tell me why you are here?'

'That is my intention,' she retorted. 'To come straight to the point, Monsieur, I want you to call off your appointment for this evening and leave Suzette alone. I don't want her sleeping with you – is that clear enough?'

'You are insulting!' Armand exclaimed. 'I hardly

know how to reply without being equally offensive. What gives you the right to dictate what I may do?'

'Suzette is my protégée,' Fernande said forcefully. 'I will not permit men like you to ruin her life.'

'Ruin her life? By taking her to dinner and buying presents for her? You are being ridiculous.'

'We both know what you demand from her in return for your dinners and presents! Suzette is mine and I insist that you cease to molest her.'

'I don't understand what you mean,' said Armand, his thoughts racing ahead to startling conclusions.

'There is no need to pretend. You understand me perfectly,' she insisted.

'Yes, I suppose I do,' he said with a sudden charming smile, 'but surely your passion for Suzette is unrequited – she had a lover before me, my cousin Pierre-Louis Beauvais.'

'If that's what you call love, then before she came to Paris she had more *lovers* than you can imagine,' said Fernande coldly. 'Why do you suppose her father beat her black and blue? She has been running wild since she was thirteen and it is a miracle that she has not been pregnant every year since.'

'And now you are instructing her in the arts of survival – is that it?'

Fernande looked at him coldly and said nothing.

'My cousin said nothing about you,' said Armand. 'He told me he thought that Suzette had another man friend.'

'More fool him!' said Fernande scornfully. 'She told him she had no other man friend, but he would not believe her. And when she became annoyed at his refusal to accept the simple truth, he at once reverted to the barbarous male type and thrashed her.'

'Perhaps,' said Armand with a shrug. 'But if you've come here to warn me off, why not the same with him?'

'There was no need to. He occupied no place of importance in Suzette's affections,' Fernande answered. 'He was a useful fool who entertained her well and bought elegant clothes for her. She recompensed him in the only way she knows how. But it seems that it wasn't enough for him to enjoy the delights of her magnificent young body: he decided that he was in love with her and demanded affection, devotion – in short, *love* – from her. And when she did not reciprocate, he became savage and dismissed himself from her life forever by attacking her with his fists and feet.'

'I believe that you exaggerate a little, Madame,' said Armand, smiling at her account, 'but I think that I understand you at last. You are teaching Suzette how to make her way in the world by making use of the marvellous endowment the Good Lord has given her – as I suppose you do yourself, if I may say so in a spirit of open-minded congratulation and without intending the least offence. She was unfortunate in her choice of Pierre-Louis, whom I know to be an emotional and short-tempered man. But, if I may say a word or two in recommendation of myself, I am easy-going, even-tempered, unencumbered by wife or family, and at least as well off as my cousin. What is your objection to me as a lover for Suzette?'

'I am delighted that we can discuss this matter in a rational and civilised manner,' said Fernande, leaning back and crossing her silk-clad knees under the black severity of her skirt. 'Men are usually stupidly emotional about such things. The reason, since you ask, is one of jealousy on my part.'

'But why on earth should you be jealous of me?'

'In the brief time Suzette has known you, she has formed too high an opinion of you for my tranquillity. I have an uneasy feeling that she is young and impressionable enough to fall in love with you. That I flatly refuse to contemplate. What is between you must end now.'

'I am grateful for your frankness,' said Armand, flattered by what he had heard, 'but I know of no reason why I should deny myself the pleasure of Suzette's friendship in order to oblige you.'

Fernande smiled at him, confident now of her ability to bend him to her will. She leaned back a little further in her chair, so that the small movement of her skirt drew his eyes to the elegance of her legs in their black silk stockings.

'My intuition tells me that you would be far more amenable if I were to oblige *you*,' she said softly.

'Ah – so you do like men after all!' Armand exclaimed with a broad smile.

'But how absurd you are,' said Fernande, returning his smile in a manner that was not merely agreeable but which also promised intimate pleasures.

'Why do you say that, Madame?'

'Because every man I've ever met imagines that the twelve or fifteen centimetres of gristle between his legs makes him the lord of creation! We women – we cloven ones – take a very different view of the worth of the extra male limb. But since men never truly grow up, whatever their age, and remain adolescents all their lives, it is necessary for us to humour them by letting them believe they are of supreme importance.'

Her mention of what lay between Armand's legs caused it to stir pleasantly. He parted his legs a little in order to draw Fernande's attention to the lengthening bulge in his trousers.

'It is your privilege to scoff at masculine aspirations,' he said, 'yet the whole of history, biology and science – to say nothing of the teachings of religion – tell us unequivocally that the male is the dominant sex of our species.'

'Ah yes, we must never overlook the dogma of Mother Church,' Fernande replied with sarcasm in her voice. 'With the priests and the scientists on your side you are convinced that you are the dominant one in this conversation. And yet I doubt if what you have to show amounts to anything much. If you dare let me look, that is.'

'Look?' Armand asked, hardly believing what he heard.

'At your tassel, of course. Although the way you have been staring at my legs and trying to see up my skirt leads me to suspect that it may no longer be in a limp condition. But no matter – you want me to see it, don't you?'

'I want every pretty woman in the entire world to see it,' he answered, with complete sincerity, 'but more to the point, Madame – why do *you* want to see it?'

'I can assure you that, except for one small consideration, it would be a matter of supreme indifference to me. But because I care so greatly for Suzette, I have a certain curiosity to see the object with which her delicate body has been penetrated – violated, I could say – but I will restrain my true feelings out of politeness.'

How then does a warm-blooded man respond when an attractive woman expresses an interest in being permitted to look at his most cherished part, whatever the reason she may give? Needless to say, during the unusual conversation that preceded this moment, Armand had been playing his regular game of undressing Fernande in his mind and imagining the elegance of her slender, small-breasted body under her tailored black suit. As a natural result, he was in a condition which made it wholly inaccurate to describe his male equipment as a *tassel*, as Fernande had rightly surmised. It stood stiffly upright, held closely against his belly by his underwear – and clamoured for his attention by a strong throbbing.

The thought of displaying it to her in this state of arousal was most enticing. And it became ever more so, if that was at all possible, when Fernande slowly undid the jet buttons of her softly-tailored black jacket and opened it. She wore no pretty silk camisole under her jacket – only the flimsiest of brassières to contain her pear-shaped breasts. The fine lace of which it was made concealed nothing. Armand gazed in delight at the small pink buds that showed through and thought of how it would feel to touch them with the tip of his tongue.

'As a token of my good will, you may look at me,' said Fernande, though Armand was certain that whatever her opinion was of him as Suzette's lover, benevolence played no part in it. But this was not the time to quibble about motives, not when Fernande was lifting her soft little breasts clear of the brassière and arching her back to make them more prominent.

'Your beauty is truly devastating, Madame,' said Armand, and he meant it, for he could not restrain a sigh of pleasure at the sight of Fernande cupping her breasts in hands adorned with gem-stones of luminous red and blue and green.

His mind was filled with delicious thoughts of Fernande baring her little breasts for Suzette to play with, and corresponding images of Fernande unbuttoning Suzette's silk blouse to uncover her plump breasts and kiss them . . . And then the two women with a hand up each other's clothes to feel between warm thighs and send little tremors of pleasure through their bodies with softly moving fingers. He pictured them undressing each other completely, Fernande and Suzette lying naked on a bed together, their thighs intertwined and their soft bellies pressed together . . .

From the arm of her chair Fernande took her handbag, a flat and elegant oblong of black suede with her monogram on it in golden cut-out letters. She rummaged in it for a moment before producing a little handkerchief of finest white Batiste linen, with a broad lace edge. Armand thought she intended to wipe her eyes gently in some strange pretence of emotion, but he was proved instantly wrong: she opened her mouth and pressed the handkerchief to it and then held out the small white square on the palm of her hand to display the scarlet oval imprint of her parted lips.

Armand was unable to take his eyes off the lace-edged handkerchief as she stood up gracefully and crossed the floor between them in four steps. She spread the handkerchief on his knee while she perched on the arm of his chair and asked him to stretch out his legs – or was she telling him, rather than asking him, for she spoke in a soft voice without inflection. Asked or told – it did not matter in the least to Armand in his condition of arousal. He spread his legs wide for Fernande to unbutton his trousers and he stared eagerly into her face as she laid bare his secrets. Her expression was one of tranquillity, bordering on mild interest.

'There it is!' he exclaimed in triumph when she pulled up his shirt and let his stiff device thrust itself out boldly through the slit of his underpants. She looked at it for some moments, making no attempt to touch him.

'Hm,' she said, a tiny sound in her throat that might have meant anything from a scornful *Is that it?* to a complimentary *Not bad!* as she surveyed his male pride with a calm that was almost unbearable.

'A certain lady of style and quality has assured me that she finds its passionate appearance enthralling,' said Armand, reinforcing his morale with the recollection of Yvonne's words.

'Some women are more easily deceived than others,' Fernande retorted. 'I see no reason for you to be pleased with yourself because you have forced this distended organ into Suzette's body. You might have harmed her – women are very sensitive between the legs. But I don't suppose you gave that any consideration.'

'It is precisely because women are so tender between their thighs that they enjoy having a man inside them,' said Armand. 'You have been married, Madame – the ring is still on your finger – and therefore you can be no stranger to the pleasures of a man lying on your belly.'

'Do not remind me of those days!' she exclaimed. 'I was twenty when my family married me off to a man ten years older than myself, a widower who had killed one wife already.'

'You married a murderer?' Armand asked incredulously.

'Truly a murderer in the eyes of Heaven, if not of the law. He made her pregnant and she died giving birth to his child. And I who was hardly more than a child myself – I knew nothing of the nature of men – he turned me on to my back and prised my legs open, night after night, to satisfy his brutal desires on my body. I pleaded with him, but he was unrelenting.'

Armand had discovered that, perched as Fernande

was on the arm of his chair, her bosom was at exactly the right height to rest his head on. He pressed his cheek against her soft bare breasts, and he was turning his head to reach her pink buds with his tongue when she pushed him away and quickly fastened her jacket. Armand was compelled to content himself with putting his cheek to the material of her jacket for the pleasure of feeling the softness underneath.

'Evidently you had the misfortune to be married to a man lacking in tenderness,' he said. 'But you cannot claim to be a child now, nor to be ignorant of the ways of men. Yet the fact is that you are an intimate friend of someone with whom I am acquainted – Marc Leblanc. How do you explain that?'

'My friendships are not your concern,' said Fernande, her cheeks blushing a fiery red. 'I doubt if you are capable of appreciating the close and very special affection that has grown up between Monsieur Leblanc and me, but I shall try to make you understand.'

'I shall be most grateful,' Armand replied, more than a trace of irony in his voice.

Happily, Fernande did not notice. She gazed at his long pink column abstractedly and in silence, while she seemed to be collecting her thoughts.

'If you are acquainted with my dear friend Leblanc, then you must know that he is only a year or two short of seventy,' she said at last. 'His interest in beautiful women is as strong as ever, but his ability to make use of their bodies for his satisfaction has disappeared. In the two or three years I have been his trusted friend, he has never once attempted to do that to me. But because he is so close a friend, I try to please him as best I can.'

'And how is that?' Armand enquired with open scepticism.

'I take my clothes off and permit him to see me naked.'

'Ah, but how poetic!' Armand exclaimed, not believing a word of what she had told him. 'I can picture the scene in Leblanc's salon – you sitting naked on one of his Second Empire chairs, while he converses with you about art and admires your beauty from afar. Or does he ask you to sit at the piano and play a little *Nocturne* of Chopin for him while he stands with a glass of cognac in his hand and watches the soft movement of your naked breasts?'

It was in his mind that, if there was any truth in her tale, then Lablanc seemed to be getting remarkably little in return for the valuable paintings he gave her.

'You are a barbarian,' Fernande said thoughtfully, 'and I knew you were incapable of understanding. Marc Leblanc is a man of exquisite sensibility. When I stand naked for him he worships me, he kneels and kisses my feet. And sometimes – just sometimes – he asks my permission to kiss my breasts.'

Armand shrugged and said, 'everyone to his own taste.'

'Oh, *you* would demand more, we both know that well enough,' Fernande exclaimed, her voice faintly scornful as she gestured towards his neglected stave. 'I've had men-friends like you in the past and I know how to deal with them.'

'I'm sure that you do,' said Armand in a knowing tone. 'I've been to your apartment and I know that you live in style.'

'Don't deceive yourself,' she said at once. 'My success is not achieved by lying on my back.'

'Then, since we are talking with such delightful frankness, dear Madame Quibon, perhaps I may be allowed to know how it is achieved,' he responded, genuinely interested now.

'By being charming,' she said softly.

Before Armand could produce a suitably sceptical reply, she moved from the arm of his chair to kneel in front of him while she draped her exquisite little lace-trimmed square over his swaying pointer. He stared wide-eyed at the bright red print of her open lips hanging round the swollen head of his eager part, and Fernande sat back on her heels to consider the effect of what she had done and then smiled up at him.

'I suppose you enjoy having this awkward thing of yours in a woman's mouth,' she asked.

'Oh, yes,' he answered, 'almost as much as putting it between her legs.'

'Soft wet lips, painted bright red – and open for you to slide in,' said Fernande, 'just like the red marks of my lips that embrace you now.'

Armand was staring as if hypnotised at the scarlet imprint of her mouth on the handkerchief. It was moving up and down his veiled ram-rod to Fernande's jerking rhythm, dazzling his mind with the deception of almost believing that her mouth was truly swallowing and disgorging him. A thought came into his mind that caused him to give a little gasp of triumph.

'And Suzette's mouth . . .' he murmured, 'it has been inside her mouth more than once.'

'Then make the most of your memories, for they are all you have now,' Fernande retorted.

Her hand flicked at him in short and fast strokes that set off a spasm in his belly announcing the onset of his ecstatic emission.

'You may do it now,' she said calmly.

She spoke in a tone that held no trace of overt domination, but which allowed no ambiguity or evasion and admitted not the least possibility of non-compliance with her wishes. Armand understood and responded with a long wail of delight to feel his essence gushing like a fountain. An expression of malicious triumph spread over Fernande's coldly beautiful face as she glanced down to watch him soak her lace-edged handkerchief.

By the time he had recovered himself, she was sitting in the armchair facing him, well out of reach, her black-stockinged legs crossed as if to protect the treasure between her thighs. Armand dried himself as best he could with the morsel of linen and lace she had left wound about his collapsing projection, then fastened his trousers. He dropped the handkerchief under his chair for later disposal, and in spite of the gratification he had just enjoyed, his mind was not tranquil at all –

it was in a turmoil of mixed emotions, principally dislike for Fernande.

He stared at her in silence, compelled to admit to himself that she had recognised – and taken instant advantage of – his susceptibility to beautiful women. And she had manipulated him cleverly, as cleverly as Dominique, perhaps, though not to awaken his interest in her own charms, as Dominique's games had been intended. No, it was to divert him from his enjoyment of Suzette, so that Fernande could have her to herself. He had not the least doubt that dear Fernande had many more little tricks in her repertoire as arousing as the first with which to entertain him – until she had drained him dry and extinguished his interest for the time being in Suzette.

And what annoyed him more than the rest was that, as an unconscious indication of her contempt, Fernande had not touched him with her bare hand for even a moment! All had been accomplished through the enveloping handkerchief she had sacrificed to his passion. *I am too vulnerable to the charms of beautiful women*, he told himself, *a weakness of character that is annoying and marvellous and marvellously annoying and annoyingly marvellous – all at the same time*.

He had known this unconsciously since he was sixteen, but he had been forced to acknowledge it to himself on the morning when Yvonne enticed him into pleasuring her on her white satin chaise-longue for no better reason than to fill an idle hour before she went out to lunch. But what am I saying, Armand asked himself – what *better* reason can there ever be than straightforward desire? And what has reason ever had to do with the pleasures men and women give each other, anyway?

Nevertheless, to be susceptible was one thing; to become a permanent victim was another. Yvonne had been the hunter and he the prey in her salon – it was Yvonne who had *him* that morning, no doubt of that, even though it was she who lay on her back. But later that day, he had been able to change all that and hunt

Yvonne as prey – she was still on her back, but with her silk-stockinged legs held vertically above her and the thin-lipped slit between her thighs fully exposed for him to play with as he chose!

It had been the slinky touch of her stockings that aroused him on that occasion, the feel of the fine black silk against his mouth and on his wet tongue. That, and the exhilaration of knowing that Yvonne had unintentionally put herself at his mercy, so that he could give free rein to every impulse, in total disregard of whatever she might prefer. Standing between her upright legs he had skewered her twice on his spike inside half an hour – compelling her to share his ecstasy in spite of her loudly expressed outrage at being brutalised, as she insisted on calling it.

In between these two performances, he had held her ankles trapped under his armpits to keep her as helpless as a seaturtle turned on its back on the sand. And he had fingered her ripe fig until it burst and spilled its juice – not just once but three times. By Armand's idiosyncratic standards, he had really *had* Yvonne that afternoon: with his fingers he had possessed her completely and, to his way of thinking, some part of her was his forever. She was so utterly fatigued afterwards that she looked pale under her make-up – almost haggard for so beautiful a woman – and she had leaned on his arm all the way down the stairs when he found a taxi for her and sent her home.

She had telephoned next day to announce her impending arrival at his apartment to resume their games, but he had been out, and he had taken no action on the discreet message left with Madame Cottier. And now he was confronted by another predator, Fernande Quibon, who stalked men and took note of their little frailties – and then pounced to devour their substance. Already she had sprung upon him once and sunk her talons into his flesh – figuratively speaking, of course. What would she do for an encore, he found himself wondering – put on her fine black gloves and drain off his strength again?

But whatever it was that Fernande might have in mind, Armand was determined that there was not going to be a repetition of her cynical manipulation of him. As with Yvonne when she came to his apartment to repeat her little triumph, the time had come for him to assert himself.

'I regret to inform you, Madame,' he said formally, 'that I am no more amenable now that you have *obliged* me than I was before. I thank you most cordially for that pleasant little interlude, but it is my intention to remain an intimate friend of Suzette and see her as often as I choose. What does your intuition tell you now?'

'It whispers to me that you are one of the fortunate who possess the priceless gift of insatiable sensuality,' she replied, not in the least put out by his manner – or at least, not showing it if she were.

'Whereas your own sensuality is strictly controlled by your reason and at your disposal to serve your plans,' said Armand. 'Well, it has been most agreeable to make your acquaintance, Madame Quibon, but I hope you will not think me impolite to suggest that it is time for your visit to come to an end.'

'Not impolite, but mistaken,' she answered calmly. 'There is much more we have to settle between us, you and I.'

'I know of nothing – I am not prepared to discuss Suzette with you,' he said.

Fernande made no reply. She stared at his face for some moments, as if finally making up her mind, then uncrossed her legs and leaned back in her chair to slide her skirt slowly up above her knees with her many-ringed hands. In spite of his determination not to be tempted again, Armand found himself gazing lovingly at the gleam of her slender thighs through the sheer black silk of her stockings. She wore no garters – her stockings were attached to black suspenders that were revealed as the edge of her skirt rose higher towards the shadowed and perfumed mysteries concealed between her legs.

167

Her skirt halted its upward glide when the hem was about halfway between her knees and her groin. Armand's heart was bounding with joy in his chest as he stared at the creamy white flesh of Fernande's slender thighs above her stocking-tops. He wanted so much to kiss them that his apparatus – even though it had been so recently and competently handled – grew again to its full potential. Fernande's sharp eyes noted the long bulge in his trousers and she smiled at the easy success of her campaign.

'You are a man with far more experience of women's bodies than should be permitted,' she said. 'What is your opinion of my legs – do you find them elegant?'

'They are exquisite,' he answered.

'I thought you must like them because the effect on you is obvious. Don't you find it a little uncomfortable, in your present condition, to be confined in those trousers? To me they seem tight and constricting.'

'What would you suggest?' he asked in a hushed voice.

'Undo your buttons again,' she said, with a knowing smile. 'Open your trousers, let your male distinction stick out. Perhaps I can think of something to do with it.'

Armand closed his eyes for a second or two to fight down the urge to do what she suggested. The initiative was slipping away from him – something must be done before she had him completely under her spell again.

'I have a marvellous idea,' he said with a grin as he began to unbutton his trousers. 'Come here and open your jacket and let me rub my *male distinction* between your breasts.'

'Certainly not!' she replied at once, outrage in her voice.

'But I have not forgotten you told me that our mutual friend Marc Leblanc is allowed the privilege of kissing them when you undress for him. Unless he has entered his dotage since I last saw him, I am certain that he does more than press a delicate kiss on them. Surely he feels them and gets out his wrinkled old dangler and presses it between them?'

To distract him from further intrusion into her private arrangements with Leblanc, Fernande put her right forefinger to her mouth and licked it until it was very wet. Armand watched in dumbfounded delight as her hand disappeared up her skirt.

'But what are you doing . . . ?' he managed to sigh at last.

'Something you will never have the pleasure of doing – I am stroking my *jou-jou*,' she told him, her eyes half-closed.

Released from the prison of his trousers, Armand's anxious component was straining upwards and quivering. And watching Fernande's rhythmically moving arm, he felt that he was drowning in an ocean of pink desire – and as he was about to go under for the last time, he clutched at an insanely flimsy idea in an attempt to save himself.

'Since you appear to be determined to force me into a sort of duel to the death to see who shall have Suzette,' he said, hardly able to keep his hands off the over-enthusiastic friend sticking out of his open trousers, 'allow me to set out the only terms on which I will accept your challenge.'

'I am listening,' said Fernande. 'Continue, if you please. But do not try to be clever with me, it's not your style. It is absurd to talk about conditions; you are merely trying to confuse me.'

She was not in the least confused, of course, she was in complete command of herself and of the situation – it was poor Armand who was confused by emotions surging through him at the delicious sight that confronted him: Fernande playing so very casually with herself. He made one last supreme effort before the twitching traitor he had bared betrayed him again and delivered him into Fernande's power.

'I propose a trial of strength,' he said, his voice shaky. 'We shall both make love to Suzette at the same time, and when her critical moment is about to arrive, we shall see to which of us she presents her little pocket to be filled.'

Fernande took her hand from under her skirt and stood up. She gazed calmly into his eyes while she bent her long back to reach down for the hem of her skirt and raise it slowly up her thighs. Armand's mouth opened in a little sigh of admiration as the tops of her black silk stockings were uncovered again for him, and then the pale flesh of her thighs above them. Higher still the skirt rose, as if it were a curtain going up at the theatre when the play is about to begin – until the moment when Armand glimpsed the lace hem of her knickers.

He had expected, for no better or more logical reason than that Fernande was wearing a black skirt and shiny black silk stockings, that her underwear would be the same colour. So it was with a start of surprise and pleasure he observed that her elegantly-cut silk knickers were of a rich dark mulberry-red! It was a colour to seize the imagination, opulent, voluptuous, and, above all, passionate.

Fernande stood still and silent, almost posing for him like an artist's model, while he had his fill of gazing in rapture, first at the delicate curve where her belly filled out the mulberry underwear, and then at the bolder little prominence between her thighs where the thin silk concealed her *motte*, and lastly at the creamy smoothness of her flesh between knickers and stockings. Armand's jutting stem shook in an agony of anticipation that brought a smile to her face.

'But how beautiful you are,' Armand whispered.

For the ten thousandth time in his life – or thereabouts – he regretted that his tiny talent for sketching had never been trained and developed properly. If only he were a painter, he could capture on canvas the luscious contrast of colours that Fernande was showing to him: the interplay of shiny black stockings, pale-skinned thighs and mulberry-red silk. And the exquisite opposition of this unveiling to the serenity of her face. How well she understood masculine foibles – he was as frantically aroused as if she had stripped naked for him, and all she had done was let him see her underwear!

But the best was yet to come, he found. When Fernande judged that he was ready to move upwards to the next stage of sensual intoxication, she hooked her thumbs into the waistband of her knickers and began to slide them down her belly, pausing to let him savour each delight to the full. First her belly-button was uncovered – a small and perfectly round dimple that cried out to be explored by the tip of a wet tongue. And when Fernande saw Armand's hands trembling on the arms of his chair, she lowered her knickers further, until she was showing him the top fringe of her patch of curls, a darker brown than he could ever recall seeing on a woman, so dark as to be almost black.

And still the best was to come! His pride was bounding so strongly that he clasped it in his hand to keep it still, and he held his breath as Fernande slid her knickers down her thighs to her stocking-tops and displayed her fleece boldly. It was not extensive, or if it was, then she kept it clipped to a small area, but the thickness and richness of colour were delicious and the effect on Armand was so powerful that he could hardly prevent his hand slipping up and down his swollen shaft to draw out a heart-felt tribute to Fernande's intimate charms.

In another moment she had taken her underwear completely off and smoothed her skirt down again to hide all he had been permitted to see. She smiled at the bewilderment that showed on his face and, in another moment, was on her knees beside him, to all intents and purposes fully dressed, her black tailored jacket buttoned and her skirt hiding her legs down to her knees. But to Armand the secret he shared with her was little short of overwhelming; the secret that under her skirt she was naked, her dark-brown curls and slender thighs unguarded from prying eyes and probing hands – if a man was bold enough to make the attempt.

And there, between her bejewelled hands, she held

out for his delectation the proof of her secret nakedness: the mulberry-red and lace-trimmed knickers she had removed. Wordlessly, Armand reached out a quivering hand to touch the charming and fragile little garment with as much emotion as if he had been touching Fernande's naked body.

'Ah, but how gorgeous,' he breathed reverently as his fingertips slid down the smooth silk and fluttered over the tiny area which had covered her thick curls and the fleshy delight that lay beneath them. And Fernande smiled knowingly and held the silk stretched taut for him to rub his fingers gently over the part that held his attention.

'You are as just as presumptuous as I expected,' she said, smiling again at his eagerness.

She understood very well, this Fernande Quibon, how to play the little game that provided her with a comfortable apartment and elegant clothes – the game of teasing men to the brink of delirium without becoming involved herself, of binding them to her without committing herself physically or emotionally. First a little encouragement to set their fantasies running, then a touch of discouragement to slow them down, followed by another little act of encouragement, and so on, until the man could bear no more and begged to be relieved of his passion – after which she could ask what she liked of him.

From Armand she wanted no financial contribution and sought no long-term acquaintance – on the contrary, her intention was to rid Suzette of his attentions. But she employed her arts on him to gain the upper hand, and he gasped loudly when she wrapped her dark red knickers round his hard shaft, taking care not to touch his flesh with her bare hand. She sat back on her heels, watching him shiver with pleasure at the soft touch of the warm silk.

'How incredible,' he sighed. 'This brightly-coloured morsel of silk that has kissed the pretty *jou-jou* between your thighs now caresses me . . .'

'You find that very exciting,' said Fernande, and she was making a statement, not asking a question.

'Ah, but you let me glimpse your *bijou*, and what I saw was enchanting,' Armand breathed, staring down at the long silk-wrapped bundle that was twitching without pause in his lap.

'You found my *bijou* enchanting?' she asked with a smile.

'Exquisite!' he assured her fervently. 'I would give anything in the world for the pleasure of kissing it.'

'You're not the first man to say that to me,' she replied, 'and my answer is always the same – *No, never, never, never!* If you were a pretty young girl, the answer would be different. I would strip myself naked and kneel over you as you sit there, with my legs spread wide for you to kiss me to your heart's content.'

'You are cruel to torment me with thoughts of delight when you have no intention of making them come true,' he sighed.

'It is not I who am cruel,' said Fernande with a thin smile. 'It is your tragic destiny: you had the misfortune to be born with this attachment. You prize it highly, I suppose, as men do in their idiotic vanity, but its presence means that your desire to touch my *bijou* will never be granted.'

The thin smile remained on her face while she pressed *this attachment*, in its mulberry-red silk covering, between the palms of her jewelled hands.

'But I have touched dear little Suzette's, and kissed it until she writhed in ecstasy and begged me to push my plunger up her and split her apart,' he retaliated.

'Rapist!' Fernande exclaimed, her face pale and contorted in anger. 'Only a vulgarian would speak of her with such disrespect. Enough! Those conditions you were trying to confuse me with, an agreement that you leave her alone – what were your terms?'

'A trial of affection between you and me, with Suzette as the prize,' he said, trying to make his voice sound strong and forceful. 'We will make love to her at the same time, we will kiss her and fondle her together,

173

each in our own way, neither of us interfering with the other.'

'That's a grotesque suggestion!' Fernande exclaimed.

'Between us we shall very quickly arouse her to the point where she will turn to one of us for the tender *coup de grâce* and we shall see whether it is your tongue or my masculinity she wants between her legs to bring on her ecstasy. If she turns to you, then she is yours and I will never see her again. But if she turns to me . . .'

'What then?' Fernande asked. 'Do you imagine that I shall be content to let her move in with you and never see her again? You are more arrogant than I had imagined.'

'Let us wait and see what the outcome is,' said Armand, who had not the slightest intention of inviting Suzette – or any other woman – to move into his apartment. 'Do you accept my conditions?'

'Of course not!'

'You are so unsure of her affections after being her lover and protector for so many months? Admit it, Madame, she stays with you not because she has any regard for you but because you provide her with a far more comfortable home than she has yet been able to find elsewhere. If my foolish cousin Pierre-Louis had offered her an apartment of her own and a generous income, who knows – perhaps you would have lost her already.'

'What nonsense!' Fernande retorted. 'Your words demonstrate the truth of what I said earlier – like all the men I've ever met you imagine that the length of gristle between your legs makes you monarch of the world and women's lord and master. But this is mere foolish self-deception, believe me. Suzette amuses herself with men, but I am the one that she adores and she will never leave me, not for your brutal cousin and not for you either, superior though you consider yourself to be.'

'And yet you are afraid to accept my terms – so which of us is indulging in self-deception?' Armand asked.

'Afraid – I?' she said, her thin black eyebrows arching up her forehead. 'You flatter yourself, Monsieur.'

'Then you accept?'

'How very absurd you are! I have seen all that you have to show,' said Fernande, and she reached between his thighs to clasp the silk-clad column standing up from his open trousers.

'Then you know that I shall be a formidable antagonist for Suzette's affections,' he replied, refusing to be overawed.

'Formidable? Never! These few centimetres of engorged flesh are all you have to offer Suzette – you cannot possibly imagine that I am impressed even, let alone anxious.'

Her brightly-jewelled hands were massaging his pike-staff through the silk.

'I have a key that fits into her lock,' Armand whispered, tremors of pleasure flickering through his belly from what Fernande was doing to him, 'while all you can offer her is another keyhole.'

'It would be the easiest thing in the world to bring on your little crisis,' said Fernande, ignoring his insult, 'but what is the point? Men are insatiable in their desires – it is hardly more than a quarter of an hour since you ruined a perfectly good handkerchief. The woman who is so foolish as to indulge a man once soon discovers that she is no more than a slave, for as long as it pleases the tyrant to whom she has submitted.'

'You have not submitted to me,' Armand sighed in pleasure. 'The deception with your handkerchief only demonstrated to me that you are incapable of passion.'

'Ha! We will settle this stupidity once and for all,' Fernande exclaimed, 'and in the way you have suggested – so that you are shown beyond the shadow of doubt how completely disposable you are.'

'When shall we settle it?' Armand asked languorously. 'If I may remind you, Suzette and I are unavailable this evening – unless you wish to join us in bed here after we return from dancing. At about two in the morning, say?'

'I see you are a comedian,' Fernande replied softly.

'Then when shall we settle our differences?' Armand gasped, unable to take his eyes off the red silk knickers through which she was stroking him.

'Right away,' she answered. 'Is that agreed?'

'Where – shall we telephone Suzette to join us here?'

'Out of the question,' said Fernande, her hands suddenly still. 'We shall go to my apartment. Agreed?'

She sank gracefully back on her heels and opened the jet buttons of her tailored jacket. Armand stared entranced as she reached behind her back to unfasten her brassière and bare her pear-shaped little breasts.

'Your apartment,' he agreed dreamily. 'Very well – I am more than ready, thanks to you. Let's go right away.'

'Certainly,' she replied, 'but first we must make absolutely sure that we agree the terms on which this idiotic duel between us is to be conducted. After you've lost – of which there can be no real doubt – it would be embarrassing and unpleasant to have you burst into tears of rage and claim you were cheated.'

'Yes, by all means let us have matters clear between us,' he murmured, his upright stem quivering. 'Point one: each of us is to have free access to all parts of Suzette's body. Point two: neither of us will deliberately obstruct any caress of Suzette by the other. Point three: if there is . . .'

'There is an area of ambiguity here,' Fernande said in a thoughtful voice as she stroked her pale-skinned breasts and their pink tips. 'That second point of yours needs some explanation. For example, suppose I am caressing Suzette's *bijou* when you take it in mind that you want to push your length of hard flesh up it. You will be unable to do so because of my fingers – yet it cannot be said that I am obstructing you deliberately. Is that also your interpretation of the rule?'

'Yes, that seems to be reasonable,' Armand said in a murmur, lacking the determination to pull her hand away from him, 'and vice-versa, of course – it cannot count as deliberate obstruction when you find it impossible to caress Suzette's peach because I have split it open and am inside it.'

'You need have no fears on my account,' she said with a thin smile as she jiggled him up and down strongly, 'you will be the one who will be shut out, not me. The idea that you will have a chance of getting *this* inside Suzette is ludicrous.'

'We shall see,' said Armand weakly as she took his silk-wrapped shaft between her hands again and stroked it. 'But I insist that you stop what you are doing now.'

'I'm sure you do,' she said softly.

To Armand, half-dazed with pleasure, it seemed that the world had turned upside-down – he was scarcely able to believe that he had spoken those words, that he of all people was asking a beautiful woman to stop playing with him!

Her hands were still, but she had not finished with him yet.

'My breasts,' she said, wriggling her shoulders a little to make her bare beauties sway. 'You never told me if you think them well-shaped, even though you tried to kiss them when I was sitting on the arm of your chair.'

Armand looked at her pear-shaped breasts and felt his extension leap between Fernande's hands.

'You accused men of being tyrants,' he whispered in delight, 'but you are the tyrant here, Madame.'

'You are beginning to learn,' she said. 'A little reward may encourage you further. What would be suitable? Ah yes, I have it – make love to my knickers, Armand.'

In spite of all that had happened between them, it was the first time she had used his name. This hint of a new intimacy had a powerful effect on Armand, as it was intended to, and he started to thrust upwards into the dark-red silk held round his stiffness by her two clasped hands.

'Does it feel nice?' she asked softly. 'Does it feel like making love to my *jou-jou?* It is as close as you will ever come to it, Armand.'

But he was immersed too profoundly in ecstatic sensation to hear her words. An incoherent cry escaped him as his body convulsed and released its tribute to her authority over his imagination. His head was thrown back and his eyes closed, but she was looking down at her mulberry-red knickers wrapped round his leaping shaft. A dark stain soaked through the thin silk as the last wet throb shook him.

'I think we've seen the last of your interest in Suzette for today,' said Fernande with a broad smile.

8

The Contest of Love

On the way to her apartment by taxi with Armand, it seemed as if Fernande was losing some of the unlimited confidence in her hold over Suzette that she had expressed earlier. That, at least, was Armand's interpretation of her increasingly hostile manner towards him. As was to be expected, she sat as far away from him as the width of the taxi-seat permitted – she was almost pressing herself back into the corner, her gloved hands deep in the pockets of her elegant winter coat of shiny black moleskin. Armand glanced down with a wry grin at the space between them, and Fernande seized the opportunity to launch her onslaught.

'It requires no great feat of imagination to guess what is in your mind,' she said in a contemptuous tone of voice. 'The moment that you are alone with a woman you think of nothing but getting your hand up her clothes, even in public and in broad daylight. I find that sort of behaviour utterly despicable.'

'Perhaps you do, Madame,' Armand answered mildly, 'but since the women with whom I frequently share a taxi find that my hand between their thighs is a very pleasurable way of passing the journey, I must with regret conclude that there is something unusual about you.'

Fernande glared at him in disdain and he continued cheerfully with what he knew would infuriate her.

'For instance,' he said, 'when I bring Suzette home, she sits very close to me so that I can kiss and caress her.'

While he said this, Armand reached casually across

the gap that separated him from Fernande and, with one finger, stroked the short and soft fur of the coat over her knee. Fernande snorted indignantly and tried to move away from him – but she could retreat no further.

'Our dear little Suzette,' Armand continued, 'whom you and I in our different ways both adore to distraction, became so wet at my touch the other evening that I truly believed she was about to enjoy a little crisis in the taxi – we were travelling along the rue de Rivoli at the time, opposite the Tuileries.'

Fernande was staring as if she were mesmerised by Armand's fingertips moving gently on her fur coat.

'You are a degenerate,' she breathed, hardly able to speak for the emotions that were choking her. 'I have no wish to hear your vile swaggering and boasting of your molestation of Suzette – you, who are not worthy to kiss her shoes.'

'You cannot surely believe that it was her shoes I was burning to kiss at that moment,' said Armand with a smile, 'but, alas Madame, I regret to say that there are constraints on what can be achieved in a taxi – otherwise I would certainly have brought our little Suzette to her moment of glory with a long kiss between her bare thighs. But as that was impossible to accomplish, she managed to hold out until we arrived at the rue de Varenne and went up to your apartment.'

'Enough!' Fernande gasped.

Her knees had moved slightly apart, Armand observed, while she stared wide-eyed at his moving fingers, her face as flushed as if he were caressing that other fur coat of hers – the little dark one between her legs. His actions had been prompted by the sudden thought that she could perhaps be as vulnerable to the ecstasies of the mind as he was himself. Back in his apartment she had inflamed his imagination to the point where she had been able to draw his rapture from him twice – and logic said that she could only understand enough to have that effect on him if her own imagination was highly developed.

Well then, it was obvious to Armand that his theory could not be left to float away into thin air, so to speak – a little experiment was required, in order to ascertain its validity. Was Fernande a cold-hearted creature who manipulated the passions of others for her own advantage, or was she a woman of intense imaginative powers which she used on others and which could be turned against her? Now that his experiment seemed to be working out well, he had no intention of abandoning it halfway – the spirit of scientific enquiry demanded that he complete his experiment with Fernande and observe the outcome.

'Happily you were out that evening,' he told her. 'Perhaps you had gone to have your pretty breasts kissed by Monsieur Leblanc? No? Well, no matter – the apartment was unoccupied and without troubling myself to switch on the lights, I picked Suzette up and sat her on the elegant rose-wood sideboard in your entrance hall. Do you perhaps have a dear friend who is an antique dealer, Madame, in addition to one who deals in valuable paintings?'

'Vandal!' Fernande responded, but her voice was noticeably shaky and weak.

'Not at all. Tell me truthfully now if you can think of any more pleasing use for your sideboard than as a resting-place for Suzette's warm bottom, with her clothes turned up to her waist?'

'No more . . .' Fernande moaned, 'no more!'

'Ah, but there was more – much more,' said Armand with relish, his fingers moving rhythmically on the short smooth fur of Fernande's coat. 'Off came her little knickers in an instant – she took them down with such alacrity that I had no time to assist her. Your rose-wood was honoured by the touch of our darling's bare flesh. You have no objection if I call her *our* darling, have you? It is, after all, an accurate description, since we both adore her.'

'This is too much – I insist that you stop at once.'

'Too much for you, perhaps,' he responded cheerfully, 'but not too much for Suzette, I assure you. I stood between her legs while she literally ripped my trousers open and dragged out the part of me which you seem to despise so heartily. What can I tell you? In an instant she had me inside her wet little notch.'

'No . . . no . . . !' Fernande gasped. 'Stop it!'

Her face was flushed pink with emotion and from the movement inside the pockets of her coat Armand deduced that her gloved fingers were scrabbling feverishly at her thighs through the material of her skirt. *Now I've got you!* he thought exultantly, *I've tickled your imagination until it is out of control. If you were alone at this moment you'd have both hands up between your legs to bring yourself the relief of a little climax. But as we are here together in the back of a taxi, there is nothing you can do but suffer the pangs of frustration – and it's a joy to watch.*

'Stop it, you say, Madame?' he tormented her. 'But our delicious Suzette didn't want me to stop it! She had her arms round my neck and was pulling me close to her while she urged me to do it to her harder. Ah, what a greedy little minx she is when she is aroused – as you know very well from your own lovemaking with her. As soon as that soft little entrance of hers becomes slippery with desire, she is insatiable for pleasure . . .'

He intended the most excruciating part of the torture he was inflicting on Fernande to be an account of how he and Suzette had reached their golden moments together, there on the rose-wood sideboard. But before he could go any further, Fernande threw her head back, gasping for breath, and her eyes fluttered shut for a moment. Armand observed the shuddering of her slender body inside her beautiful coat, and concluded with a smile that he made a start towards evening the score between them. It stood at two to one, in her favour, but she would be so furious at being challenged and beaten at her own game that it was almost as good as two-all.

And most certainly it was *her* game in which he had scored a point, for he had not touched her – not that she would have let him, he knew – but he had not even touched her to the limited extent she had touched him, back in his apartment, when she had shielded her hand from contact with him by wrapping his hard flesh in her handkerchief and then in her silk underwear. The smile of satisfaction was still on his face when Fernande recovered and her dark brown eyes flicked open to glare at him unforgivingly.

'So that's how it's to be,' she said in a threatening mutter. 'Very well – the struggle between us will be without rules or mercy. You have deliberately brought this upon yourself – do not complain when you start to suffer.'

'But there *are* rules!' Armand objected at once. 'We agreed them between us before we left my apartment. There will be no complaint from me so long as they are respected. We shall make love to Suzette together – neither of us interfering with the other – until she is aroused enough to turn to either you or me to finish her off, you with your fingers or tongue or I with something more naturally appropriate for pleasuring pretty young women.'

Fernande said nothing, but her eyes spoke eloquently of the fate she wished for Armand and his *naturally appropriate* item. And he, convinced that she would cheat and break the rules to give herself the advantage, gave some thought to how he had been able to excite her sufficiently to bring on her crisis – the key was to talk about making love to Suzette. To be able to incapacitate Fernande in that way might serve him well later on, when the contest between them for the affections of Suzette – or at least for her desirable young body – began in earnest.

'To recapitulate, Madame,' he said. 'We have agreed not to tell Suzette how the winner is to be decided, since that would put in her hands the power of consciously choosing between us. We want her passions to decide the issue, not her opinion on which of us is likely to maintain her in superior comfort. And so it will be whichever of us that Suzette turns to for her final ecstasy who is the winner – and has full possession of her in future. You accepted those rules before. If you have changed your mind, please say so, and I will leave you here and now and make my private arrangements with Suzette as I find convenient.'

'No, no – it is agreed,' said Fernande, with bad grace, at the end of this long speech of his. 'My only wish in this imbecilic agreement is to see Suzette reject you and throw herself into my arms to share her ecstasy with me.'

In the entrance-hall of Fernande's apartment they took off their hats and coats. Armand made a show of running his fingers delicately along the shiny top of the rose-wood sideboard – and when he saw the flush that brought to Fernande's cheeks, he bent down and kissed the polished wood.

'Observe,' he said, smiling broadly at Fernande, 'this is the very spot honoured by the touch of Suzette's little blonde muff. That alone is sufficient to transform this piece of furniture into a family heirloom to be treasured.'

'Gloat while you still can,' said Fernande, tight-lipped.

'I shall still be gloating, as you choose to call it, in an hour from now, though I doubt if you will,' he retorted.

He was intent on presenting to her an appearance of complete confidence – though in effect he had secret anxieties as to the outcome of the curious competition he had so lightly proposed an hour ago. Fernande smoothed down the skirt of her tailored black suit and looked at herself in the mirror on the wall, while she patted her glossy dark hair.

'I'm ready,' she announced. 'Are you?'

'Of course – but are you sure that Suzette is at home?'

'She's here,' Fernande answered flatly, 'getting herself ready to go out with you this evening. She's been at it since she got up this morning – primping and preening herself, as if it made the least difference whether she beautifies herself and puts on her most elegant clothes or not. The moment you had her alone you'd abuse her body for your selfish pleasure even if she were unwashed for a week and had hairy legs and was wrapped in an old potato sack.'

There was an undercurrent of uneasiness in Fernande's voice that brought a faint smile to Armand's lips – evidently she too was not feeling completely confident of victory.

'I compliment you on your vivid imagination,' he said with a smile, 'though I must protest at your lack of understanding of my personal tastes.'

'Your personal tastes! They are those of plundering and destructive men throughout history,' she retorted. 'I have no doubt of that.'

'Tell me something, Madame,' said Armand, smiling sweetly at her, 'how clean and sweet-smelling was Suzette when you first found her in a back-street bar and brought her home for your pleasure? My guess is that her legs were hairy then – and she had hair under her arms, perhaps. Did you stop to bath her before you took her to bed? Or did you throw her down on her back and push her legs apart just as she was?'

'Barbarian!' Fernande exclaimed angrily, and Armand found it possible to chuckle as he followed her into her elegant sitting-room.

Suzette was sitting on the sofa, under the Bonnard painting that Armand had admired, the naked woman in red shoes looking out of a window over the roof-tops of Paris. For a moment the painting held his attention, bringing back fond memories of the night when Madeleine had stood at her sister's window in her chiffon negligee. He had stood close enough to press his thick mast against her bottom while he opened her negligee and traced with his fingers the smooth flesh of her breasts.

There was a smile of delight on his face as his gaze fell from the painting to Suzette on the crimson and grey-striped sofa. She was wearing not precisely a negligee but a pretty kimono of orchid-pink satin, embroidered in a Japanese pattern of chrysanthemums, and her bare legs were curled under her in a way that showed most of her charmingly plump thighs. The whole effect – her kimono, the way she sat, her almost blonde short hair – all combined to make her appear very young and defenceless.

Seeing her like that, Armand found no difficulty at all in understanding why so worldly-wise, so beautiful, and so elegant a woman as Fernande felt the same ardent desire as he did himself to ravish and consume Suzette – as if she were a ripe fruit to be squeezed and sucked and drained of all its sweet juice. To understand was one thing, but to stand aside was another – and for a hypocrite like Fernande who made her living by titillating men she claimed to despise, never! She had made it clear to him, and with unnecessary candour, that he and she were competitors. Or rather that he was an interloper in her private Garden of Eden and that she intended to chase him out forever.

Suzette was polishing her fingernails to a bright shine with a little buffer of chamois leather. When she looked up from her manicure to see Fernande and Armand standing together before her, her hazel eyes opened wide and her nose wrinkled in surprise. But she smiled in greeting and offered no comment. Armand kissed her hand, and Fernande bent to kiss her cheek, already staking her claim to firmer proprietorial rights than his. Suzette swung her legs down from the sofa and put her bare feet on the carpet, and to Armand's regret, flicked her kimono over her thighs to cover them.

He took a seat beside her on the sofa, although not too close, for he had no wish to be accused by Fernande of trying to cheat by starting while she was absent – she having gone to fetch a bottle of champagne and glasses. Yet even so, Fernande gave him a long stare of doubt and suspicion when she returned and set down her laden silver tray. And indeed, she had reason to be suspicious, thought Armand with a secret smile at her discomfiture; if it had been he who had gone to get the wine, leaving Fernande alone with Suzette, then he too would have found it impossible not to be disturbed and jealous.

The simple and sufficient reason for Fernande's fears

was that Suzette was evidently just out of the bath – about her warm body there clung the faint and deliciously naive fragrance of *muguet du bois* bath essence. And to Armand, as to Fernande, it was equally evident that Suzette's beautiful body was totally naked under her loose kimono. It would have been the easiest thing in the world to have slipped a hand into the wrap-over top and stroked her plump breasts – and as easy again to have put a hand into it below the sash around her waist and felt between her bare warm thighs.

Fernande seated herself on the sofa on the other side of Suzette, perceptibly closer to her than Armand was. He offered to open the bottle, but Fernande insisted on displaying her independence by unwiring the cork and twisting it out herself. It came out with a loud pop and the wine frothed over, spilling on to the carpet before she had the neck over the glasses. The three of them took a glass each and Suzette stared curiously from Armand to Fernande, to see if either of them intended to say anything.

'To love,' said Armand, determined to annoy Fernande if he could, and raised his glass.

'To *real* love,' Fernande countered at once, raising hers.

'And to Suzette,' Armand added.

'Above all, to Suzette,' said Fernande with fervour.

'What *is* going on?' Suzette asked, her head turning from one side to the other as she stared first at Fernande and than at Armand.

'Nothing at all for you to trouble yourself with,' Fernande replied quickly, wishing to prevent Armand from giving his version of events. 'The fact is that your new friend and I have reached a certain arrangement between us . . . well, how can I explain it. Give me your complete trust, my darling. Close your beautiful eyes and let matters take their course for the next half hour. I shall take very good care of you, I promise – you do trust me, don't you?'

Suzette nodded and reached out to take Fernande's hand, while Armand emptied his glass and leaned back to watch through half-closed eyes. Suzette was lying back on the sofa, her head on Fernande's shoulder, her eyes open and looking at her with love and confidence. She held Fernande's jewelled hand for a while, listening to what was being whispered into her ear, and then slipped her friend's hand into the bosom of her kimono and rubbed it over her hidden breasts. There was a look of bliss on Fernande's face as she caressed her friend lovingly, her dark head bending to bring her mouth to Suzette's.

Armand heard a muffled little thud as Suzette's empty champagne glass fell from her hand to the carpet and rolled under the sofa. He reached out to touch her thigh, and a moment later he felt her fingers running delicately over the buttons of his trousers, searching for an opening. He parted his legs and undid his buttons for her – and when she probed inside his trousers to clasp his hard bolt and squeeze it, he felt under her kimono, to touch her bare thigh and stroke it upwards to the blonde-flossed peach he knew was waiting to be plucked. He caressed it – with fingers that were trembling – and heard her moan into Fernande's open mouth.

Almost at once, Fernande broke off the long kiss and raised her head to see what Armand was doing to affect Suzette so profoundly. At the sight of his hand disappearing under the orchid-pink satin of the kimono, she uttered a loud and quickly suppressed gasp of outrage. Then seeing no way to oust him from the citadel except by taking possession of it herself, she slid to her knees on the carpet, between Suzette's outspread legs, and used both hands to undo the sash round her waist and spread the kimono wide open.

'Ah, *chérie!*' Suzette sighed, her fully exposed body lolling back on the sofa and her eyes closed to better feel the caress of Fernande's experienced hands from throat to thighs. Armand watched in delight, drinking in all the beauty that Suzette was offering, his shaft leaping in her clasped hand in an effort to gain her attention. Fernande's fingers, laden with bright gem-stones, traced the hollows and curves of Suzette's voluptuous body, the sight arousing Armand so furiously that he thought he was about to spray his desire into Suzette's warm hand.

When Fernande was certain that she had triumphed over Armand and that Suzette was completely hers, she sank down on her bent legs until her coldly beautiful face was poised above the wispy curls between Suzette's legs. Her scarlet-nailed thumbs parted the soft folds which the curls did nothing to conceal, and murmuring 'darling, darling, darling' she lowered her head further, until she could press the tip of her wet tongue into Suzette, and draw from her a long soft sigh of pleasure.

Not that Armand believed that he was defeated, of course: he was deliberately letting Fernande take the lead in these early stages of the contest – using her as the pace-setter in a marathon race, so to speak – before he started to display his real abilities. While Fernande's loving attention was directed towards the pretty *jou-jou* between Suzette's plump thighs, he edged closer on the sofa and turned so that he could take Suzette's face between his hands and pull her eyelids gently open, so that it was him she saw while he kissed her soft mouth. And through a kiss that lasted for what seemed an eternity of delight, his hand roamed over her bare and chubby breasts.

Unable to allay her suspicions, even though she believed that she had won the victory already, Fernande glanced up and saw what Armand was doing to Suzette. Immediately she left off her deep caressing and knelt upright between Suzette's parted legs. Armand turned his head to see what she would do, his cheek pressed close to Suzette's hot and flushed cheek and his hand still in possession of her right breast.

With graceful deliberation, Fernande opened her tailored suit to display her alabaster skin and her small breasts in their flimsy lace brassière. She shrugged off her jacket and slipped one narrow strap off her shoulder – so that she could pull down the lace cup and fully expose a pear-shaped breast. Suzette gave a long contented sigh, let go of Armand's jerking wand and sat up on the sofa. She took Fernande by the hips and leaned forward to press her mouth to the pink bud of the breast that had been uncovered.

Thinking that the loose and open kimono hid too much from him, Armand eased it off Suzette's shoulders and pulled it down. Evidently she was of the same mind as he – that any kind of concealment of her body was unnecessary in the present circumstances, and she let go of Fernande's hips so that he could pull the kimono off her arms and let it fall about her. As she leaned forward, now totally naked, to caress Fernande's buds with her tongue, Armand stroked her back and was delighted by the feel of her satin flesh under his palms.

When she was close to dissolving into ecstasy under the touch of Suzette's tongue, Fernande took Suzette's face between her hands and gently pulled it away from her breasts. She rose to her feet, a little unsteady through the force of the emotions aroused by Suzette's mouth. As her skirt fell about her legs to reveal that she was naked except for her black silk stockings, Suzette gave a little moan of pleasure and whispered, 'But where are your knickers, chérie?' as she reached out to touch Fernande's thick fleece of dark curls.

'They are ruined and I threw them away,' Fernande whispered back. 'Your friend Armand made love to them – for him there exists no distinction between a woman's body and her clothes. If you give him a pair of your gloves you will see him making love in them with as much ardour as if he were lying between your legs. He cares for nothing but his own cheap satisfactions.'

While she slandered Armand in this way, she was standing with her feet apart, her curls dark and rich against the slender whiteness of her thighs, and Suzette was loosening the lace suspender-belt round her waist and rolling down her silk stockings. Armand's hands found their way under Suzette's soft armpits and then round to clasp her plump breasts as, with bated breath, he observed over her shoulder Fernande's polished legs emerging from the fragile black sheaths of her stockings.

Suzette touched and parted Fernande's dark curls, and her little hand turned over, palm upwards, to hook gentle fingers into the fleshy lips she had uncovered. Fernande's long *ah* of delight was echoed by an equally profound sigh from Suzette – which was inspired by Armand stroking down her belly and between her parted thighs until his fingers probed her secrets gently and found her hidden bud. The sighing and murmuring of the two women mingled in a long hymn of joy, both of them shaken by the little spasms of pleasure flickering through their naked bodies from the caressing fingers between their legs.

The soft flesh under Armand's fingertips was thrillingly wet and from its rhythmic pulsing he guessed that Suzette's crisis was only moments away – but Fernande guessed it too and moved to hold it back. She turned quickly, to seat herself on the sofa, and draw Suzette towards her so that Armand's fingers lost touch with their wet little plaything. While the women embraced each other in a long kiss, Armand slid quickly out of his clothes and was naked, his elongated spike thrusting fiercely upwards.

By then Suzette had turned completely towards Fernande, presenting to Armand her gleaming expanse of back, with dimples he had not before noticed, above her gleaming cheeks, and the rich fullness of her bottom itself. He was gasping with eagerness as he pressed himself tightly against her, to force his engorged shaft between those magnificent cheeks and underneath her, so that it was held trapped between her flossy-haired delight and the striped cushion of the sofa.

She was not so utterly overwhelmed by the delights Fernande was giving her that she was unaware of what Armand was doing, for she leaned forward in order to thrust out her bottom and press it against his belly. Her rounded hips began a slow and rhythmic rolling that slid her wet and open nectarine along his imprisoned shaft. Armand groaned in incipient ecstasy and held her by the waist while he thrust to and fro, so aroused that he no longer cared where his frothing champagne spilled when the cork flew from the bottle.

But the new rhythm of Suzette's pleasure warned Fernande that something was happening that she had not initiated. She put her chin on Suzette's shoulder and stared down the length of her back. 'Ah, would you!' she gasped, seeing where Armand's sturdy part was concealed, and at once she dragged Suzette off the sofa and down on to the carpet. Released from under its soft burden, Armand's staff sprang up like a Jack-in-the-box, so furiously that it smacked against his bare belly and stood shaking in angry frustration.

Down on the floor Fernande had Suzette flat on her back and was lying on her, face to face and dark-haired mound to fair-wisped mound, as if to shield her from Armand's devouring eyes. By a great effort of will he sat where he was for a time, watching Fernande moving on the girl's body to give herself the enjoyable sensations of breast against breast and belly against belly. He knew he could afford to be patient – these were no more than the preliminaries of love: soon Fernande would turn her attention away from Suzette's panting mouth towards those other wet lips between her thighs.

And meanwhile, how delicious it was to observe the contrast of the skin-tones of the two women. Suzette had the golden glow of youth about her – her charmingly plump body gleamed with health and vivacity – while Fernande's faultless skin was pale and smooth as alabaster. Armand stared avidly at her long and sinuous back and at the delights of her bottom, for her face-down position on top of Suzette enabled him to see this enchanting part of her for the very first time.

The small cheeks were taut, satin-smooth and enchantingly round and they were sliding in an unbelievably voluptuous way up and down, to the gentle rhythm in which Fernande was rubbing herself against Suzette's pomander. To watch this unhurried rolling excited Armand so powerfully that he found it necessary to take hold of his twitching haft, to stop himself from leaping on Fernande and plunging it between those elegant cheeks and discharging his desperate passion into whichever of her soft apertures he struck first!

Sighing in her pleasure, Fernande put her palms on the floor and raised herself on straight arms, so pressing her loins on Suzette's with more weight. Armand sighed too, and his hand slid slowly up and down his pommel at the sight of Fernande's elegant little breasts dangling just above Suzette's round and plump ones. And here again, it was the comparison that brought a smile of unalloyed delight to his lips – small pink buds hovering above swollen red buds – Armand told himself fervently that it would be a genuine foretaste of Paradise if it were only possible to cram all four buds into his mouth at the same time.

At this moment Fernande glanced up from the pretty face of the girl beneath her to stare at Armand. His swollen fore-limb jumped in his hand at the new contrast presented to his eyes – and, even more important, to his furiously active imagination: the superb expressions on the women's faces. Suzette's mouth was wide open to show her wet tongue, her hazel eyes shining with the gluttony of a nineteen-year-old for more and more intense pleasure while Fernande, twice her age, had an expression of delicate concentration on the method of providing that pleasure.

Fernande looked at Armand's flushed face and his hand slowly stroking his engorged shaft and her tranquil expression was transformed to a grin of malevolent triumph. She guessed that it would take very little to make him squirt his frustration over his belly in defeat, and to hasten the process she rolled Suzette on to her side and kissed down her body, pausing between kisses to glance up at Armand with a smile of mockery and a look in her dark-brown eyes that said as plainly as any words *Don't you wish you were doing this to her?*

When her lips touched Suzette's *petit palais* at last, Fernande gave Armand one last taunting glance before she thrust her wet tongue into it. He stared down at the back of her head, at her glossy black hair against the warm flesh tones of Suzette's belly – this was the moment for which he had been waiting with such agonised patience. Silently, though by now Fernande was too engrossed to pay any attention to him, he slid down from the sofa to the carpet and lay behind Suzette. One of her parted legs was draped over Fernande's shoulder, and Fernande was nuzzling and kissing between her thighs.

From time to time Suzette shuddered and cried out softly at the sensations coursing through her, sometimes for a moment she squirmed away from Fernande's mouth for a brief respite from pleasure that was so intense as to be almost painful. Armand ran his hands over the plump cheeks of her bottom, presented so fully to him, and stroked down along the crease between them. Her body twitched when he fingered the warm little knot of muscle he found there, less than a handbreadth away from the tender spot where Fernande's tongue was at its work.

The intoxicating thought came into Armand's head that there was nothing to stop him from entering Suzette's luscious body by this back door! But he was deterred from doing so by the certainty that Fernande would claim the credit for what happened after that to Suzette – and there would be no way of telling who was right, for Suzette's sense of judgement was too swamped by sensation to be taken as reliable. A different approach was needed, and he pressed himself against her perspiring back, his arms round her body, so that he could grasp her plump breasts and squeeze them hard to get her attention.

'Lie on your back for me, Suzette,' he suggested. 'I have something long and hard between my legs which will give you greater pleasure than Fernande's tongue can.'

His murmur was loud enough for Fernande to hear – as he intended – for he had it in mind that during their taxi-ride together he was able to induce a climax in her by creating word-pictures of making love to Suzette, and it seemed to him now that if he could repeat his little success, Fernande might be immobilised for long enough to give him a chance to slide quickly into Suzette. And then, while Fernande screamed and clawed at his back, he would gain the victory by bringing on Suzette's crisis with short hard jabs.

Obediently enough, Suzette began to turn, but whether she would have gone all the way and opened herself for him to plunge into was a question that never was settled. The thrills that shook her body were so overpowering that she was tottering on the very brink of the precipice – a millimetre more and she would hurtle over into the unfathomable abyss of ecstasy. Fernande had played with Suzette for enough nights and days to understand and appreciate the capabilities of her succulent young body, and she knew that Suzette's crucial moments were no more than a heart-beat or two away. She fought to reassert her power of control over the girl by raking her sharp fingernails down the insides of her thighs as she pulled her mouth away from her.

'Don't stop now – don't stop!' Suzette shrieked, left frantic with sensation.

'Then beg me!' Fernande answered her. 'Plead with me to take pity on you and finish you off! Say, *I love you, Fernande,*' and she stared hard into Armand's eyes to savour her triumph over him.

But Suzette's emotions were much too far out of control to understand what was required of her – her beautiful body was a wet and gaping sexual maw that clamoured to be filled with ecstasy. She jerked away from Fernande and threw herself over Armand's body, forcing him on to his back – a position he took up without the least resistance. His happy impression was that Suzette was about to snatch the victory from Fernande and award it to him by spiking herself on him. But instead, she pushed his legs apart and sucked his pulsing length into her hot mouth, and rubbed her wet nest against his knee with the rhythm of desperation.

His hands groped for her breasts, but she was too

awkwardly placed for him to reach them. Her hot tongue lapped round the bulging velvet head of his stilt and his back was beginning to arch in an impending explosion of ecstasy. He smiled blissfully up into Fernande's face, staring down at him over Suzette's shoulder, its expression one of incredulity and rage. He looked directly into Fernande's dark brown eyes and taunted her by murmuring words of encouragement to Suzette. Words ostensibly addressed to Suzette, that is – though their true purpose was to inflame Fernande's sensibilities and drive her into an unshared crisis of desire.

'Oh Suzette, how I love the touch of your soft mouth on me . . .' he murmured.

'No, no – this is intolerable!' Fernande moaned.

She caught hold of Suzette by the hips and attempted to drag her away from him, but Suzette's mouth clung like a leech to him and he moaned in rapture to feel her pointed fingernails digging into the soft part of his groin and then nipping at his pompoms, to send ripples of delicious pain through him. His hugely swollen pride was straining upwards, over Suzette's licking tongue, trying to cram itself into her throat, and he knew that in another moment the explosion would be set off that would annihilate him.

But it was Fernande, not Armand, who was annihilated first. It was her back that arched convulsively and her eyes that rolled upwards! She let go of Suzette, her hands flying to her own parted thighs, where her fingers dabbled in the open pink furrow between her dark curls. Armand smiled and abandoned himself body and soul to Suzette's intimate ministrations – but he had reckoned without Fernande's rapid powers of recovery. Barely an instant before the handle of his detonator was depressed to set off his explosion, she gripped Suzette by the shoulders and dragged her away from him by main force.

Armand sat up with a long sigh of exasperation – perhaps he had been mistaken about Fernande's climax. Perhaps what he had seen was no more than a brief flicker of passion through her belly, leaving her as aroused and determined as before, or even more so. He was in time to see Suzette rolled over on her back between him and Fernande.

'You have not won yet!' he gasped.

'But *you* have most surely lost,' she replied, her hands gripping the insides of Suzette's thighs to hold them apart.

'You are mistaken,' he said. 'It was you who submitted then, not me. We are even now – twice each.'

Fernande was smiling thinly to observe how the male limb that stood upright between his thighs shook with pent-up desire.

'And now I am ready to take the prize,' she said, 'whereas you in another moment will squirt your futile aspiration into the air. The truth is that you are so aroused that you wouldn't last long enough to satisfy Suzette even if you put your ridiculous thing in her. The one who gratifies *her* first wins – that was the condition you set.'

Her assessment of Armand's pitch of arousal was so near to the truth that he almost despaired. But in her eagerness to express her scorn for a rival she believed already beaten, she failed to take into account that Suzette was in a similar condition to Armand. And Suzette had an impetuous nature – she had been so intensely aroused by the simultaneous and yet different attentions of her two lovers that she was in torment for the ultimate satisfaction. She was begging to be licked, rubbed, kissed, fingered, bitten, pierced – anything at all that would put a climactic end to her exquisite sufferings!

Her pleading drew the eyes of Armand and Fernande away from each other and down to her. She was twisting and turning on her back, flinging out her arms and legs, clutching at Armand and Fernande. She pulled up her knees and spread them wide, offering herself fully, her hands clenched feverishly on her own plump breasts. And then, too impatient to wait any longer for a response from her staring lovers, she put her hands between her spread thighs, where her open pink slit showed between wisps of apricot-coloured floss. At once, both her middle fingers were inside and she stroked herself with breathless speed, her bottom jerking off the floor in a frantic rhythm.

After a moment or two of wide-mouthed watching, Armand and Fernande looked up from those flickering hands and stared into each other's eyes. Without a word spoken, an understanding was reached between them – they each took one of Suzette's wrists and pulled her hands away from their exciting little task of mercy. Suzette rolled from side to side on the carpet, pleading for satisfaction in gasps and sighs and broken little words, but still giving no indication at all of which of them she preferred to precipitate her crisis – him or her!

And thus, while victory and defeat were poised on a knife-edge, Armand and Fernande stared into each other's eyes over the naked prize that writhed between them, waiting for her to gasp out the name of the one she wanted. Suzette's physical need was so intense that it pervaded the entire room, almost as if the atmosphere were charged with electricity before a blue-white flash of lightning splits the air. And when their bodies had become fully charged with this electricity of the soul, Armand and Fernande were drawn involuntarily towards each other across Suzette, their faces approaching closer and closer.

Both were breathing heavily, each could feel the hot breath of the other – so close and so exciting that Armand had the strange impression that his hardness was embedded in the softness between Fernande's thighs. The invisible vibrations of sexuality that radiated from Suzette engulfed them both and temporarily overrode their prejudices – her contempt for him, his dislike of her. But still they had not touched each other, even though, above Suzette's squirming belly, their faces were only a centimetre apart.

And then – eternally unbelievable moment that it was, a moment utterly outside time itself and not part of the ordinary reckoning of this world at all – the wet tips of their tongues met in a caress that was minimal and yet more intimate than if he had penetrated her. It was not Armand's unfocused desire alone seeking the touch, and not even Fernande's, but a sudden psychological compulsion that gripped them both and commanded their caress.

Beneath them, Suzette cried out and raised her hips and shuddering loins from the floor to receive a kiss or a touch that would end her suspense. But Armand and Fernande had forgotten her as the passions raging in them brought their open mouths together at last, and their tongues flickered over each other in wet and gasping delight. All their physical sensations, all the most voluptuous feelings they had ever experienced in their lives, all their hopes and longings, all the tenderness of which each was capable – everything was concentrated at that moment in their tongues, fluttering exquisitely together.

Suzette's whimpering and writhing on the carpet between them thrust itself as a distraction into their trance of ecstasy. It was as if their souls had merged and they could read each other's minds: at the selfsame instant each of them put a hand between Suzette's splayed legs and stroked quickly up along the inside of a thigh until their hands met at her plump *jou-jou*. At this new contact they paused as if they were entranced, the touch of each other's fingers more exciting than the touch of that tender part of Suzette they had both made love to with such passion in the past.

Suzette was so open and slippery with desire that their fingers slid easily into her, to where her swollen little bud awaited them. Their fingertips caressed it together, with the same profoundly sensual rhythm as the caresses their tongues were exchanging, and Suzette shrieked as her climax struck her like the blow of a fist and huge spasms shook her from head to foot. She cried out in time with the contractions of her belly, her back arching off the floor to ram herself against the fingers that were bringing her sweet release.

Over her squirming body Armand and Fernande had

been made drunk by her ecstasy, and when Suzette needed no more of their caresses, they found a new and delirious intimacy. While their tongues continued to kiss, their hands, slippery with Suzette's passion, were searching blindly for each other across her body, limp now except for an occasional and mild after-tremor of rapture. Though neither Armand nor Fernande dared formulate the thought, they were feeling for the secret and most cherished parts between each other's thighs.

Armand's groping hand touched warm and satin-smooth skin, then thick curls, and then tender and slippery flesh. He sighed as if his heart was breaking with happiness and, only moments later, his fingers penetrated unchecked into the sanctuary that Fernande had denied he would ever touch. He heard the little rasp in her throat and held his breath in celestial joy when her hand touched his stem for an instant, and withdrew. Would she clasp him? Could she bring herself to do so? Was it more difficult for her to touch his pride with her fingers than to touch his tongue with her tongue? Armand's fingertip slid gently over her secret bud while he waited.

Yes! She touched him again, and this time her fingers met round his stalwart shaft, though only for an instant, before releasing it again. *Patience . . . be patient for just a little longer . . .* he told himself, his emotions so intense that he was hardly able to breath. Then the hand hovering close to his belly found his stiffness again and clasped it, timidly at first, and then resolutely. Fernande had, it seemed, made up her mind at last, for she began to pleasure him with rapid flicks of her wrist.

Armand rose unsteadily to his knees, and she rose with him, on the other side of Suzette, to offer their bodies to each other. They stared into each other's eyes so deeply that they both felt that they had penetrated right to the other's soul. Different, incompatible, contrary and opposed though their characters were, they recognised silently that they had something in common: a shared streak of perverse sensuality that Suzette, in spite of her greed for pleasure, was unable to match or share with either of them.

'Fernande – you are adorable,' Armand gasped.

'Armand . . .' she murmured.

He swayed towards her, to seal with a long, hot kiss their unformulated agreement, and Fernande swayed towards him, her red-painted mouth open to receive the homage of his tongue. But the pressure of sensation that had been building up inside Armand since they had arrived at the apartment to begin their tender battle over Suzette – and even before that, when he was tormenting Fernande in the taxi – had reached a point which was beyond what his over-strained nervous system could sustain any longer.

'Ah, yes,' Fernande murmured sympathetically, recognising the familiar signs.

Armand's eyes widened and went out of focus, and he stared blindly into nothingness as the dam burst, and the foaming torrent that it released poured down over Suzette's naked belly. He tried to hold on to Fernande, hoping to make her share his pleasure, but his strength was fast draining away from him through his wildly leaping part and his hands fell away from her. He sagged forward across Suzette, and she twitched and murmured incoherently under him, until he found himself lying with his chest over her wet belly.

He had slipped out of Fernande's hot palm, but though the incredible moments of ecstasy were past, the golden memory caused him to tremble and retain his hardness. Fernande stretched herself on her back on the floor, an expression of rapture on her face such as Armand had not seen before, her legs apart to offer him her wet little pouch. The last throbs of his pleasure were fading as he put his hands on her slender thighs and, with great tenderness, pushed them wider apart and stared in stupefied delight at her dark-haired secret.

He touched it gently and spread the long pink lips to see their gleaming moistness. He had opened her like a flower, like the soft petals of a rose.

'Fernande, Fernande . . .' he whispered.

He put his hands under her bottom and sank his fingers into the taut flesh of the smooth cheeks and dragged her round on her back, until he had her lying with her bent and parted legs over Suzette's belly and his shoulders were between her thighs. Under his caressing fingers her secret bud was as hard as the buds of her breasts and he put his head down between her legs and kissed it. She began to sigh loudly as his forefinger penetrated slowly into her wet depths, deeper and deeper.

He wanted to push his distended male pride where his finger was and slither in and out until Fernande screamed with pleasure and he spurted his strength into her. But, highly aroused though he was, he knew that to be a futile dream, a fantasy that would never be realised – Fernande's response would be the reverse of what he desired.

She moaned as he thrust his wet tongue into her and flicked at her bud. As her excitement mounted towards its crisis, she blindly reached out a trembling hand to touch Suzette's face, and Suzette took hold of her many-ringed hand and pressed it to her lips and kissed the soft palm and fluttered the tip of her tongue against it. Fernande pushed her thumb into Suzette's mouth and Suzette sucked it hard, holding her wrist tightly to slide the thumb rapidly in and out between her wet lips.

She was pinned on her back to the floor by the weight of Fernande's legs and Armand's chest over her chubby belly, but even so she managed to raise her shoulders and prop herself on an elbow to watch her dearest Fernande's crucial moments. Her hand travelled slowly up Fernande's body to her breasts and plucked at their hard pink buds. Overwhelmed by the sensations that were surging through her from Suzette's manipulations and from Armand's attentions between her thighs, Fernande wailed and her belly fluttered in and out to the hot spasms of her climax.

9

Secrets Revealed

To hear that the woman he adores to distraction has become so far reconciled to her unfaithful husband that she has permitted him to pass a night with her in the same bed – that would discompose any lover. For this is the awakening of the anguish of jealousy: to see in the mind's eye another man lying naked and with a stiff bolt next to the adored one, his hands feeling her soft little breasts. And agony of despair: to imagine her spreading her slender thighs for the intruder's prying hand to caress her pretty *jou-jou!*

That the man in question is still her husband and has, by the reckoning of both State and Church, a firm right to these intimacies with her – this is no consolation at all to the aggrieved lover. Indeed, it might be said to add insult to injury. And what makes the whole miserable imbroglio even more wretched is to hear the dismaying information of the adored one's flagrant act of betrayal with her own idiot of a husband from her sister, in casual conversation.

All this compounds together to produce an experience that is disenchanting in the extreme. It goes without saying that Armand wanted to talk to Madeleine and demand to be told whether her sister's story was true or not, though he had little real hope that Yvonne had lied. But Madeleine was out of Paris that day and not expected back until late in the evening, and by the time evening came, Armand had quenched the fire of his passions with the assistance of Yvonne herself.

The upshot was that he went to bed relieved that a bitter lovers' quarrel between himself and Madeleine had been postponed at least, if not averted. When he woke up the next morning and thought things over, he was fairly well resigned to losing Madeleine, if the worst happened – or, at best, to sharing her charms secretly with her husband. He telephoned to arrange a meeting with her, a meeting at which matters could be brought to a satisfactory conclusion between them. But even at ten in the morning, she had already gone out, according to the servant who answered, and she had left no word of the time she expected to return.

By ten o'clock that evening Madeleine had not returned his call, and when he tried again, he was told that she was not yet back. At that, he shrugged, convinced that their love affair was truly over. As it happened he had other plans for the next day, for when a man's heart has been broken beyond possibility of recovery – shattered and trampled underfoot by the one he adores – then he has great need of the solace other women can provide. That is to say, Armand planned to take Suzette Chenet out to dinner that evening and afterwards avail himself of the very considerable consolation of her youthful charms.

Naturally, he still had it in mind to telephone Madeleine to hear what she had to say, even if it was only goodbye, but before he had time to carry out his intention, Fernande Quibon had arrived at his apartment and forced her very unusual attentions upon him. That led on to the fascinating question of which of them was best entitled to enjoy the pleasures of Suzette, whom Fernande claimed as her protégée.

The rest of the day was devoted very pleasurably to settling that intricate question, not that it could be said to be finally settled – not in any real sense – since he and Fernande eventually reached a compromise and shared the girl between them. After they had ravished her by hand on the carpet in Fernande's sitting-room, they went to bed and held her naked between them while they played with her and with each other.

Sometime during the night Armand had been half-woken by the little murmurs and sighs of one of the women being pleasured by the other. He was squeezed between two soft naked bodies and with the curtains drawn across the windows it was too dark to see who was who. Not that it mattered which of the women was bringing the other to a gasping climax – for it was the seventh or eight time for each of them since they had got into bed.

Not that Armand had been neglected, but lying half-awake in the dark, listening to the soft little cries and moans, his drooping part demonstrated its persistence by growing long and hard yet again. He was lying on his side and both women had a leg over him, and one had an arm across his waist to caress the other's warm and furry *minette*. A moment later the rumpled bed shook softly under him to the convulsions of ecstasy and Armand knew that, drained as he was, he had to do it again.

The warm body in front of him turned lazily over with a sigh of content and the soft cheeks of a bare bottom nestled against him. The woman behind him withdrew her thigh from over his waist and turned away, pressing another warm bottom against him. Armand reached out blindly to touch smooth female flesh – and with gentle fingers he parted the wet lips below the soft cheeks and steered his ready spindle inside.

Whoever it was he had enfiladed, she gave a sup-pressed little shriek – but he was not able to tell from the cry alone whether it was Suzette or Fernande. And he did not want to find out! It would have been easy enough for him to identify his partner – he had only to reach over her body and feel her breasts – if they were plump and round, he was entrenched in Suzette, if they were small and pointed, it was Fernande. But it was delicious *not* to know, and he kept his hands away from the softly shaking body into which he was plunging in a steady and unhurried rhythm.

He found it highly arousing to imagine that Fernande had become so drunk with pleasure that she was letting him pierce her. It was not likely perhaps, but that was not important – in men like Armand the power of fantasy is very strong and it was causing the fleshy staff he slid in and out to grow thicker and harder, second by second. He sighed and moaned to himself while he pictured behind closed eyes the long slender body of Fernande, naked and pale-skinned, stretched out before him for his pleasure, and soon enough he persuaded himself that it was indeed Fernande's dark-haired slot in which he was revelling.

The exertions of the preceding hours had depleted his strength so much that it took him a long time to arrive at the desired destination. He rocked backwards and forwards until eventually he was rewarded: the bald-headed priest he had set in the pulpit twitched and delivered the sermon which the rapt congregation had waited for so patiently. To be sure, it was not the usual high-flown harangue – it was no more than a two-word little sermon that was stuttered out, for the priest had used up nearly all his remarkable eloquence earlier, but it was a benediction that had Armand jerking and panting in release.

After that he slept soundly, and if there were any more tender passages between the naked women who flanked him in the bed, he was undisturbed and unaware of them. When he woke up again there was enough daylight under the curtains to show him that his two partners were fast asleep, Suzette huddled out of sight beneath the creased satin sheet, only the top of her head showing, while Fernande was completely uncovered, lying on her back with one arm under her head. Armand stayed still and contemplated her elegant naked body for some time.

Her slender thighs were together and it was impossible to see more than the tuft of curls between them, of a shade of brown so dark as to be almost black. Armand stared and wondered if those thighs had in reality opened for him during the night – was it into her secret enclosure that he had penetrated from behind? Even if it were, he was certain that she would never admit it to him – and probably not even to herself. The secrets of the night would remain hidden forever.

Careful not to wake her or Suzette, he eased himself out of the bed and found his gold wristwatch on the dressing-table. It was very nearly eleven o'clock already. His clothes were strewn over a chair and it was the work of a moment to scoop them up and leave the bedroom silently. The bathroom mirror did not flatter him – there were dark circles under his eyes and black stubble on his cheeks. He splashed his face with cold water, put on his clothes and left the apartment to look for a taxi at the corner of the rue de Varenne.

Madame Cottier was busy cleaning and sweeping when he arrived home. She gave him the grin of comical understanding she reserved for these occasions when he stayed out all night, made hot milk for him to drink with his croissants instead of coffee and packed him off to bed to recuperate. He did not wake up again until after six that evening, ravenously hungry. He showered and shaved and went out for a sustaining dinner.

For all these perfectly understandable reasons, these unexpected interventions by Destiny, as it were – making love to Yvonne's slender silk-stockinged legs when she visited his apartment, then allowing himself to be seduced by Fernande's mulberry-red silk knickers, and then participating with her in the ravishment of dear little Suzette and discovering that he and Fernande could be friends after all – with so many important events taking place it was no cause for surprise that he had not had time to get in touch with Madeleine and meet her to acknowledge the end of their love-affair.

After a fine dinner and an excellent bottle of red wine, he was in the mood for a stroll – it was a fine autumn evening with a brisk and bracing little breeze along the Boulevard that put a spring into the step of the passing couples. After twenty minutes or so of this, Armand went into the next bar he came to and, over a glass of cognac, thought about Madeleine. After his second glass he reached the conclusion that she had treated him very badly. Good manners and common decency surely required that she should inform him that she had decided to go back to Pierre-Louis.

But no, there had been no straightforward, if regrettable, farewell – instead she had avoided him for three days, neither speaking to him when he telephoned nor returning his calls. In all honesty, he had to admit that he had not tried to telephone her every day – other considerations had claimed his attention, but he was able to say with his hand on heart that he had meant to. And there was no reason on earth to prevent Madeleine from getting in touch with him. She owed it to him to do so!

Although Armand had started the evening in a commendably philosophical frame of mind, by ten o'clock he reached a state of high indignation at the way Madeleine had behaved towards him. He went to the telephone on the wall at the back of the bar and racked his brains until he recalled Yvonne's number. When a maid answered, he demanded to speak to Madame Beauvais, only to be told yet again that she was not there.

'Listen to me, and listen well,' he said slowly. 'Go and tell her that unless she comes to the telephone by the time I have counted to twenty, the next thing she will hear will be me hammering on the door – and I shall refuse to go away until I have spoken to her. Do you understand me?'

'Yes, Monsieur,' the maid answered, sounding slightly put out. 'A moment, please.'

There followed a long wait. Armand leaned against the wall, holding the receiver to his ear while he struggled one-handed to get a flat Turkish cigarette from his gold case to his mouth and light it. He guessed the maid had delivered his ultimatum and that Madeleine was in anxious consultation with her sister Yvonne as to how best to handle the matter. The twenty seconds of his threat passed and turned into a minute, and then two, but for all his patience, the voice that eventually spoke to him was not Madeleine's but Yvonne's.

'Armand!' she said, and she sounded absolutely furious. 'How dare you interrupt my dinner-party with your idiotic calls – get off this line at once!'

'Not until I have spoken to Madeleine,' he said stubbornly. 'The sooner you persuade her to come to the telephone, the sooner I shall leave you in peace.'

'She isn't here – the maid told you that!'

'I don't believe you,' he answered. 'Your maid's been telling me that for days now.'

'But it's true! Madeleine is not here.'

'Then where is she?'

'Where she should be – with her husband.'

And with that, Yvonne hung up. Armand had another glass of cognac while he pondered whether Yvonne's information was more likely to be true or false. Then he telephoned the Beauvais apartment. A servant answered and told him that Madame was not there – thus confirming his suspicions that Yvonne had been telling him a pack of lies. He asked to speak to Monsieur Beauvais and learned that Pierre-Louis was away from Paris, with no set date for his return.

At that, Armand's indignation knew no bounds. He rushed out into the street and into a taxi and recklessly urged the driver to go even faster as they sped perilously through the late evening traffic of the Grands Boulevards to the Place de la Concorde with its strolling couples and obelisk, and up the long lamp-lit vista of the Avenue des Champs-Elysées. By ignoring all threat to life and limb, and by promising the driver double fare, Armand was ringing Yvonne's doorbell not more than a quarter of an hour after leaving the bar.

The maid who opened the door knew who he was, of course, and tried to tell him – with the greatest regret – that she had instructions not to admit him. But Armand was in no mood to be thwarted by a domestic. He pushed his way into the apartment and suggested to the maid that she should go and tell Madame Beauvais that he had arrived – as promised on the telephone. Otherwise he would have no choice but to break into Madame Hiver's dinner-party.

In a short time Yvonne came storming into the

entrance hall, her nostrils flaring in fury. She wore a spectacular frock of dull gold that covered one shoulder and left the other bare, so that her left breast was completely concealed and her right was displayed almost down to its tip. But for once Armand was in no mood to pay any attention to the pleasures of high fashion.

'Again Madeleine refuses to see me!' he exclaimed. 'I who have worshipped her as her adoring lover. It is too much. Do not try to stop me, Yvonne, I am going to drag her out of your party by the hair.'

'Armand, for Heaven's sake calm down,' Yvonne said quickly, in fear that her friends might be subjected to a scene of unpleasantness. 'Madeleine is not here – she left days ago.'

'Left? Then where is she?'

'With Pierre-Louis, of course.'

Armand seized Yvonne by the shoulders and shook her so hard that her long pearl-drop earrings jiggled wildly and the perfection of her glossy dark-brown hair was slightly ruffled.

'No, you're not going to fob me off a second time,' he told her indignantly. 'She can't be with him because I know that he's gone away. Tell me the truth now – where is she?'

'Keep your voice down,' Yvonne exclaimed, with a nervous glance over her bare right shoulder at the closed door behind her. 'Come in here for a moment.'

The small room into which he followed her was furnished with a handsome walnut desk and well-stocked bookshelves – it was evidently Jean-Roger's retreat on the occasions when he stayed in the apartment with his family.

'It is no use trying to silence me,' Armand warned Yvonne. 'I am not in the mood to be either reasonable or discreet.'

'Impossible man!' said Yvonne, her temper starting to smoulder. 'Can't you get it into your head that Madeleine doesn't want to see you? You were her lover for a few weeks, and now you're not – it's as simple as that. Do you imagine that you own every woman who lets you make love to her?'

As Armand reached for her shoulders to shake her again, Yvonne stepped backwards to avoid his hands and found herself with her back against the study wall. She could retreat no further. He shook her until her pointed breasts bounced under her thin gold frock.

'Where is Madeleine?' he asked in a voice so determined that she saw it was useless to procrastinate further.

'She has forgiven Pierre-Louis,' she said. 'They've gone away together on a second honeymoon.'

'I don't believe it!' Armand gasped. 'Where has he taken her? I must know.'

'Why? You intend to pursue them? Be sensible, it's over.'

'Where has he taken her?'

'What does it matter? They will be back in a few weeks.'

'How could she go away without a word of goodbye?' Armand demanded in outrage. 'And Pierre-Louis – we have always been the best of friends – why did he not say anything of his plans to me? He was anxious enough for me to come and plead with Madeleine for him, not so long ago.'

The smile that appeared on Yvonne's beautifully made-up face was thin and supercilious. 'Well, you have no one to blame but yourself for what has happened,' she informed him. 'Pierre-Louis finally convinced Madeleine that his affair with the little girl from the Left Bank was finished by explaining that you have taken her off his hands and are her new friend.'

'My god – he didn't tell her that!' Armand gasped.

'But he did, my dear. You can well imagine that Madeleine's opinion of you changed instantly – and not for the better – when she heard that you are sleeping with Pierre-Louis' cast-off. In the circumstances, you could hardly expect tender and tearful goodbyes from her.'

'He is a traitor!' Armand exclaimed in anguish, 'A

bad and untrustworthy friend – I shall never speak to him again.'

'You've been a complete idiot and you've got no more than you deserve,' Yvonne commented coldly. 'Now leave here at once and stop disturbing my evening.'

Her sneering words and the scornful expression on her face annoyed Armand beyond reason. With one short step forward he trapped her against the grey-striped wall, his belly pushing hard against hers.

'Stop that.' She said sharply.

He smiled down insolently at her and clasped an arm round her waist to hold her still – while with his other hand he dragged the diagonally-cut top of her evening frock off the one shoulder it covered – so revealing both her breasts naked.

'Let go of me before I scream,' she threatened furiously.

Armand handled her fleshy delights vigorously and plucked at their prominent buds.

'Scream your head off for all I care,' he said. 'Your friends will come rushing in and find you like this. I shall say that you sent for me because you found the evening boring and needed to be amused.'

Before she could make any sort of reply, he closed her mouth with a long kiss. Soon he was forcing his tongue between her lips and though she resisted for as long as she was able, he felt her begin to shiver against him.

'But why . . . ?' she whispered when he released her mouth from the kiss at last. 'Why are you doing this to me?'

Without bothering to answer, he reached down between her knees and slipped his hand under her frock. She caught hold of his wrist and stopped him as he touched the smooth bare flesh above the tops of her silk stockings.

'No, I beg of you, Armand – not now and not here! Tomorrow – I will come to your apartment, I promise.'

'Yes, tomorrow,' he said. 'Come early – I will do things to you that will astonish and enrapture you.'

'At eleven,' Yvonne said quickly. 'I will be with you by eleven and stay all day – I give you my word.'

But hope was deceptive – she had not dissuaded him in the least from his intention. Even while she was making her promise to him of greater pleasures tomorrow if he would forego the prospect of snatched pleasure today, Armand was using his superior strength to force his hand higher and higher between her thighs, against all the downward pressure of her arm. She squeezed her legs together as best she could, but her feet had been carelessly apart when he had pinned her to the wall, and it was too late to close them now his feet were between them.

She made herself almost knock-kneed in the attempt to get her thighs together, but Armand's questing hand crept higher and higher under her frock. When at last she felt his fingers slip into the open leg of her knickers and touch the soft skin there, she gave a long sigh of defeat and let go of his wrist.

'Please don't, Armand,' she implored him in a voice that was very nearly devoid of hope. 'Wait until tomorrow – I'll let you do anything you like tomorrow.'

His only response was to run his fingers through the thick curls of her fleece. There was no point any more in attempting to hold her thighs tightly together and, when his fingertips stroked the soft lips of her *bijou*, all her resistance came to an end. She let her muscles relax and her thighs open to a less strained position – and a moment later she felt the tip of a finger easing its way into her.

'You told me that you find it exciting to feel helpless,' said Armand, a grin twisting his handsome face. 'Well, you are helpless now, dear Yvonne, as you were when you came to my apartment, and I held your legs up in the air to keep you flat on your back while I played with you – as I am doing now.'

Between her thighs Yvonne could feel two fingers stretching her open to get at her bud, and she gasped at the sensation of a third finger insinuating itself into her moistness.

'If someone should come looking for me . . .' she whispered.

'Then whoever comes in will have the pleasure of seeing your pretty breasts bare and my hand up your frock,' he replied.

He went on caressing her deftly with one hand while he was unbuttoning his trousers, then he took her hand and pushed it inside the slit of his underwear. 'Feel that Yvonne!' he ordered. At first she was unwilling to accept this forced collaboration, but the strength and stiffness of the warm shaft of flesh that was twitching against her hand soon overcame her reluctance. 'Oh well,' she sighed, and shrugged her bare shoulders in a little gesture of acquiescence as she took hold of his pride and slid her hand up and down its solid length.

Armand's mouth found hers again and his tongue fluttered on her tongue in very much the same way that his fingers between her legs were fluttering over her sensitive little button. She sighed into his mouth when he raised her thin golden frock to her waist and she trembled against him in excitement when she felt him fumbling quickly under her clothes, and he had her elegant satin and lace knickers halfway down her thighs.

She thrust both hands into his gaping trousers, to extract his pommel and guide it up between her legs. Her portal was open and ready for him and he pressed straight in. The visitor's first advance took him over the threshold and into the grand vestibule, so to speak, of Yvonne's *petit palais*, at the second advance he glided masterfully halfway along the royal passage, where he was made to feel very welcome, and then the final advance brought the swollen-headed guest right up to the innermost sanctum.

By then Yvonne no longer cared whether anyone might come looking for her and find her being pleasured against the study wall. Armand was moving in and out strongly and he had slipped his hands behind her to enjoy the shape and texture of her bottom. While she pushed her loins rhythmically against him to meet his thrusts, he opened the bare cheeks under her raised frock and pressed a fingertip into the tight and warm little node between them.

Yvonne squealed faintly and bumped her belly against him faster and harder. Each time she jerked forward she felt his hardness slither into her, and each time she pulled back, she felt his finger sink a little deeper. And Armand – what of him? With both finger and rampant part he was experiencing the fierce palpitations of pleasure inside Yvonne's body – the regularly timed contractions, front and back, of the two velvety channels that embraced him and held him captive as her prisoner of love.

She was moaning into his open mouth and her long scarlet finger-nails were clawing at the sleeves of his jacket. Armand was panting and his rhythm quickened until she shook like a leaf in his grasp, then a long spasm took her at the instant his triumphant desire gushed into her in thick jets. Thus flooded, Yvonne expressed her ecstatic appreciation in little screams, until Armand recovered himself sufficiently to become fearful that she would be heard. But finally she was quiet again – she sank back against the wall with a long sigh of satisfaction.

'You are a monster,' she said, staring curiously up at him.

She traced the line of his thin black moustache with a fingertip – a gesture that many women made.

'A monster,' she repeated. 'Suppose Jean-Roger is alarmed by my long absence, and searches until he finds us in his study? How will you explain to him why my new Paquin frock is pulled down to my waist and my knickers are round my knees? He is not a jealous man, as I think you know, but he would be extremely displeased to find that his dinner-party for two members of the government and a newspaper proprietor – not to mention their dreadful wives and mistresses – has been endangered by your inconvenient appetites. He might do something drastic to you.'

'Ah, your husband is here this evening? That did not

occur to me,' said Armand, stepping away from her quickly and doing up his trousers. 'Why on earth didn't you warn me?'

'Would it have made any difference?' she asked, pulling up her underwear and wriggling her shoulder back into the slanting top of her frock at the same time. 'Besides, I enjoy it when you treat me brutally – you can't imagine how refreshing a change it is from the licking and fawning I usually get. And to tell you the plain and honest truth – Jean-Roger's dinner-party has been excruciatingly boring and I really did need to be amused. And who better than you? *Au revoir*, Armand.'

The next day was Sunday and it never for a moment entered Armand's head that Yvonne would keep her promise to visit him. Not that it *was* a promise in any true sense – merely a frantic and unconsidered offer to divert him from what he was doing to her. Yet before eleven o'clock in the morning she was on the telephone to say that she was putting on her hat and coat and would be with him in a quarter of an hour. She rang off before he had time to reply, so that he was left standing with the receiver in his hand and an expression of surprise on his face.

On Sundays the amiable Madame Cottier did not come in to tidy up the apartment and Armand was required to make his own coffee. After Yvonne's telephone call he cleared his breakfast tray from the sitting-room and rushed to shave and shower before she arrived. Apart from people going to Mass or for a very early lunch, there would be hardly any traffic in the streets to hold her up, he knew, and he had scarcely dried himself and splashed sweet-smelling *Eau de Cologne* over his body before he heard the doorbell.

There was no time to dress – she was ringing repeatedly and impatiently. There was not even time for the decency of pulling on his pyjamas again – the bell gave him time for nothing but to shrug himself into his silk dressing-gown and hurry to the door, tying the sash about his waist as he went. And there stood Yvonne in a leopard-skin coat and a tall toque hat of the same rich yellow, white and black fur.

She stared at Armand with an expression of contempt on her beautiful face, taking in everything from his hastily brushed hair to his bare feet showing below his dressing-gown.

'I see,' she remarked acidly. 'You are conceited enough to believe that I have come here for you to maul about and so you do not take the trouble to get dressed. You are convinced that I shall fall into bed with you the instant you reach out for me – or do you think you can simply push me against the wall and violate me again?'

All this was said in a loud and accusing voice out on the landing, where Armand could hear steps coming down the stairs from a higher floor.

'Please, Yvonne, come inside,' he said quickly, trying to take her arm, but she flung his hand from her.

'Let me make clear something that may surprise you,' she said. 'I have not the slightest interest in you as a lover and do not intend to permit any repetition of yesterday's appalling behaviour. You can dismiss completely whatever dreary fantasy your vulgar little mind has conjured up about me. I am here on a very confidential matter of family concern.'

Standing there in the doorway, puzzled by what was going on, Armand said a courteous *bonjour* over Yvonne's shoulder to Monsieur and Madame Bonfils making their way down the stairs from the top floor. Both raised their eyebrows at the sight of Armand in only a dressing-gown, talking to so elegantly dressed a visitor at his door. Madame Bonfils, who was forty and fat and dressed without style, pursed her mouth in disapproval, but her husband waited for her to walk on ahead and then winked at Armand behind Yvonne's back.

When the Bonfils vanished down the next flight of stairs, Armand apologised profusely to Yvonne for the negligence of his dress – or rather, his undress. Her expression remained sceptical while he explained how it had come about – not as a slur on the modesty of her

217

person, but in his hurry to prepare himself on short notice for her most welcome visit. Eventually she allowed her ruffled feelings to be calmed, at least to the extent of crossing his threshold and entering the sitting-room, although she kept her hat and coat on, saying that her business with him would take only a moment or two.

She seated herself in the armchair where Fernande Quibon had sat when she came to dispute the possession of Suzette with Armand. And when Yvonne crossed her silk-stockinged legs under her leopard-skin coat, an image came surging up from the depths of Armand's memory of how Fernande had sat in that same chair, slowly undoing the jet buttons of her tailored black jacket and then opening it wide. *What a moment that was*! he thought, and he crossed his own bare legs tightly under the thin silk of his dressing-gown, to prevent his permanently enthusiastic part from asserting its presence.

He could even remember the thought that had come into his mind at that enchanted moment when Fernande had displayed her pink-tipped breasts to him – how marvellous it would feel to touch those buds with the tip of his tongue. But alas, these pleasant reminiscences were scattered by Yvonne's voice demanding that he answer a most humiliating question – *did he understand why Madeleine had gone back to her husband*?

'According to you, Pierre-Louis told her that I have become closely acquainted with his former girlfriend,' said Armand, shrugging. 'These little annoyances happen in life, as I am sure you have had occasion to know.'

'Good, good – at least you understand why she broke off her love-affair with you,' said Yvonne, addressing him as she would an idiot with a limited grasp of reality, 'but the time has come for you to ask yourself this – why has Madeleine returned to her husband instead of taking another lover?'

'Another lover!' Armand exclaimed indignantly. 'Who?'

'Do you suppose you are the only man who has been interested in her since she left Pierre-Louis? You cannot be that vain!'

'Tell me his name!' Armand demanded vehemently

'I could tell you half a dozen names, but I must admit in all truthfulness that my sister is faithful to one man at a time. You, and you alone, have been privileged to be her lover – though you have not been the only contender.'

'It's Vincent Moreau, isn't it?'

'I see that you are determined to evade the most important question for as long as you can,' said Yvonne, staring coldly.

'There is a disagreeable look on your face that warns me you are here to tell me something spiteful that I do not want to know,' he replied.

He was right, of course – there was a malicious little smile on Yvonne's face. Now that the great moment of revelation was at hand, she was determined to enjoy it to the uttermost. She leaned back in her chair and peeled off her fine black suede gloves with a slow deliberation that infuriated Armand.

'Get on with it,' he could not stop himself saying, though he knew it was a mistake to show his irritation.

'Ah, certainly,' she said, 'but it is very warm in here – not that you would feel it, being completely without proper clothes on. Perhaps a window could be opened?'

'Impossible,' he answered, glad that there was something he could refuse her.

Yvonne shrugged and unbuttoned her fur coat, to reveal a knee-length frock of black and white taffeta. She slipped the coat off her shoulders and took her time in arranging herself comfortably, the skirts of her coat spread out to display the crimson silk lining, her gloves lying across the handbag on her lap – and when she was ready to explode her bombshell, she smiled with malevolent sweetness at Armand.

'Madeleine has gone back to Pierre-Louis because she is pregnant,' she said calmly.

Armand said nothing. He was considering the implications.

'Well?' she prompted him. 'Have you nothing to say?'

'No, nothing,' he answered.

His reaction did more than disappoint Yvonne – it aroused her resentment. She wanted to enjoy anguish, futile rage and turmoil, bitter words, violent emotions, shouts, threats, vows, high drama and low melodrama – anything but this calmness.

'You realise that you are the father,' she accused him.

She succeeded in making it sound as if he had committed an offence so wickedly unnatural that no decent member of the human race would ever speak to him again.

'Who says so – you or Madeleine?' he retorted.

'There is no point in trying to deceive yourself any longer. Why do you suppose she invited Pierre-Louis to visit her last Tuesday and stay all night? By then she had known for at least ten days that she was pregnant. When her stupid husband is eventually told, he will believe the child was conceived that night – and is his.'

'But why? I do not understand this,' said Armand.

'You are almost as stupid as Pierre-Louis,' Yvonne said maliciously. 'Neither of you deserves her. For reasons that I do not understand, Madeleine is in love with her husband. She knew her marriage was in danger of total collapse when he found himself a girl-friend – the first of many, she feared. And being a practical woman, she took steps to save the situation.'

'You are suggesting that she became pregnant deliberately?' Armand asked in astonishment.

'Of course she did – do you think she is a fool? In a few weeks' time she will inform Pierre-Louis of her condition – and he will be beside himself with joy to learn that he is to be a father at last, after eight years of marriage.'

'The duplicity of women!' Armand exclaimed.

'A necessary defence against the faithlessness of men,' was Yvonne's immediate retort. 'None of this would have come about if Pierre-Louis had loved Madeleine as she loves him.'

'I have been used yet again,' said Armand in a sudden mood of exasperation. 'It seems that I am destined all my life to be exploited by women for their own devious purposes.'

'What conceit – exploited indeed! The pleasure of making love to my sister was a most generous reward for your modest contribution towards preserving her marriage.'

'Do not try to belittle me,' Armand said indignantly. 'You have experienced my abilities as a lover – and you are well aware that there is nothing either modest or miserly about the pleasure I give.'

'You flatter yourself,' she replied dismissively. 'You did more to me with your fingers than anything else. I could have done as much for myself.'

Armand cast about in his mind for some insult to destroy her haughtiness. In his mind he had already done so, by summoning up the recollection of how he had held her helpless on her back with her silk-stockinged legs in the air while he forced her into a succession of climaxes. But in a battle of words he felt he might come off the loser and so he chose the most primitive male form of retaliation he could think of.

'I think you should leave now, Yvonne,' he said, 'but before you do, there is something I must remind you of – something which gave you great satisfaction yesterday.'

While he was speaking he flicked open the loose knot of his sash and parted his dressing-gown to expose the menacing device standing up from between his thighs.

'You are disgusting!' she exclaimed.

She stood up at once, gloves and handbag in her hand, and reached behind her for her fur coat, to remove herself from the scene of the insult. Armand also sprang to his feet, threw his striped dressing-gown off altogether, and seized her round the waist. Hampered as she was by coat, gloves and bag, Yvonne was easy to spin round on her high heels and force head-down over the arm of the chair she had been sitting in, her face against the cushion and her rump in the air. Armand stood close behind her firmly with a hand on the small of her back.

'How dare you treat me like this!' she shrieked.

He grinned and put his other hand under her black and white frock and up between her legs. His grin became a chuckle as he touched the bare flesh above the tops of her silk stockings, so smooth and so vulnerable to his fingers.

'Don't you dare touch me, you degenerate criminal,' Yvonne said furiously. She struggled hard enough for her leopard-skin hat to fall from her head on to the chair cushion.

Armand forced his bare foot between her slim ankles and kicked her legs apart without a thought for whether he bruised her pale skin or not. When he had her knees well separated, he felt higher, until his prying fingers touched lace and then the silk of her underwear. Yvonne became very abusive as she writhed on her belly across the chair-arm. She tried to kick backwards at his legs – and other more easily damaged parts – but he was too close. With exquisite slowness, his fingers found their way into her loose underwear, to touch the short curls and soft folds between her thighs.

He flipped her rustling taffeta frock up over her rump and found that little more than a crepe-de-chine chemise – so thin as to be almost transparent – concealed the beauties of her slender body from him. At once he wrenched the fragile garment upwards, without the least care for whether he tore it or not, and laid his left hand flat on the pale warm skin of her narrow back and her pliable spine, to keep her face-down. By now the blood was pounding in his veins and his stalk was growing harder by the second. To hasten the pleasurable process, he clasped it firmly in his hand and massaged it while he stared at Yvonne's pretty knickers.

They were of the same fine crepe-de-chine as her chemise – a most delicate shade of pure ivory-white, with lace trimming and insets that had taken a skilled seamstress hours to accomplish. But of course, at such a moment all this elegant needlework went for nothing. Armand's eyes grew round with delight as he observed how the narrow strip of silk and lace between Yvonne's thighs was stuck in the cleft of her smooth-skinned cheeks, and at the sight his twitching stem excelled itself in size and stiffness and leaped in lusty vigour.

'Once again we find ourselves together in an unconventional situation, my dear Yvonne,' he said.

He was rubbing his fingers lazily up and down the lacy strip to enjoy the warmth of her crease through it.

'Yesterday you put your back against a wall for me,' he continued mockingly, 'and today you lie belly-down over my arm-chair. Evidently we have an affinity for each other.'

'Let me up,' she responded, adding words which are never used by married women of good family – and not even known to many of them.

Her head-down position had pulled her knickers tightly up between her legs and the thin satin strip between them was caught not only in the cleft of her bottom but also in the long furrow of her secret emplacement, where it held the lips open a little. Armand contemplated this enchanting sight for a while, then hooked a finger behind the satin and eased it out, only to press his thumb into her. Her angry cry amused him and, to enrage her further, he pulled her flimsy little knickers halfway down her thighs.

'I have discovered what this affinity between us consists in,' he said, fondling the satin-smooth cheeks he had exposed.

'This is indecent – stop these imbecilities and let me up at once,' she ordered him hoarsely.

'There is something about you, Yvonne – a certain arrogance, shall I call it? But *arrogance* implies a claim to superiority which I find lacking in you, so perhaps we should call it a sneering contempt for others? But whatever name we give it, the truth is that your attitude invites violence – it begs to be humbled rudely! In short, I propose to abuse you.'

He parted the cheeks of her bottom and rubbed the ball of his thumb over the puckered little knot of muscle there. For a moment he was tempted to violate Yvonne beyond her darkest fears and imaginings by ramming his stanchion into this small opening, but he held himself in check, and even resisted the temptation of pushing a long forefinger into it. Instead, he rubbed the swollen head of his eager part along the deep split of her fuzzy peach.

With her knickers looped around her thighs, he was unable to push her legs very wide apart and, to prepare her for his grand entrance, he opened her tender pink lips with his fingers, probing into her with one finger, and then with two, searching out her hidden bud. Yvonne began to shake and jerk her rump up and down to his fingering. And when his fingers became wet with the slipperiness of arousal, it occurred to him that, yet again, he was being exploited. Yvonne had deliberately provoked him because she enjoyed the drama of imagining herself a victim of rape – but a victim who was in control!

Highly excited though he was, he had no reason to oblige so disagreeable a person as Yvonne. He took a step back from her and gave her bare bottom a hearty smack.

'Up you get, Yvonne,' he said, sounding as nonchalant as any man could who was standing naked with his trembling stock only a hand-breadth from a beautiful half-naked woman, 'I'm meeting a dear friend for lunch in half an hour and I must get dressed. She does not like to be kept waiting.'

Astounded, baffled, and confounded by this withdrawal of Armand's interest at the very instant she was awaiting his solid penetration into her open receptacle – and hobbled by her knickers round her knees – Yvonne turned to glare at him. Her furious gaze fell from his grinning face to the stiffness that was rearing up impudently from between his naked thighs, and she collapsed sideways over the padded arm of the chair. Armand stood with hands on hips, trying to guess what she would do to retrieve the situation, a situation which she evidently found humiliating in the extreme.

In some inexplicable way – at least, inexplicable to Armand – Yvonne's rolling tumble over the chair-arm hitched her frock well up round her waist and brought her to rest sprawled on the seat, her silk-clad legs sticking out awkwardly and the dark-haired tuft of curls between her legs well displayed. She put her long-fingered hands over her eyes, as if to hide her shame – an emotion with which she had not the least familiarity since the age of eleven – and Armand could see that she was watching him through the gaps between her fingers. *Well, Madame*, he thought, *I am sure you are about to surprise me in some way.*

Surprise him she did – lying in this immodest position she began to moan and shriek, to sob hysterically, and then to threaten Armand with every form of punishment imaginable for his vicious and hideous assault on her innocent person. Life imprisonment with hard labour was the very least – after that she proposed transportation to the prison colony of Devil's Island, and then the ultimate indignity of decapitation on the guillotine itself. After a while Armand was unable to prevent himself from laughing heartily.

'Vicious assault you call it!' he said when he at last stopped laughing. 'All I did was feel your bottom. Do you regard it as so superior that no hand may touch it without your written permission? It's nice enough in its way, though rather less plump than I prefer.'

She stared at him wide-eyed in disbelief that anyone dare attribute less than perfection to her. Armand knelt beside her legs and gave her tuft of curls a casual tweak.

'As for this well-used thing,' he continued, 'tell me what in your opinion makes it special?'

Yvonne snatched her hands away from her face and glared at him open-mouthed, temporarily and uncharacteristically at a loss for words. Armand took advantage of the brief paralysis of mind his offensiveness had induced to drag her crepe-de-chine knickers the rest of the way down her legs and off. A moment later her had her legs splayed wide and was on his knees between them. *So you want to feel yourself violated*, he thought, staring boldly into her dark-brown eyes. *Alas, dear Yvonne, I am not your mechanical toy to wind up and set going, and it will not be how you hope*!

His hands were under her bottom, grasping and squeezing the bare cheeks, while he bowed his head to vibrate the tip of his tongue in her belly-button. Yvonne gasped and regained the power of rational speech to exclaim, 'But I don't want you to do that! No, no, no, Armand!' when she felt his fingers penetrate her and play over her bud, while from underneath, his thumb pushed itself into the hot little aperture between her cheeks. Armand had remembered how quickly an assault on two fronts had aroused her the evening before – if a fingertip had affected her so strongly then, what might a stiffly-held thumb do?

'No!' Yvonne panted as she rose upwards away from the thumb that intruded into her puckered little knot, only to press her bud against the fingers that flickered over it, and 'No!' again as she sank down to escape the fingers, only to jam the thumb deeper into her. 'No!' as she jerked up again and 'No!' as she fell back, 'No!' and 'No!' until her cries and movements became rhythmical and purposeful. And it was then, when Armand could hear her gasps of pleasure, that he took his hands away.

'If you don't want me to, then I won't,' he said, completely disregarding the truth. 'You know I respect you too much to force you, Yvonne.'

'But you were willing to force me yesterday,' she gasped in her disappointment, and her bare belly jerked upwards in little spasms to raise her loins hungrily towards him.

'It was wrong of me,' Armand confessed, 'and I hope that you will forgive me.'

The row of ivory buttons down the front of her frock ran all the way from the low neck-line to the hem. Armand turned his attention to exploring them, pretending to be too absorbed to hear Yvonne insisting that there was nothing to forgive, she explained that his desperation when he held her against the wall had touched her heart. She assured him that he was wrong to think that she despised him, and in any case, she had no objection whatsoever to being played with if he wanted to. By then Armand had made the interesting discovery that her buttons were not ornament, but were made to be undone.

While Yvonne was squirming her on the chair in frustration, he started at her hem-line and, after undoing eighteen buttons, found that her frock fell open in two long flaps. He pulled her chemise right up round her neck to stroke her breasts and kiss them – even in repose their russet tips were more prominent than on most women and now that she was aroused they stood proudly to almost the thickness and length of the top joint of Armand's little finger. He licked them until he heard her gasping again, then stopped.

'Open your legs for me, Yvonne,' he suggested, to prolong her torment, and sat back on his heels.

She grasped the chair-arms for support and raised her silk-stockinged legs to the level of his head, and let her heels rest on his shoulders for a moment, so that he felt the smooth leather of her high-heeled shoes against his skin. Then as he watched in delight, her legs swung slowly apart, as if the doors of a beautifully-made cabinet were being opened. Back and back they moved until the sinews showed in her groins and taut muscles were stretched along the insides of her thighs. She sank lower until she was almost lying on her back, her legs propped on the chair-arms at right-angles to her body.

'But that's marvellous,' Armand breathed.

He was staring into the wet pink centre of her delight, held open by the pull of her legs. Her secrets were revealed to him; she was offering herself to him to see, to admire, all was his to use however he wished, all was for his pleasure. He was unable to resist leaning forward to let the tip of his tongue slip between the velvety petals of the full-blossomed vermilion rose that was offered to him.

'Oh, yes, Armand, oh yes!' she began to moan.

He tantalised her until he felt her body shake in the long tremors that precede and herald a climax – then he raised his head to smile up into her dark-flushed face. He had threatened to humble her, and he had kept his word. Her expensive black and white frock was undone and crumpled beneath her like a rag, her beautiful chemise was twisted about her armpits, her leopard-skin hat was lost and squashed flat somewhere beneath her back – even her mauve-flowered garters had slipped down to let her silk stockings droop and wrinkle about her legs.

But as ever, Armand's plans did not take into account his own susceptibility. He stared down in triumph at Yvonne, and he was gloating at how he had reduced her cold and elegant beauty to dishevelled and frantic desire. He watched how her breasts rose and fell to the irregular rhythm of her breathing, how her smooth belly was palpitating, how her legs were spread so wide for him that her sinews were straining. He looked up at her face to make her quail at his victory, and he saw that her brown eyes were shining in incipient ecstasy – she *knew* that he was about to penetrate her.

She was right. With a total lack of scruple, Armand's hot and throbbing shaft betrayed his resolve. He flung himself at her, aligned his stiffness with her wetly glistening split and pushed strongly to sheathe himself in it. He held her by the hips and, with one long hard push, sank the whole length of his distended flesh into her belly until his dark curls were crushed against hers and he was lying over her. She hooked her legs over his shoulders and he plunged and gasped in rapture, making her bare breasts jolt up and down her chest to his deep thrusting.

The idea in his mind – in so far as there was place for any such thing in those moments of delirium – was that Yvonne formed part of a marvellous legacy he had received from Pierre-Louis. Destiny had arranged that his cousin's simple act of infidelity had brought beautiful Madeleine naked to Armand's bed, then chubby-breasted and boisterous Suzette had given herself to him, and in the wake of Suzette came the bizarre delights of his encounter with Fernande, and now, following directly from his love-affair with Madeleine, her sister's lascivious body had been put at his disposal.

In effect, Pierre-Louis had unwittingly provided him with four women to enjoy. And in return he had provided his cousin with an heir! To Armand that seemed reasonable – and then all reason deserted him as the moment of his crisis arrived and he stabbed passionately into Yvonne's slippery depths. Her head jerked up off the chair and she screamed, and there followed a seeming-eternity of ecstatic sensation as he emptied his hot passion into her. Her body bounced on the chair under his hectic strokes, while the rhythmic contractions of her belly gripped him tight and sucked him in greedily.

At last their wild spasms slowed and stopped, and they both collapsed, his satisfied betrayer still deeply wedged in her.

'Oh Armand, what have you done to me!' Yvonne panted.

She took his face between her hands and kissed him.

'I've fallen in love with you,' she confessed in surprise and delight. 'I love you, Armand!'

He kissed her and murmured a routine, *'Je t'adore, Yvonne.'* It flattered his male pride enormously when women murmured broken little endearments to him after he had pleasured them. He did not comprehend, of course, that the reason why Yvonne had so elaborately enticed him to make love to her was that Madeleine had asked her to take him off her hands. In this Madeleine had merely copied the tactics of her husband – after she learned how he had disposed of his girlfriend by arranging for Armand to be alone with her in circumstances which guaranteed that he would make love to her – his desires being as imperious as they were.

By asking her elegant sister to play the part of Suzette

in a second comedy of which Armand had, without knowing it, the leading role, Madeleine had rid herself neatly of a lover whose devotion had become inconvenient at a time when she wished to return to her husband. It was fortunate indeed for Armand's self-esteem that no suspicion of any of this devious behaviour by the sisters entered his head. Nor did it occur to him, lying there at his ease on Yvonne's warm belly in the after-glow of ecstasy, that her words of endearment meant anything more than, that was very nice, *chéri*!

But as all the world knows, human nature is capricious and unreliable – and therefore unpredictable. To her astonishment Yvonne was experiencing unfamiliar emotions which she took to mean that she was in love with Armand. It would perhaps be nearer the truth to say that her self-willed nature had been first outraged and then infatuated by the off-hand and perverse manner in which Armand had used her for his pleasure. He knew her to be possessive and manipulative, of course, but he did not yet guess that he was going to be exploited as never before by Yvonne's consuming love.